DON'T

GET

CAUGHT

KURT DINAN

sourcebooks
fire

Published by Sourcebooks Fire, an imprint of Sourcebooks, Inc. P.O. Box 4410, Naperville, Illinois 60567-4410 (630) 961-3900 Fax: (630) 961-2168 www.sourcebooks.com Library of Congress Cataloging-in-Publication data is on file with the publisher. Printed and bound in the United States of America. VP 10 9 8 7 6 5 4 3 2

For Eric, who made me a reader,

and Jen, who made me a writer.

CHAPTER 1

Rule #1 in any quality heist film is *Don't get caught*.

So I'm quiet as I slip out my bedroom window, cross the roof in the cool darkness, and drop from the garage onto the wet grass. Overhead, my parents' lights may be off for the night, but this is a terrible idea any way you look at it. It's stupid, irresponsible, and borderline suicidal. But I'm going anyway.

Blame every movie hero I idolize, blame Tami Cantor, blame Mr. Watson's stupid classroom banner. Blame whomever and whatever you want. This is poor decision making at its finest. But I'm still going.

I stay to the sidewalks because lurking in shadows would only make me look suspicious. In the shadows, I'm a potential burglar, but on the sidewalk, I'm just another sixteen-year-old kid out for a walk—"on my way to a friend's house, Officer" if I get stopped by the cops.

It's Heist Rule #2: *Be cool.*

Like, bank vault combination changed at the last minute? Be cool.

Someone on your crew double-crosses you? Be cool.

Security guards show up unexpectedly? Be cool.

It works for Vin Diesel stealing cars in *The Fast and the*

Furious. It works for George Clooney robbing casinos in *Ocean's Eleven.* It works for Timothy Hutton on *Leverage.* Even John Travolta, back before he got all bloated, played it cool when the Russian mob wanted him dead in a movie called—wait for it—*Be Cool.*

So if it works for them, it has to work for me, right? You might as well just go ahead and add me to the list— Vin Diesel, George Clooney, Timothy Hutton, prebloat John Travolta, and Max Cobb: cool personified.

The only problem is "cool" and "Max Cobb" go together about as well as sharp knives and dull minds.

It's more like, three-day weekend coming up? Sit at home watching movies with my parents.

Score in the forty-ninth percentile on the ACT three times running? Scream into my pillow until I'm hoarse.

Be best known for passing out in front of the class in ninth grade? Contemplate fashioning the bedsheet into a Snoopy-themed noose.

Screw those people who say, "Be yourself." Being myself has only gotten me a stupid, boring life. So for once, I'm doing the opposite. Tonight, there's no Max Cobb or, as Tami Cantor called me, Just Max. As in "Oh, don't worry about him, that's just Max."

No, tonight I'm Not Max, which means keeping cool. I refuse to play it safe and turn back like Just Max begs me to. Instead, Not Max keeps a steady pace, forcing himself not to flinch at every passing car, his heart quickening when the lights of Asheville High School appear in the distance.

AHS is an ancient building that was constructed about the time Pangaea split to form the continents. If it weren't for the soccer, baseball, and football fields nearby, you'd think you were looking at a decaying mental institution, which I suppose all schools are in a way. My destination's the water tower sitting on the edge of school property. With its massive rusting legs stretching into the night sky, the tower's *Asheville High—Home of the Golden Eagles* can be seen by the entire town. I'm halfway across the soccer field, walking in the weird gray light of the full moon, when I catch movement out of the corner of my eye.

"Max?"

My heart almost explodes through my chest. It's a girl's voice, but I can't see whose.

"Max? Is that you?"

She's coming toward me now.

Screw *Be cool.*

I sprint away, running with no clear destination. I need gone, away from this stupid decision before something bad happens.

Not Max…what the hell was I thinking?

After only twenty feet, I'm panting like a two-pack-a-day smoker. I might as well be running in thick mud. So of course, slow ass that I am, whoever she is catches me. And not just catches me, but tackles me from behind, driving me to the soccer turf. Then I'm flipped over, flat on my back, and looking up into the face of Ellie Wick from my Introduction to Philosophy class. She's straddling my chest with her black spandex yoga pants and grinning as big as the moon.

"Hey, Max! You got an invitation too?" she says. "Isn't this awesome?"

Heist Rule #3: *If questioned, be evasive.*

"Invitation?"

Ellie's face pinches. "Maxwell Cobb, you know darn well why you're out here. It's the same reason I am."

"I don't know what you're talking about. I was just out for a walk."

Ellie pins my arms to the ground. She's freakishly strong for someone so small. "Here, I'll help you," she says. "Repeat after me. Say, 'I'm here because of the Chaos Club, Ellie.' I'm not letting you up until you admit it."

You have to love a girl who considers chest-straddling a punishment.

You have to love it even more if that girl is Ellie Wick and you've liked her since seventh grade. But even if I'm all for Ellie staying on top of me all night, we have a ten o'clock date to keep, so I enjoy the contact for a few more seconds before saying, "Okay, I'm here because of the Chaos Club."

Inside, my hormones give me the finger.

"See how easy that was?" she says, standing up. "Come on, we don't want to be late. We're about to become a part of history."

As we start across the soccer field for the gate, I look at Ellie from the corner of my eye. With her blond hair and big green eyes, Ellie's as wholesome looking now in eleventh grade as she was back in middle school. Well, by *now* I don't mean *now-now* because Ellie certainly doesn't look wholesome at the moment. In fact, she looks lava hot. Black spandex tends to have that effect on me.

"So where was your invitation?" she says. "Mine was under my windshield wiper after school."

"Taped inside my locker," I say. I don't tell her that even with my name on the envelope, I double-checked the locker number to make sure it was actually mine.

"They really can get anywhere," Ellie says. "It's like they're ghosts. It's so awesome."

Awesome is the right word for the Chaos Club.

In just the last two years, the four-decade-old organization has:

1. Stacked tires all the way up the flagpole.

2. Filled a guidance counselor's entire office, floor to ceiling, with water balloons.

3. Hacked the district's website so anyone visiting was redirected to BarnYardLove.com.

4. Punished the school board for banning *Slaughterhouse-Five* by projecting pictures of them with Hitler moustaches on the scoreboard during the homecoming game.

There's even a website dedicated to documenting their pranks.

But making the Chaos Club even more awesome?

Its membership is anonymous.

Its movements are untraceable.

And no one's ever been caught.

So the big question is, why in the world was I, Max Cobb—Mr. 2.5 GPA, Mr. No Social Life, Mr. I'm So Lame the Career Interest Survey Recommended "Worker" As My Future Profession—chosen to receive an envelope with this message inside:

10:00 tonight at the water tower.
Tell no one.

CHAOS CLUB

I sure as hell don't know.

But I do know that as we cross the dark parking lot, Not Max is fifty yards from finding out.

CHAPTER 2

Heist Rule #4: *Be suspicious.*

Like, someone on your crew acting out of the ordinary? Be suspicious.

Museum security system switches off without any complications? Be suspicious.

Breaking into the mansion goes too smoothly? Be suspicious.

Because when the characters in heist films don't follow Rule #4, things go to hell and people go to jail.

But just one look at who's waiting for us at the water tower and I know I don't have to worry about Rule #4. Because there's no way these three people are in the Chaos Club.

"Dude!" Dave Wheeler shouts across the parking lot at us. "You too? Excellent!"

"Isn't he on house arrest?" Ellie whispers.

"I think the charges were dropped. Supposedly, the surveillance video disappeared."

"He's a friend of yours, right?"

"Sort of."

Which is probably the only safe way to be friends with Dave Wheeler.

Back in junior high, Wheeler and I used to hang out, but Mom quickly (and correctly) pegged Wheeler as a "bad influence" and put an end to our outside-of-school friendship. Now the only time we really talk is in fourth period, Weird Science, where Wheeler's my assigned "nature buddy," as Mrs. Hansen calls it. Whenever the class goes outside, which is three times a week, Wheeler and I partner up on assignments, meaning I search for the insects or write a nature poem while Wheeler pretends to dry hump trees. Normally, I'd be pissed at such unequal work distribution, but since Wheeler is determined to graduate dead last in our class, the arrangement is probably for the best.

We meet Wheeler mid–parking lot, his arms out like Ellie and I have just returned from a decade in a North Korean prison camp. He has a tangle of hair that makes him look like he lives in the woods behind the school and is wearing a white Superchunk T-shirt with "I broke my back in a trust fall" printed across the front.

"Holy shit, Ellie Wick," he says. "You're about the last person I'd expect to see here."

"You'll find I'm full of surprises, Dave."

"Yeah, like that outfit. If that's what's currently fashionable for churchgoing girls, I may have to start attending. Do your parents know you're in public in those clothes?"

Ellie puts a finger to her lips and says, "What the Reverend and Mrs. Wick don't know can't hurt them."

Wheeler claps once and points a hard finger at Ellie.

"Now that's what I like to hear! And you," he says, turning to me. "Why didn't you tell me you'd gotten an invite?"

"The note said not to tell anyone."

Wheeler's eyes go wide. "Shit, it said that?"

"Oh my gosh," Ellie says. "You told someone?"

"Totally," Wheeler says, "I tweeted it and posted a picture of the note on H8box. Everyone probably knows by now."

Ellie stiffens and blinks like her brain's rebooting.

"Relax! I'm kidding! Even I'm not that dumb. Come on over and join the party."

And that moment right there pretty much exemplifies why it's best to just "sort of" be friends with Dave Wheeler.

Up ahead, Kate Malone, who's also in our philosophy class, sits on the curb, earbuds in, graffiti-ing her jeans with a black Sharpie. Her current work in progress on her clothes notwithstanding, Kate's one of the best artists in the school. We're talking guaranteed-full-ride-to-college good. Oh, and she's also the only girl in the universe whose boobs I've seen.

I'm not joking.

"Hi, Kate," Ellie says. "Isn't this exciting?"

Malone pops her earbuds out and drapes them over her shoulders.

"So are you here to ensure we don't have any fun, Ellie?" Malone says. "Maybe you want to search me, make sure I don't have any books with swear words in them?"

Oh man.

Remember when I said the school board banned *Slaughterhouse-Five*? Well, Ellie's dad is not only the minister at the Baptist church, but he's also on the school board. When his Hitler-moustache picture appeared on the football scoreboard, Ellie fled the student section in tears. But right now, Ellie somehow keeps her smile and says, "Nope, nothing like that. Tonight's about joining the Chaos Club."

"Why do you think that? Because of the card? Did yours say the same as mine?"

Malone stands up, and now I see "Fear of a Female Planet" freshly inked on her jeans. From her back pocket, she pulls a black Chaos Club card with red lettering.

"That looks just like mine," Ellie says.

"Mine too," I say.

"Mine three," Wheeler says.

Simultaneously, all of us hear someone approaching us from behind. We all turn to see who this person is, and—

Person isn't the right word. Goon is more like it.

Tim Adleta is a junior like the rest of us, but to most people, he's known as Dim. Not that anyone calls him Dim to his face—at least not anyone who wants to avoid being identified by dental records. Adleta has started varsity lacrosse since freshman year, leading the league in scoring every season. He also has a monkey on a bicycle where his brain should be. He lumbers toward us, his knuckles dragging on the asphalt.

"Is this what your card looks like?" Malone says once he joins the circle.

Adleta grunts a response. I'm not exactly sure if there's a word in there because primate isn't my second language.

"See, none of our cards say anything about joining the Chaos Club," Malone says.

"What else could they possibly mean?" Ellie asks.

"I'm not sure, but look at us. Honestly, do we seem like Chaos Club members?"

It's nice to know someone else believes in Rule #4 too.

"Well, maybe that's how the Chaos Club's stayed around for so long—by playing against expectations," Ellie says.

"Maybe, but the tower's spotlight is off too. When was the last time that happened?"

I look up into the dark sky. How hadn't I noticed that?

"So you really think this is a setup?" Wheeler says. "Why would they do that?"

"I didn't say it's a setup. I'm just saying it's weird."

"Yeah," I say, the cautious Just Max speaking. "I was thinking it was weird too."

"So what should we do?" Ellie asks.

"Yeah, what's your solution, Kate?" Wheeler says, smirking. "Pull off your shirt and take pictures?"

Malone shoves Wheeler so hard and fast he never sees it coming. He stumbles back, his feet hitting the curb, dropping him on his ass. Then Malone's face is six inches from his.

"Apologize."

Wheeler puts both hands up.

"I said apologize," Malone growls.

"Yeah, Christ, I'm sorry," Wheeler says.

"So never again, right?"

"Yeah, sure, no problem."

People think Kate's gay because she has short hair, ripped arms, a rainbow patch on her backpack, and works at the Asheville Climbing Center, teaching people how to rock climb. But her sexting scandal last year involved pictures she sent to a boy, not a girl, so it's sort of confusing. After what she just did to Wheeler, I'm sure not going to be the one asking about her sexual orientation, I know that.

She continues glaring at Wheeler for a moment longer before finally backing off. Adleta snorts what may be a laugh. I'd be able to tell if I looked at his face, but gorillas view direct eye contact as a sign of aggression.

"What if we poke around?" I say. "Maybe there are instructions or something. We were invited here for a reason, right?"

I'm surprised when no one scoffs at the suggestion.

"Great idea, Max," Ellie says. "You come with me."

When we're around the corner of the fence and away from the others, Ellie takes out her phone and starts texting. I try to see what she's typing, but her fingers are too fast.

"My parents," she says. "They think I'm at the library studying."

"But the library closes at nine on Thursdays."

"That's not something Mom and Dad would think about. They trust me too much."

"It sounds like maybe they shouldn't."

"You're definitely right about that."

On the far side of the water tower, the woods are just an arm's reach away and block out any moonlight. It's chilly for September, and I regret not bringing a jacket.

Ellie moves in close and squeezes my arm, saying, "I'm glad you're here."

My mouth is a balled-up gym sock.

"Why's that?"

"Because knowing other people makes it more fun, you know?"

Make that two balled-up gym socks.

We keep walking the perimeter of the fence, pointlessly looking around for clues. From the other side of the water tower, I hear Malone tell someone to shut up. Dollars to doughnuts it's Wheeler.

"I thought it was crummy what Tami said in class today," Ellie says. "I felt bad for you."

"It wasn't a big deal."

"No, no one deserves that. Especially you."

Each Thursday in philosophy, we have Big Questions of Existence, when Watson divides the class into two sides to debate whatever topic he chooses to torture us with.

Today's question: Is every life valuable?

The topic was handled with the sensitivity and respect

you'd expect from a class of teenagers. Admittedly, I didn't pay too much attention. Instead, I was busy completing an extra credit assignment due in English second period. Normally, I'm not a big extra credit guy, but my grade sort of demanded it. Besides, it's not like I could turn down this assignment: Concoct a Scheme in Which Gatsby and Daisy Live Happily Ever After. My idea involved Gatsby killing that bitchy tennis player Jordan Baker, then framing Daisy's asshole husband, Tom, for the murder. It's this type of thinking that goes a long way toward explaining my empty social calendar.

So while I was busy arranging for Tom Buchanan to spend the rest of his life locked up in prison, Watson called on Tami Cantor.

(Quick—ever known a nice person named Tami? Exactly.)

Tami, doing her best to live up to the reputation of every Tami in recorded history, said, "Look, some people just aren't as important as others. Not everyone can be somebody. There have to be nobodies too. I'm not being mean. It's just statistics."

In the commotion that ensued, Tami decided to raise her position on the Bitch Power Rankings by saying, "Look, I don't mean *nobody* in a bad sense. Nobodies can be good people. They're just not very important. Like Dan over there. He's nice and people like him, but he's not special or anything."

I looked up from my notebook, wondering just who Tami was talking about because there isn't any Dan in our class.

Then I saw where she was pointing.

And everyone was looking my way too.

This is my life.

"My name's Max," I said.

Tami did a perfectly executed *whatever* shrug that made my face burn.

"We've been in classes together since kindergarten," I said.

Tami huffed and said, "Well, that just sort of proves my point, doesn't it? And don't get so defensive. I'm not saying you're a bad person. You're just kind of there. You're just Max, and there's nothing wrong with that."

Here's the ethical question Watson should offer next week: Is it technically murder if you kill someone without a soul?

The dismissal bell rang seconds later, but Tami's comment about me being a nobody, being Just Max, pinballed around my brain all day.

Now, fifteen hours later, here I am.

"Wait, you don't believe Tami, do you?" Ellie says as we approach the fence gate.

"Uh, no, of course not."

"Look, she's the nobody, Max. The only reason people like her say things like that is because—" Ellie stops and points. "What's that?"

Stuffed in one of the diamond-shaped holes in the fence gate is an envelope. Ellie almost comes out of her shoes to get it.

The front reads: *Initiates.*

"Should we call everyone?" Ellie says.

"No, you found it—you get the honors."

Ellie tears into the envelope like she's expecting a Wonka Golden Ticket inside.

Out comes another black Chaos Club card, and Ellie reads the back before turning it my way.

Climb up.

CHAPTER 3

When we get back to the others, Wheeler's throwing rocks at a streetlight, Malone's on the curb, comatose with her music, and Adleta's off by himself, probably calculating long division in his head. So much for everyone looking for clues.

"We found something," Ellie says. "Come see."

As the card makes the rounds, Ellie bounces hard on her toes. Malone's the last to read the instruction to climb. Then she looks up at the dark tower.

"I don't like it," she says.

"Why not?" Ellie says.

"Because now it definitely screams setup."

"You're just being paranoid," Wheeler says.

"It's called being smart," Malone says. "Maybe try it sometime."

Wheeler opens his mouth to say something, but his bruised ass keeps him quiet.

"They could be up there right now listening to us, waiting to see what we'll do," Ellie says. "We could be on a time limit."

"Yeah, or someone could be up there waiting to throw us over the railing," Malone says.

"Why did you even show up then?" Wheeler says. "No, don't get all pissed again. I'm serious. If you're just here to hate, why come at all?"

Instead of clobbering Wheeler into next week, Malone just makes a frustrated face and shakes her head.

"I'll tell you what," Ellie says. "Why don't we take a vote?"

"Because this isn't a majority-rules deal," Malone says. "If someone doesn't want to go up, they don't have to."

"Right, but we were invited here as a group, so we should act as one. Let's just see what everyone else thinks. I'm for climbing, and I'm guessing you're against it, Kate, so that leaves you three. So what do you think, Tim? Should we go up?"

Adleta shrugs and says nothing. And to think adults complain that kids today have no social skills.

"I'll put you down as undecided," Ellie says. "What about you, Dave?"

"Hell yeah I'm in," Wheeler says. "Be a part of the club that once suspended Stranko's car over the theater stage? I'm climbing that tower even if they want me doing it naked."

"Thanks for that visual," Ellie says. "Max?"

Great, as the tiebreaker, I have to choose between curiosity and skepticism. Fearlessness and logic. Not Max and Just Max. Not to mention, between Ellie and Malone, which could be the difference between being kissed or being punched.

"Well," I say, stalling, "I am little suspicious, to be honest. Like Malone said, it's all just very weird."

Ellie goes eerily still.

"But," I add quickly, "we weren't chosen at random to be here. And the envelope does say *Initiates*. So there's that."

All four just stare at me.

You can hear crickets, and I mean literal crickets.

"Dude, what's your point?" Wheeler says.

"Yeah," Malone says, "shit or get off the pot."

And somewhere in the far back corner of my head, I hear Tami Cantor calling me a nobody and the rest of the class laughing with her.

"Let's go up," I say. "Ellie's right—this could be our chance to be a part of Asheville history. Maybe there's another note."

Ellie looks happy enough to kiss me.

Malone, not so much.

"Whatever," she says, "but don't say I didn't warn you."

"Are you coming?" Wheeler asks her.

Malone looks up at the tower and taps her finger against her leg. Then her shoulders drop, and she reaches into her pocket.

"Okay, but I'm recording this just in case."

Ellie leads everyone back to the gate where we found the envelope. She gives the gate a shake, and surprisingly, it opens.

"Creepy," she says.

With six massive legs reaching into the night sky, the water tower is like an enormous metal insect preparing to stomp the high school. A ladder runs up the closest leg, and a safety gate extends twenty feet up the ladder's base to prevent anyone—read: teenagers—from climbing. The safety gate isn't locked either.

"So who wants to go first?" Ellie says.

Adleta grunts and starts up, a teenage King Kong climbing the Empire State Building.

Wheeler turns to Malone and says, "Ladies first."

"Like I'm going to let you stare at my butt the whole way up."

"You can't blame a guy for trying."

Wheeler begins climbing, and Malone follows. Ellie puts her foot on the first rung and looks back at me.

"You look like you're going to throw up."

"I'm not a fan of heights," I say.

"Oh, don't be silly. You'll be fine."

I may not be a fan of heights, but I especially hate ladders. I always think the rung I'm on is going to break away and send me plummeting. Climbing this ladder in the dark, the rungs sticky for some reason, only worries me more. But despite that, I'd be lying if I didn't say how awesome this was. The higher I climb, the harder my heart pounds from the adrenaline. I feel like a jewel thief scaling a skyscraper at midnight on his way to steal the Hope Diamond. Then I make the mistake of looking up at Ellie in her tight pants climbing just ahead of me. My foot misses the next rung, and I awkwardly stumble. I have to wrap both arms around the ladder to keep from falling. Just what I want on my death certificate: death by yoga pants.

Up ahead in the darkness, Wheeler goes into a mock newscaster's voice, announcing, "Five Asheville High School students fell to their deaths last evening when—"

"Shut up," Malone says.

The climb takes only two minutes but feels like an hour by the time the ladder ends at the base of a metal grating no more than four feet wide. If a strong wind blows, a waist-high railing is all that's there to keep me from hurtling to my death.

"Wow, this is higher than I thought," Ellie says, looking out over the lights of the town.

Malone, recording everything with her phone, says, "I wish I had my climbing gear. I'd love to rappel off this."

"What was it Jesus said, Ellie?" Wheeler says. "'I think I can see my house from here'?"

And me, I want down. And not just down, but to roll in the grass and kiss the earth. Then, as I'm about to wuss out, Ellie's hand is in mine and she's leading me along the platform.

"Come on," she says. "Let's look for the next clue."

Her hand is soft and warm, and if the platform gives away right now, I can die a happy man.

"You get to open the next envelope if there is one,"

Ellie says. "Or maybe it'll be like in the movies, and there'll be a cell phone that rings and—"

My foot kicks something metal, sending it clanking and skittering across the platform before dropping into the night.

From the other side of the tower, Malone says, "What was that?"

I look down at my feet and see four more of what I've just booted—spray paint cans.

And in one horrifying moment, I realize why the rungs were sticky when we climbed.

Red paint covers my hands.

Oh shit.

I lean back for a better view of the water tower to see what's been spray-painted there. The wet paint trails down from certain letters like red teardrops.

Double shit.

Heist Rule #5: *When in doubt, run.*

But we don't get that chance.

Suddenly, the water tower lights blaze to life, illuminating the newly painted message for the entire town to see.

Assville High School—
Home of the Golden Showers

Both Malone and Wheeler say, "Shit."

Ellie says, "Wow."

Adleta says nothing.

And then a voice booms from a bullhorn below, where red-and-blue lights flash in the parking lot.

"This is the police. Come down immediately."

So much for *Don't get caught*.

CHAPTER 4

Officer Hale identifying himself as the police is a misnomer—sort of like the adult who rolls out the balls for us in gym class calling himself a teacher. It's accurate only in the most technical sense. Hale's the school security officer we're supposed to go to if we're being bullied or if we want to rat on someone. But he can't arrest anyone. And he doesn't have a gun. Which are pretty much the only reasons to become a cop in the first place, right?

Instead of driving us to the police station, Hale parks in front of the school administration office and death marches us into a conference room, where he orders us to give up our home phone numbers.

"And don't lie to me," he says. "Because I'll know."

So like any budding criminal, I lie. My parents are already going to kill me, so I might as well postpone the execution as long as possible.

Within twenty minutes, the conference room is filled with parents, each of them standing behind their delinquent children. I'm the only unclaimed kid, but Ellie's parents stand so close to me, I'm hoping they'll be mistaken for my parental representatives.

From across the table, Wheeler's mom gives me a small,

sad wave. Dave's the bane of her existence. Her other two sons are fine, upstanding young men who earned full rides to college. Dave, not so much. I once asked him about this, and in a moment of actual maturity, he said, "Who wants to be like everyone else? Sometimes you have to break out and do it your own way."

Yeah, and sometimes people go too far in trying to do that, Just Max scolds me as we sit awaiting our execution.

Minus a couple weird noises Wheeler seems to be making with his mouth, the room is eerily quiet, so it's a relief when Mrs. B finally arrives. Mrs. B, or Mrs. Barber in the real world, has been the principal here for twice as long as I've been alive. As far as adult authority figures go, Mrs. B's one of the most tolerable, and I'd be fine suffering through this embarrassment if she were the only administrator here, but no, Stranko's with her.

My parents graduated from this very high school with Stranko twenty years ago, and all you need to know is that Stranko was voted Most Likely to Be Accused of Police Brutality. Cop, vice principal—there's really no differ-ence. Supposedly, Stranko's been waiting for Mrs. B to retire so he can take over, but every year she returns, and you just know it makes Stranko want to scream his throat bloody. To make matters worse, Stranko hates me. It turns out he takes it personally if you quit his summer lacrosse camp two days in. And yes, you read that right—in my search for some purpose, I tried lacrosse. Feel free to laugh hysterically. Everyone else sure did.

"Well, good evening, everyone," Mrs. B says. "This certainly isn't the preferable way to meet, is it? Kids, whatever happened to causing trouble during school hours? It's way past my bedtime."

Everyone laughs politely. Minus Stranko.

"To keep this orderly, I'd like to hear from Officer Hale first, then the students, before opening the floor to everyone else," Mrs. B says. "Officer Hale, will you get us started?"

"Yes, ma'am. At approximately ten o'clock, I received an anonymous text reporting vandalism occurring at the water tower located on school grounds. Living close by, I drove over immediately. I quickly discerned something was amiss because the tower lights were off. When I parked, I could hear voices from up top. I ordered them down, and here we are, presently."

"Wait," Wheeler says, his head cocked, "you do know you're not a real cop, right?"

Mama Wheeler rolls her eyes in an exhausted *See what I have to live with?* way before smacking Wheeler's head.

"Thank you, Officer Hale," Mrs. B says. "And for the defense?"

Ellie looks shamefaced at the table.

Malone's face scrunches up like she doesn't know how to start.

Wheeler picks at his fingernail with a paper clip.

And Adleta looks like he's just been wheeled out from electroshock therapy.

"Well?" Mrs. B says. "Anyone?"

"We were set up," I blurt.

I glance around the table, just as surprised by my outburst as everyone else. I slouch in my seat but fail to disappear completely.

"Would you care to elaborate?" Mrs. B asks.

Malone gives me a nod of encouragement, and when my silent prayer for a sudden embolism isn't answered, I open my mouth. What follows is a ramble about the Chaos Club notes we received and the instructions to climb the tower. It's sloppy storytelling at best, but the longer I talk, the easier the words come. I finish with, "Right after we saw the golden shower thing, Hale showed up. And that's it."

Mrs. B looks like she believes me. But Stranko's glaring at me with such intensity I have to look away.

"Where are your parents?" he says to me, then turns to Hale. "Did you call his parents?"

"He said they were out of town. I left a message with his guardian."

"Out of town?" he says to me.

"They left yesterday for Seattle for a broadcasting convention. Dad's one of the speakers. I'm staying with a family friend."

"Seattle, huh?" he says. "And who is this person supposedly watching you?"

Stranko sounds like he's going to call bullshit on me. And when he does, the first thing he'll do is leave the room and call my house. Then it's RIP Not Max.

"I asked who's watching you," Stranko says.

And right as Not Max is about to fold, the universe gives me the first real break of my life, and in a moment of perfect timing, the conference room door opens.

Here's the scoop on Uncle Boyd:

1. He's not my real uncle but Dad's oldest friend.

2. He calls himself an artist, although I'm not sure his so-called sculptures qualify as art.

3. And finally, and most importantly, Uncle Boyd sees me as the son he's never had, meaning I can trust him.

Hopefully.

"Sorry I'm late, Mrs. B," he says. "I didn't get the message about Max until a few minutes ago. I must've had the radio up too loud."

Boyd's wearing ripped jeans and a paint-splattered Rage Against the Machine shirt. He comes up behind me and nods to Stranko.

"Howdy, Dwayne. Been a while."

Stranko flinches like a bee's just flown by his face.

"With students in the room, Boyd, I prefer to be called Mr. Stranko."

"I'll do my best, Dwayne. I mean, Mr. Stranko. Sir."

"So Max is staying with you, Boyd?" Mr. B says.

"For the next few days, yeah. It doesn't look like I've been doing a very good job watching him. I apologize for that."

Stranko's looking all *bullshit* again but doesn't say anything.

Mrs. B says to Boyd, "Max here was just filling us in on the evening. Max, do you have any evidence to back up your story?"

I hold out my invitation and the *climb up* message from the gate. Stranko lays both on the table before taking pictures with his phone.

"Is there anything else?" Mrs. B asks.

"I have a video too," Malone says.

Kate unlocks her phone, then passes it over to Mrs. B. Stranko and Hale crowd behind her, but they only make it through fifteen seconds of us on the tower talking about looking for another clue before Mrs. B turns it off.

"I don't think I need to see any more," she says. "Is there any other information you'd like to share?"

All five of us collectively shrug.

"I'm sorry, I don't mean to interrupt," Malone's mother says, "but this Chaos Club, is it a school-approved organization?"

"Absolutely not," Stranko says. "We would never sanction such behavior."

"Well, apparently you can't stop it either," she mutters.

Ellie's mom raises her hand slowly and just above a

whisper asks, "Can someone please tell me what a golden shower is?"

The room fills with an awkward silence, all of us wondering how to explain being peed on for pleasure to a woman who probably bathes in a swimsuit. And yes, Mrs. Wick is probably that naive. She only wears skirts and is the secretary at the town's Methodist church, where Mr. Wick's the minister. I'm not sure how they spend that much time together without wanting to kill each other. Jesus must be one heck of a marriage counselor.

"I've never heard of a golden shower either, Mr. Stranko," Wheeler says. "Could you please explain it to us, sir?"

Stranko turns such a wonderful shade of red I think he might start bleeding from the eyes. I have to pinch my leg hard to hold back from laughing.

"Let's focus on the issue at hand, please," Mrs. B says.

"What I want to know is if our kids are in danger," Wheeler's mom says. "I mean, isn't this bullying? These kids were targeted."

"More like stupid," Adleta's dad huffs. "Putting their futures and scholarships in danger by being dumb enough to fall for a prank like this. It's goddamn embarrassing."

If it's possible, Mr. Adleta is even bigger than Tim. He stands at almost military attention, his fingers digging into Tim's shoulders like he's trying to snap his collarbone. But all you really need to know is that when Tim was in third grade, Mr. Adleta was banned from Tim's soccer games because he wouldn't stop screaming at the refs. *Third grade.*

Mrs. B says, "No, Mrs. Wheeler, I don't think your children are in danger. But this is the first time I can remember students being set up in this manner by the Chaos Club. Am I right, Mr. Stranko?"

Stranko must be some sort of Chaos Club historian because he launches into a summary of their history, quoting pranks from their website. He finishes by saying, "I can assure all of you that we're doing everything we can to eliminate this group, whoever they are."

Then he taps the phone clipped to his belt.

Heist Rule #6: *Be observant.*

Malone's mom says, "So what all this really means is that no one knows why these kids were targeted, and that there's nothing you can do to stop it from happening again?"

"Ms. Malone, I can assure you these students are safe. But you're right. I have no explanation for why they were chosen," Mrs. B says, and looks at us. "I want each of you to promise to come to me if you're contacted again. Will you do that?"

We tell her we will, and Stranko adds, "Or come to me."
Yeah right.

"So what happens now?" Reverend Wick says. It's the first time he's spoken tonight. As a school board member, this has to be pretty embarrassing. Not Hitler-moustache-embarrassing, but embarrassing nonetheless.

Mrs. B teepees her fingers under her chin for a moment, then says, "On one hand, it's clear to me these students are not responsible for the water tower vandalism. Do you agree, Mr. Stranko?"

Stranko nods but without much confidence behind it. You get the feeling he almost he wishes we were the culprits.

"On the other hand," Mrs. B says, "we have a very clear policy regarding trespassing on school grounds that was spelled out at the beginning of the year. That is something that must be addressed. So tomorrow after school, you will each take part in painting over the message on the water tower. I believe two hours working in the sun may help deter you from coming onto school property again after hours."

"How is that fair?" Adleta's dad says. "You even said they didn't do it. To punish them for that is crap. And Tim's going to miss practice then. I don't see how—"

"Or," Mrs. B says, staring at Mr. Adleta, "I suppose we could simply turn them over to the Asheville Police Department and let them handle the trespassing violation. You could transport them to the station, could you not, Mr. Hale?"

The stare down doesn't last long. Mr. Adleta mumbles something under his breath that causes Ellie's mom's cheeks to redden.

"And, David," Mrs. B says to Wheeler, "I'd appreciate it if you could refrain from posting pictures of the water tower to that website you frequent. Is that possible?"

"Anything for you, Mrs. B," Wheeler says.

They're talking about H8box, a smart-ass website for posting and commenting on pictures and articles that pulls in more than two millions hits a day. In school, Wheeler may underachieve to global proportions, but on H8box, his twisted vision of the world has made him a god. If you need someone to take a picture of a crowded street at night in Singapore or want an advanced copy of a movie not out for weeks, Wheeler and his H8box connections are your guys.

Mrs. B stands and says, "If there's nothing else, we all have an early morning tomorrow."

We all follow her lead and stand. Boyd, probably worried I'm about to make a break for the door, puts a light hand on my arm. But it's not necessary. I'm enjoying this. Who'd have thought juvenile delinquency would be such a thrill?

Stranko says, "Tim, you and your dad wait for me in the hall. Got it?"

I imagine Adleta running the stadium steps for the rest of his life, and before I can stop myself, a small laugh escapes my mouth.

"Is something funny, Cobb?" Stranko says. "Maybe you should understand something before you ridicule it. You could have learned a lot from the lacrosse team if you were man enough."

And had a lobotomy, I think.

Stranko's still sneering as he's on his way out with the Adletas when he points to Malone.

"Send me the video you shot tonight. I want it as evidence."

And here Stranko taps his phone again.

Something then clicks in my brain. Stranko is investigating the Chaos Club.

Just call me Sherlock Cobb.

Ellie passes by with her parents, and for a second, our eyes meet.

"We need a plan," she whispers.

Before I can respond, her parents have her out the door, probably to exorcise the demon that led her to this blasphemy. Boyd and I follow them and are close to a clean getaway when Mrs. B calls out, "Max? Boyd? Will you two stay a minute, please?"

Boyd mutters, "Ah, hell."

The rest of the room clears out, and Mrs. B motions for us to sit down beside her at the table.

"Boyd, it seems like just yesterday that we were having meetings in here with your parents about you."

"I was sort of hoping not to be back, Mrs. Barber. No offense."

"None taken," Mrs. B says, smiling. "Work keeping you busy?"

"Plenty."

"Has Pat Kreider contacted you yet?"

"We're supposed to have a meeting next week. Thanks for the recommendation."

Mrs. B waves it away.

"So, Max," she says, "we've never really spoken before, have we?"

"No, ma'am."

"Well, I'm sorry it has to be under these circumstances, but we might as well make the best of it. I'm sure you know your parents attended school here, but did you know your father once used a coat hanger to break into my car for me when I locked my keys inside?"

It's not a story I've heard, but as far as Dad's pseudocriminal abilities are concerned, well, he and Boyd are friends for a reason.

"Jump ahead twenty-five years later, and here's his son, the apple not falling far from the tree," she says. "Do you think that, like your father, you'll only use your abilities for good, or will this be the first of many unfortunate visits to my office?"

"I don't plan on being back."

"Oh, you're welcome back, Max. Let's just hope it's for something positive next time. And, Boyd, you'll pass all this on to his parents?"

"Absolutely. Max and I'll be having a long discussion about this on the way home."

But the only talking Boyd and I do is when we're pulling out of the parking lot in his truck, Guns N' Roses blasting on the radio.

"Thanks for saving my ass," I say.

"Hell, when I was your age, I used to wish I had someone half as cool as me on my side. It's nice to do some good for once. You okay?"

"Surprisingly, yeah. More than okay, actually. I just feel stupid."

"About getting tricked, getting caught, or getting lectured?"

"All of the above."

"Yeah, that sounds about right. You get used to it though."

Boyd smokes a cigarette and leaves me alone for the rest of the ride. I put my feet on the dash and close my eyes, smiling to myself as I replay the night. Ten minutes later, we're parked on the street a few houses down from mine. I thank him again as I climb out.

"This is just between the two of us, right?" I say.

"You got it, man."

"Thanks, Uncle Boyd."

"I gotta say, I'm sort of proud of you, doing something dumb like this," Boyd says. "It's unexpected. Good for you."

Which is pretty much why I went in the first place.

I don't expect Mom and Dad to be sitting on my bed in full war paint, ready to take hatchets to me, but I still breathe a sigh of relief when I reenter the house through my window and see my bedroom is empty. That's the nice thing about being boring—it gets to where even your parents overlook you.

When I climb into bed, you'd think I'd be able to relax now that the shock of getting caught has passed.

But you'd be wrong.

Relaxing is the last thing on my mind.

Because if I've learned anything tonight, it's that having

the guts to not be a nobody—that taking risks and being Not Max—feels good.

No, scratch that.

It feels great.

What doesn't feel good is knowing someone set me up and I was dumb enough to fall for it.

Just Max may have put up with that, but Not Max sure as hell won't.

Ellie's right—we need a plan.

It's Heist Rule #7: *Always get payback.*

CHAPTER 5

The worst thing about school the next day isn't how the school newspaper website headline reads *The Water Tower 5*.

Or the photoshopped picture of the five of us in prison-orange jumpsuits accompanying the story.

Or the constant calls of "Water Tower Five!" in the halls.

Or how someone Sharpied it on my locker.

No, the worst part is that I respond to it by hiding my ass in the theater. Before school, between periods, during lunch, I sit in the dark theater, embarrassed, worrying that a group of students will come in and stand in a circle around me, mocking my very existence and stupidity.

Can you say delusions of grandeur?

And believe me, I know how pathetic I sound. Not Max would punch Just Max in the groin for behaving this way. Less than eight hours ago, I was full of gung ho confidence, ready to destroy my enemies single-handedly. Now I'm considering faking a stomachache so I can go home early. But I can't help it. I didn't think there was anything worse than being a nobody, but it turns out I was wrong. Being thought of as an idiot is way worse. Add that to the shame I feel for being a coward, for disappearing instead of walking the halls with a *screw you* swagger like any one of my movie heroes would do, and my descent into loserdom is complete.

Coming a close second in the Worst Thing about School the Next Day list is the perp walk Warden Stranko forces us to do from his office to the water tower after school. He marches us through a corridor of students in the parking lot, everyone laughing and pointing at us in the safety helmets we're forced to wear. Like an inmate entering the prison population, I keep my head down as I walk and ignore the ridicule. It's not easy though, especially with the entire lacrosse team waiting for us at the tower. As we get close, Geoff Varelman, the senior captain, says to the others, "Any of you guys smell piss? Because I smell piss. It reeks of piss."

Clearly, Varelman has a bright future as a prison yard storyteller.

At the base of the tower, Stranko orders us to step into crotch-strangling harnesses with ropes and clips around the waist.

"Latch on when you get up top," he says. "We don't need a lawsuit if you fall to your death."

"That's very caring of you, sir. Thank you," Wheeler says.

"Just get your butts up there."

We climb the tower in the same order we did less than twenty-four hours earlier. This time though, it's not excitement I feel but constant humiliation. The student mob has followed us from the parking lot to the tower, chanting "Water Tower Five!" the entire way.

"This sucks," Wheeler says.

"You certainly have a way with words," Malone says.

"And you certainly have a way with photography."

"Enjoy this climb, Wheeler, because I'm throwing you off the tower as soon as we get to the top."

But once we're on the platform overlooking the parking lot, Malone doesn't send Wheeler to his death, at least not right away. We're all too busy looking down at the growing crowd of students pointing up at us and filming us with their phones. I can't help but wonder if the Chaos Club is down there too, mixed in with the others, admiring their accomplishment. If they are, there's no way of knowing it. What I do know is that the audience below is made up of a who's who of personal tormentors.

Stranko and his lacrosse team for Adleta.

Tami Cantor for me.

The tsk-tsking youth groupers from Ellie's church.

And Libby Heckman for Malone.

If I haven't mentioned her earlier, Libby's one of Malone's former friends and, like Kate, one of the best artists in the school. More importantly though, she's the reason every boy in this school has a picture of Malone half-naked. Last spring, Malone made the epic mistake of sending a topless picture of herself to a junior named Troy Huff, Libby's ex-boyfriend. When the inevitable *let's give this relationship sent from the heavens a ninth chance* occurred two days later between Libby and Troy, the picture of Malone wearing only an open robe appeared on everyone's phone. Libby wasn't exactly secretive about being the sender. And if you must know, yes, I've looked at that picture. Okay, more than a thousand times. It's not something I'm proud of.

The only one of us without a ridiculer below is Wheeler. It's not that he doesn't have enemies. Far from it. It's just that they're all afraid he'll recruit a ninja from H8box to fly around the world to lop their heads off.

"I guess we should get started," Ellie says, picking out a brush from the bag lying on the catwalk. Beside the bag is a single can of blue paint we're supposed to use to cover the "Assville High School—Home of the Golden Showers" message.

Malone pops the lid and dips her brush in, but before she can start, Wheeler says, "Wait, everyone hold up your brushes and smile in that direction."

Standing on the far side of the parking lot where Wheeler is pointing is a lone figure aiming a camera at us with a lens that looks like it could photograph a tick on the moon.

"Who is that?" Ellie asks.

"Mark Richardson," Wheeler says. "He's shooting a picture for H8box."

"But Mrs. B asked you not to do that."

"Right, but she didn't say anything about someone

else doing it, did she? Semantics, man. They'll get you every time."

We all hold up our paint brushes in Mark's direction and pause for a picture before dipping our brushes and slathering the water tower with blue paint. I'm standing next to Ellie on the end, which, if I have to risk my life up here, is the best place to be. Up until last year, Ellie's parents forced her to wear long skirts to school. She eventually won the battle to dress more like a normal teenager, but in her parents' minds, that means loose jeans and shirts buttoned high. Still, if anyone can rock the Puritan look, it's Ellie.

What's awesome is the paint we're using isn't a perfect match for the original blue. The district will inevitably have to pay someone to repaint the entire tower, which is a small but excellent consolation.

"So you made it back into your house without getting caught?" Ellie says.

"Luckily. What happened to you?"

"I just got a—quote—stern talking to—unquote—about temptation and the importance of our family's reputation."

"But they didn't ground you?"

"No, my parents don't do that. I think they're afraid I'll become like other PKs."

"PKs?"

"Preacher's kids. Haven't you heard? We're the biggest drunks, druggies, and sex fiends out there. Did Stranko call your parents yet?"

"No, not yet," I say. "I'm betting it'll come in the next couple days."

"Well, if he tries, he's not going to have much luck."

I raise my eyebrows.

"You know how I'm an office aide second period? Today I changed your parents' phone number in the system to the childcare room at my dad's church. It's only used on Sunday mornings. So if Stranko does call, the phone will just ring and ring."

"You did that for me?"

"Sure. Why not?"

It's official. I'm in love.

From somewhere down below, someone shouts, "Hey, you missed a spot!"

Clever.

"You know what pisses me off?" Malone asks. "Knowing the Chaos Club is probably down there laughing at us."

We all stop painting and look over the side again.

"I'm going to find 'em and kill 'em," Adleta growls.

"And who exactly are you going to kill?" Malone asks. "No one knows who's in the Chaos Club."

"Oh, someone knows. I'll find out who," Adleta says.

"How? By beating people up until you get a confession?"

"It's an idea."

"Yeah, a dumb one."

"Like you're one for good ideas. What's your answer? Text everyone another nudie?"

Malone holds Adleta's eyes a lot longer than I'd be able to. Or maybe he's holding her eyes. Regardless, I haven't heard Adleta say that many words in all the years I've known him.

"Look, everyone just needs to chill out," Wheeler says. "This isn't a big deal."

"That's easy for you to say," Ellie tells him. "You don't care about how this'll look to prospective colleges."

"Or how Stranko's going to make your life hell during practice," Adleta says, then adds, "with your father's blessing."

"Or what it's like to give everyone another reason to make fun of you," Malone says.

"Okay, okay, I get it," Wheeler says. "But let's remember that if Ellie hadn't given that quote to the paper about how we didn't paint the tower, they would've thought we were the Chaos Club. We'd be gods. But noooo, now we're just assclowns."

"You're used to being an assclown though," Malone says.

"Yeah, but on my terms, not someone else's."

"What I can't stop wondering is why us?" Malone says. "Of everyone the Chaos Club could pick for this prank, why the five of us?"

"Because we're stupid," Adleta says.

"Thanks for sharing. But seriously, hasn't anyone else thought of this?"

I have. A lot. If there's anything positive about my self-imposed isolation in the theater, it's that I've had a lot of time to think. And all those thoughts haven't been bad.

I feel different, like whoever went up the tower isn't the same person who came back down. And I do have an answer for Malone. I'm just not sure how to answer her without someone tossing my body over the railing. But regardless of the shameful way Just Max had me hiding out today, Not Max has definite opinions on what needs to be done in this situation, and he's not about to shut up. So while I'm nervous to say anything, I have to.

"We were picked because we're easy targets," I say.

Malone stops painting and looks at me.

"Excuse me?"

"We're easy targets," I repeat. "Adleta's right. We were stupid. We made it easy for them."

"How am I an easy target?" Malone says. She's not holding the paintbrush like a knife, but considering her tone of voice, she might as well be.

"Because of what happened last year with your picture. It made you a victim, so of course you'd want to join the Chaos Club."

Now Malone's coming at me, ready to paint me blue, and I back up with my hands out.

"Whoa, hold on," I say. "We're all that way. We all have reasons we'd fall for that invite. I went because I don't have shit going on in my life. Ellie's in the same boat as you, but with her dad and the book thing."

"What about him?" Malone says, pointing to Wheeler. "How's he a target?"

I don't have to answer because Wheeler does it for me.

"Are you seriously asking that question? An invitation to join a club known for pulling pranks and, by their very name, causing chaos? They could've written 'This is all a setup' on the card and I still would've shown up."

"Okay, that was dumb of me," Malone says.

All of us have stopped painting now, and from the base of the tower, Stranko shouts up, "Get back to work!"

"Asshole," Wheeler says.

"You don't know the half of it," Adleta says. "So what about me? How am I a target?"

Actually, the answer to Adleta's question is simple. But answering him is hard. No one wants to die young.

Still, Heist Rule #8 says, *Recruit a strong crew*, and no one is stronger than Adleta. Literally.

"People have been talking about you behind your back ever since you screwed up in the tournament game last year," I say, then brace myself. If death comes, I hope it's quick and painless.

But Adleta doesn't murder me.

At least not yet.

"What do people say?" he asks.

Wheeler says, "That you have anger-management issues that would make the Hulk jealous."

"Is that so?"

"Sorry, dude. It's the truth."

Last year during the state lacrosse regional semifinals, Adleta, doing his best impersonation of his father, screamed at a ref and got thrown out of the game. The team was already playing shorthanded, and losing him sealed their fate. I didn't see the game, but supposedly, his dad had to be restrained by security from murdering the ref, then Tim.

"Why does getting thrown out of a game make me an easy target?" Adleta says.

"Because when you feel powerless, you'll do anything to feel better about yourself."

Thank you, Psychology 101.

"You may be right, but that's not why I showed up."

"Then why did you?" Malone asks.

Tim doesn't answer; instead, he turns his back and resumes painting the tower.

"So let's say you're right, Max," Ellie says. "What if all of us were chosen because we were easy targets. What are we supposed to do about it?"

It's all been leading up to this. If you've never seen *Ocean's Eleven*, there's a scene where Danny Ocean, the group's mastermind, gets everyone together and pitches the impossible heist of robbing three casinos in one night. I'm no Danny Ocean, but I did watch that scene three times today on my phone in study hall, planning for this moment. *Steal from the best*—that's my motto. It's time for Not Max to step up.

"I think we're all pissed about what happened to us," I say. "And we should be. We look like idiots up here, and no one's going to let us forget about that. But I think the

Chaos Club messed up. We're not the type of people to just roll over and take it. I might have been, but I'm not going to be anymore."

"Me either," Adleta says.

"Yep," Wheeler says.

"I agree," Ellie says.

"So, revenge?" Malone asks.

"No, not just revenge," I say. "That's too shortsighted. I don't want to just get back at the people who pranked us. Anyone could do that." I throw in a dramatic pause here—the result of watching way too many movies. "What I want is to nuke the Chaos Club out of existence, to be the ones to end their secret society forever."

Go big, right?

Ellie claps her hands once.

"Excellent!"

"Abso-freakin'-lutely, dude!" Wheeler says.

Even Adleta's smiling.

And, of course, Malone's shaking her head no.

"Nice goal. But like you said, we don't even know who they are."

"Right, I have a plan for that. But before I get into it, what I'm thinking could get us in a lot of trouble. If I explain everything and someone wants out, that's cool."

"Oh, I like the sound of this," Ellie says.

Of course she does. It was her whispered "we need a plan" last night that really made me take this seriously. If getting to spend time with Ellie means having to risk

Stranko's wrath and possible grounding by my parents until I'm eighty, then I'll take that chance.

"How do we start?" Wheeler says.

"We need as much info on the Chaos Club as we can get," I say.

Heist Rule #9: *Know your enemy.*

"Do you have a plan to do that?" Malone asks.

"I do."

And I tell them my idea. It's so ridiculously dangerous that once I'm finished explaining, even Wheeler is slack jawed.

Ellie finally breaks the silence by bursting into heavy laughter. Soon all of us are in hysterics at the absurdity of the proposal. From the base of the tower, Stranko shouts repeatedly at us to get back to painting, but we ignore him.

"Game on," Ellie says between gulps of air, her eyes full of tears. "Game. On."

CHAPTER 6

Ellie calls it Operation Stranko Caper and gives each member of the Water Tower Five code names related to his or her role.

Adleta is Goon.

Malone is Shadow.

Wheeler is Potatoes.

Ellie is Crybaby.

And I'm Bleeder.

But at the moment, waiting for zero hour while standing in the back hallway where I can view the busy cafeteria, I'm feeling more like Puker because I want to sprint to the bathroom to vomit up my guts.

And to think this was all my idea.

Here's Heist Planning 101:

1. Identify your target. In this case, the target is Stranko's phone. Clearly he's investigating the Chaos Club; the pictures he took in the office prove that. Who knows what other evidence against them he might have?

2. Formulate a plan. It took a week of observing Stranko during school (all of us) and after (thank you, Adleta)

to realize he's most separated from his phone during lunch duty. It sits on a table on the stage next to where Stranko polices the cafeteria. Now if he were to be pulled away from the stage...

3. Practice, practice, practice. The five of us rehearsed our roles for more than a week. The plan isn't the most complicated, but we only have one shot at this.

Our final run-through of the plan lasted two hours on Saturday, with Ellie and Wheeler the most excited. Even Adleta, who's probably risking at least a thousand push-ups every day for the rest of his life, liked the idea. Malone, go figure, predicted failure.

"It won't work," she said. "Maybe in a movie, yes, but not in real life it won't."

"No, they won't see it coming," I said. "No one expects things like this to happen and especially not from us. We're trying to stay out of trouble, remember? Why would we risk getting suspended?"

"Max is right," Adleta said. "There'll be too much going on for Stranko to realize what's happened. It's going to work."

"What if we get caught?"

"Then we do what you should do whenever you get busted," Wheeler said. "We lie our asses off."

I don't mind Malone's concerns. In fact, I appreciate them. The more I'm around her, the more I depend on her skepticism. Every heist crew needs someone to point out the weaknesses in a plan. Malone's perfect for that. She's also tech-savvy, a brilliant artist, and athletic as hell. A jack-of-all-trades really. Or more like a jill-of-all-trades.

A heist can go wrong for any number of reasons, the worst of which is the double cross. You can just never be sure if everyone is really on your side or if they're working an angle. I don't necessarily think anyone in my crew is behind the setup at the water tower, but the hint of doubt is there. Still, why would someone set us up to get busted and include him or herself in the busting? It makes no sense.

However, if one of the crew did it, my bet is on Adleta. He's the one I know the least. If he's setting us up for an even bigger fall than the water tower, the Stranko Caper is the perfect time for a double cross. But Heist Rule #10 is *Trust your crew*, so that's what Not Max is going to do.

We picked Monday for our heist because that's the school day where everyone, even the administration, just slogs through until the final bell. At the time I was excited, but now it's nausea city. Reality sucks that way. But I'm not going to back down and hide in the theater again like I did the day after the water tower. Not that I could put a stop to our plan if I wanted to. Everyone's in position. The pin's pulled and the grenade heaved. All I can do is try not to get my head blown off.

On stage, Stranko reads something on his phone, then

places it on the table beside him before returning to his surveillance. In a lot of ways, thinking of him as a prison guard is dead-on. The entire building is a prison, with the staff as guards, students as prisoners, and rules that dictate when we can stand up and leave, talk, and even go to the bathroom. The school even has security cameras, which are positioned in all corners of the cafeteria. I've seen the room with the video monitors though, and I'm not as worried as I might be in a newer school. The monitors here are in black and white and the images blurry, like it may be the first security system ever created—maybe used back in the Garden of Eden where God watched a grainy image of Eve heisting that apple.

Then, right on cue at 11:45, Crybaby, sitting at her usual table near the front of the cafeteria, pushes her tray aside and puts her head down in her arms.

Step One, the Split, has begun.

Crybaby's friend, Vickie, is the first to notice the weeping and puts a hand on Ellie's shoulder, leaning in to check on her. Crybaby goes for the Academy Award then, shoving away her friend's hand and now quaking, refusing to lift her head. It isn't long before three girls are rubbing Crybaby's shoulders, begging her to tell them what's wrong. And still she refuses to lift her head.

It's beautiful.

Ellie was right—all those skits she was forced to

perform in front of the church honed her acting chops. She could make a killing as a professional grifter.

Vickie, panicking now, searches the cafeteria for help, and her eyes fall on Mrs. B and Stranko at their posts on the stage. She runs to Mrs. B—no girl would ever go to Stranko with an obviously girl-related problem—who wastes no time hurrying to Crybaby.

Others in the cafeteria notice the drama at this point and watch as Mrs. Barber convinces Crybaby, her face scarlet and tearstained, to accompany her to the office. The two leave the cafeteria, successfully splitting up Mrs. B and Stranko, who's about to fall victim to:

Step Two: the Diversion.

Fake it till you feel it.

That's what I tell myself as I swallow hard and take a deep breath.

Then I step into the cafeteria holding over my head Stranko's greatest possession: the lacrosse state championship trophy. Stranko doesn't have any children, but if he did, I'm pretty sure he'd save the trophy first if there were a fire. He carts that stupid thing out at every start-of-the-year meeting as an example of Asheville's excellence. Only ten minutes earlier I waltzed into Stranko's coaching office in the athletic wing and took the trophy I now hold high over my head.

There's no turning back.

I'm on a suicide mission as I approach the first set of tables while trying to remain calm. Which is impossible. Every step I take is one step closer to the complete batshit chaos that we've planned. I weave my way toward Stranko at the front of the stage, a few heads turning toward me but no one important. My throat gets drier with each step because I'm about to find out Adleta's real intentions. If he really is working with the Chaos Club, he'll screw this up on purpose. If that happens, there's a good chance I'll spend the next year being traded for cigarettes in jail.

I'm watching the lacrosse table, waiting, when Goon, right on cue, stands up, points, and shouts, "What the hell?"

The team members jerk their heads my way, and I'm filled with complete crap-your-pants fear when I see the menace in their eyes. But none of it matches the pure hatred on Goon's face. He's on his feet, stalking toward me, fists at his sides and the rest of the team following, hungry to tear my head off for daring to touch the symbol of the lacrosse team's dominance.

I never should have trusted him.

"Wait, no—" I say, backing up.

"You're dead."

His anger is so authentic, so primal, that I freeze, wishing I'd told my parents I loved them this morning because I'll be spending the next decade in a coma.

That's when Goon winks.

And I understand.

I should never have doubted him.

"Dead," Goon shouts, and he comes faster now.

My feet unstick from the floor, and I backpedal a few steps before turning and running for my life, the trophy tight in my hands. I zigzag around tables, with Goon's bull-like grunting close behind. I hear other footsteps too, and I know the rest of the lacrosse team is salivating at the chance to kill. Kids leap up to watch the excitement, and I race for Potatoes's table.

Stranko leaps down from the stage now, shouting, "Cobb, get over here!"

It's worry, though, not anger in his voice. Sure, I'm about to get murdered in front of hundreds of witnesses, but God forbid the championship trophy gets damaged.

The entire cafeteria rises to its feet, cheering. Stranko angles to cut me off, and I turn toward the front of the stage. Goon closes in a few feet behind me now, ready to maul me when he gets the chance.

It never happens.

The second I pass Potatoes, he jumps up from his chair directly into Goon's path and yells, "I'll save you, dude!"

I don't get to see Potatoes get stampeded and eventually tossed onto the stage like a…well, like a sack of potatoes, hence the name…but I hear the collision as he smashes into the table. Or possibly through the wall. I want to look back—this may be the last time I see Wheeler alive—but I don't have time.

Wheeler's the crew's maniac, the person who doesn't give a shit for personal safety and is willing do whatever's necessary to make the heist work. In Wheeler's case, the possibility of a hospital stay and therefore missed school was all it took for him to accept the job.

I run to Stranko for safety and hold out the trophy. He jerks it from my hands, pulling it close to his chest like it's the Holy Grail. Then Goon tackles me, crushing my spine and sending me across the tiled floor. We rehearsed the tackle in my basement using pratfalls Ellie learned in theater class, but Goon, fully embracing his role here, crashes into me like he's trying to take off a lacrosse opponent's head. My body screams in pain, or maybe that's me. I'm pinned to the floor, my cheek wet from what I'm guessing is blood. If so, it'd fit my code name.

I manage to lift my head up just enough to see Potatoes, angling through the crowd toward Shadow, sitting alone in back, with the illegal cell phone data extraction device Potatoes borrowed from one of his H8box friends.

Step Three, the Grab, is complete.

Or not.

I can't be sure the Grab is a success because I'm under a pile of lacrosse players swinging blindly, doing more damage to each other than to me. Over their shouts, Stranko yells for them to stop, although with not as much urgency as I would like. Goon smothers me with his weight, pulling his punches and wrestling more than anything. He has my knee pinned against my ear and smiles widely, like this is the most fun he's had in his life.

"I can't breathe," I eek out.

Goon lets off a bit, but it isn't until other teachers arrive to stop the fight that the chaos ends. The fight's over, but the shouting in the cafeteria seems louder than ever.

Goon whispers, "Time?"

"Yeah."

He pushes backward, and the players on top of us fall away. I'm supposed to act hurt, with lots of limping and groaning, maybe even pretend to pass out. But acting isn't necessary because my entire body throbs like one massive exposed nerve.

"Get up," Stranko snarls, practically yanking my arm from its socket.

I stumble to my knees, then, achingly, to my feet. Varelman and the rest of the lacrosse team breathe hard, fists clenched at their sides like they still might come at me. I risk a quick look to Shadow sitting hunched over her laptop. Potatoes is nowhere to be found.

"You're finished here," Stranko says.

"But I was only—"

"Shut up." He turns to Goon and says, "Return the trophy and get your ass to my office."

I'm led away to cheers. I can't tell if the students are on my side or are calling for my beheading, but Stranko's opinion is clear.

"I'll have you expelled by the end of the day."

"I didn't do anything."

"Shut your mouth."

If being a jerk keeps Stranko's focus on me instead of what I hope is happening right now in the cafeteria, he can say whatever he wants. He drags me through the hall to his office, his grip so tight he's almost grinding bone. His administrative office is beside Mrs. B's, and just as we're passing, she and Crybaby, whose eyes are puffy from her crying fit, emerge.

"What happened?" Mrs. B says.

"Cobb decided to get cute and race around the cafeteria with the state lacrosse trophy. I'll handle it."

Mrs. B's face remains calm as she looks at me.

"Max?"

"But he told me to do it," I say, pointing at Stranko.

His grip goes from tight to crushing.

"What did you say?"

"You sent me a note."

Both administrators look confused. Mrs. B steps back into her office, saying, "Let's discuss this in here. Ellie, return to lunch. If you need to talk more, I'm here."

But Crybaby doesn't leave.

"Mrs. Barber?" she says. Her voice is so thin and innocent I have a hard time keeping a straight face. "I think I know what Max is talking about."

Mrs. B sighs and waves Ellie into the office with us. Crybaby and I are on one side of the principal's desk, with Mrs. B and Stranko on the other.

"Do you want to call your parents first, Max?" Mrs. B asks.

"There's no reason to. I didn't do anything. I got a note from him to bring the trophy to the cafeteria."

"I didn't send you a note," Stranko snarls.

"But I have it right here."

I take the purple office note from my pocket and hand it to Mrs. B.

She reads, "Bring the lacrosse trophy to lunch. I want to teach you something."

"That's not my handwriting," Stranko says. "He forged this."

Mrs. B gives me a look that says, *Well?*

I go all Lifetime Movie on them, making my eyes bug out and trying to sound as pathetic as possible when I deliver my scripted line.

"But Mrs. Hansen gave me that note!"

Crybaby had me practice that line, coaching me on how to sound desperate. I don't dare look at her now because I'll start laughing.

"So Mrs. Hansen is out to get you? Is that it?" Stranko smirks.

"No, she just—"

"That Mrs. Hansen wanted to get you in trouble?"

"No, but—"

Then, Crybaby, right on cue, "I took the note to her."

Stranko's jaw almost drops off his skull.

"Second period," Crybaby says. "This was one of the

notes I delivered that period. It was in with the others. She told me she didn't have Max until fourth, but when that happens, I just say to give it to him when he shows up. Mrs. Hansen said she would."

I'd easily pay a thousand dollars for a picture of the shock on Stranko's face during Crybaby's explanation. His mouth is open, but nothing's coming out.

"You didn't find this note the least bit suspicious, Max?" Mrs. B asks.

"Why would I? It's an official pass. Besides, I don't want to get in any more trouble."

"What would be the point of having you bring me the trophy?" Stranko says.

"I have no idea. Maybe you thought I'd feel some sort of pride if I carried the trophy and I'd join the team."

"Why would I want that?"

"Because you told me the other day how much I could learn from the lacrosse team."

This time, I'd pay two thousand dollars for a picture of Stranko's face.

"I swear I didn't write that note, Mrs. B," I said.

This is the truth.

"Do you have any idea who did?"

"No."

And this is a lie.

The bell rings, signaling the end of lunch. If all is going according to plan, Malone has uploaded the contents of Stranko's memory card to her computer and Wheeler has the phone back on stage. That's a lot of ifs.

"Max," Mrs. Barber starts, "this is the second time you've fallen for something like this. There's a fine line between being legitimately tricked and simply being gullible. Your decisions, especially this one, are well on the side of being gullible. You have to be more careful."

"Yes, ma'am," I say.

Stranko may have a stroke right in front of me.

"However, it sounds like you and Mr. Adleta caused quite an unnecessary scene, and that can't be dismissed as easily. What do you think, Mr. Stranko? Does a day of in-school suspension seem fair?"

Stranko shakes his head.

"I want him gone for a week at least."

"That may be a bit much," she says. "What about work crew instead? They wrecked part of the school; they'll clean part of the school. We'll make the punishment fit the crime."

"Fine," he spits. "But we add Dave Wheeler to that list too."

"That's fine. And I'll have to call your parents about this, Max. They are in town this time, right?"

"Yeah, but here," I say and pull out a pen. "Can I have one of those Post-its?"

On it, I write Mom's and Dad's work numbers. Another day of the school calling the unmanned phone in the church nursery is just asking for trouble.

"You can get them at those numbers. They're usually not home until late."

"Thank you, Max," Mrs. B says. "You both can go. Thanks for your help, Ellie."

"No problem, Mrs. Barber."

We walk out of the office and into the hall, and it's only when we're around the corner that the both of us break into hysterics.

Step Four: the Getaway. Complete.

"The *Ocean's Eleven* team couldn't have done it any smoother," Ellie says.

"You were quite the actress, Crybaby," I tell her.

"No, Crybaby was a one-timer. Call me Puma."

"What?"

"Puma. That's my official code name. And you're Mongoose."

"I thought I was the Bleeder."

"That's for today only. You're Mongoose from here on out."

It's a lot catchier than Not Max. And hell, Ellie can call me Bloody Diarrhea for all I care.

"So, Puma, huh?"

"And don't you forget it," Ellie says.

Before I can respond, she goes on her tiptoes and kisses me on the cheek.

"Gotta get to class," she says and, catlike, is gone.

CHAPTER 7

"So what can we steal next?"

Ellie's question, of course.

The five of us are debriefing—something that occurs in every heist film after a mission is complete and everyone is back at headquarters. In this case, headquarters is my basement seven hours following the Stranko Caper, and the debriefing is more of a celebration than a review of the heist.

"Dude, the way we pulled that off, could you imagine the epic pranks we could do if we really were in the Chaos Club? No one could stop us," Wheeler says.

"Yeah, we're the ones who should've been in the Chaos Club," I say.

"And Stranko never saw any of it coming," Malone says. "I watched all of it from the back of the cafeteria, and no one had any idea what was going on. It was amazing. Tim tackled you so hard I thought you were dead."

"My ribs are still killing me," I say.

"Sorry," Adleta says.

"No, I just wish I could've seen what happened after you took me out."

"Yeah, you missed Wheeler gank the phone," Malone

says. "I swear he could be a professional thief, the pickup was so smooth."

"Because he threw me right into it," Wheeler says.

"Again, sorry," Adleta says.

Malone continues, "When Wheeler dropped the phone in my lap, I got so paranoid, I put it up my shirt so no one would see it."

"That's so hot," Wheeler says.

Malone laughs and hands him a small black box the size of a deck of cards, the phone-cloning device he borrowed from a friend on H8box.

"And this thing is great. Dangerous but great. It downloaded everything in about a minute," Malone says.

"So no problems?" I say.

"No problems."

"And no problems getting the phone back to the stage?" I ask Wheeler.

"Nope."

"Aww, I feel like I missed all the fun," Ellie says.

"No, you were great," Adleta says. "I watched you crying at your table and really thought you were upset. If you hadn't pulled that off, the plan wouldn't have worked."

"Thanks, but next time I want to do something more dangerous."

"No problem," I say. "Adleta can Hulk-smash you, and I'll get to stay in one piece."

"Deal," Ellie says.

Having everyone here has calmed me down. From the

moment I got home, I've imagined answering the front door and Stranko Tasering me before hauling me off to jail, where real criminals perform unspeakable acts on me. Of course, if Stranko does show up, he'll have to get in line behind my parents, who have grounded me for a week after talking to Mrs. B. I didn't argue the punishment and kept quiet throughout the *you've got to use your head better* lecture. The only reason they let me have the others over tonight is that I used the magic words: class project. If you haven't learned yet, starting a sentence with "I have this big class project…" hypnotizes parents to immediately let you do whatever you ask—break curfew, fire a bazooka, buy a monkey online, you name it.

And a quick word on my parents: If you're hoping for *A Child Called "It"*–like abuse or emotional scars that'll have me seeing a team of psychiatrists through adulthood, you'll be disappointed. My parents are smart, mostly calm, and—I say this with some guilt—trusting. Dad's a news producer at Channel 4 ("Your home for hometown news!"), and Mom works for an agency finding jobs for people who don't have them. The worst thing I can say about them is they've raised a revenge-driven teenager who's secretly plotting to ruin lives. But isn't everyone doing that?

"Did you guys bring what I asked?" Malone says.

We all fish into our pockets for flash drives while on the couch Malone fires up her laptop. Her wallpaper is a girl in black boots, black-and-white striped tights, and a black dress who's spray-painting "Riots, Not Diets" on a brick wall. All of us, even Adleta, crowd around her.

"Okay, so there's good news and bad news," Malone says. "The bad news is there really wasn't anything helpful in the phone's memory. A bunch of sports news apps, all the Angry Birds games—which, weird, right?—and zero photos. He's completely boring."

"But we saw him take pictures," Ellie says.

"And he's on that phone all the time," Adleta adds.

"Which leads me to the good news," Malone says. "There's nothing on his phone because he stores everything in his cloud, and I downloaded everything in there."

"Have you looked through it yet?" I ask.

"I skimmed it, but I didn't have the time to read it all. It would take a week."

"That long?"

"*Obsesssive*'s the word I'd use to describe it."

Once the files are transferred, I see what Malone means. On my laptop, the folder labeled Chaos Club expands into five subfolders: History, Evidence, Witnesses, Suspects, and Pictures. A quick scroll through each reveals at least seven hundred files total.

"See what I mean?" Malone says. "It's way too much for any one person to sift through."

"I'll do it," Ellie says. "I don't really have the time, but I'll make it. I want the Chaos Club dead."

It's the harshest I've ever heard Ellie sound. She must see the look I give her because she says, "No, it's true.

And not just for the water tower, but for last year. I couldn't care less about them calling my dad a Nazi. I might even agree with them. But kids are still doing that whole *Seig Heil* thing to me in the hall. Someone even keyed a swastika into my car door last week. We had it buffed out, but the outline is still there. I mean, it's bad enough being known as a goody-goody, there's not much I can do about that, but I'm being blamed for something I wasn't a part of. No one hears the fights I get into with my dad about censorship or how the earth isn't only six thousand years old or how we should be teaching more than abstinence in health class, but I also have to deal with finding pictures of Hitler in my locker. I blame the Chaos Club for all that."

An awkward silence falls on the room until Malone says, "I'm sorry. I didn't know."

"None of you would," Ellie says. "You're not people who would do that. But the ones who would and do need to pay."

A moment later, a muffled ring tone sounds out. Wheeler fishes into his jacket pocket with his left hand and the ringing stops.

But in his right hand, Wheeler's still holding his cell phone.

So two phones?

Malone and I understand at the same time.

She grabs Wheeler's left hand before he can pull it from his pocket.

"Hey, wait," he says.

Malone goes into attack mode, practically climbing onto Wheeler to get at his jacket pocket. He struggles, pinning his hand against the opening, but Malone pinches his earlobe between two fingernails. Wheeler lets out a shriek that would make a six-year-old girl proud and jerks his hand from his pocket to cover his ear.

Malone thrusts her hand into his pocket, and a second later she's holding up the hidden phone.

Stranko's phone.

"You idiot," Malone says.

"Look, I know it looks bad, but there were too many teachers around, and I got to thinking about the damage we could do, so…" Wheeler trails off.

"So you kept it," Malone finishes, pissed.

"We're screwed," Adleta says.

"Look, it wasn't my plan to keep the phone, but I couldn't get it back to the table and thought about leaving it in the bathroom or something, but then I got to thinking—"

"Which is never a good sign," I say.

"—that everything's on here," Wheeler says. "Malone's right—there's nothing about the Chaos Club on the phone, but his contact list is a gold mine. It's all here—Stranko's home phone number, address, teacher's numbers, people he emails, everything."

"I downloaded all that too," Malone says.

"Yeah, but this is his *phone*. We can call from it or send texts; they'll all look like they're coming from Stranko."

"Until he has his service discontinued," I say.

"But until then, think of the havoc we could unleash. You don't blow an opportunity like this. That guy's been a pain in the ass for years. We have an obligation to every kid he's terrorized. His balls are ours now. We need to squeeze them until they explode."

"Ewww," Ellie says.

"You have to get rid of that," I say. "If you get caught with it, you'll get expelled. And once he figures out how you got it, we'll be expelled too."

"Dude, he's not going to find out. I disabled Find My Phone and turned off the location services. I'm not dumb enough to bring it to school either."

"But you are dumb enough to walk around with it," Malone says.

"That was just for tonight. I was going to show all of you that I had it. Seriously, I'm going to hide it in my house tonight. Come on, trust me. We might need it later. Besides, he uses a cloud app for storage. If he discovers anything new about the Chaos Club, it'll upload into the cloud. It's like having access to his brain."

"And if he changes the password?" Adleta asks.

"Then the phone is useless and I get rid of it. But that's a big *if*. I doubt Stranko thinks someone stole his phone. He probably just thinks he left it somewhere."

"He's not stupid," Adleta warns. "An asshole, yes, but not stupid. I've known him too long. We can't underestimate him."

"Tim's right," Malone says. "We need to be careful with Stranko. Ever since this started, I've been thinking a lot about him. I don't think he knows how awful he is. In his mind, I'll bet he believes he's helping the school by being such a tight ass that discipline keeps things under control. It's like when we read *The Lord of the Flies* our freshman year; none of those kids thought they were doing the wrong thing, even though they were. I think Stranko's just doing what he thinks is best for the school."

"Like that's an excuse for being a prick," Wheeler says.

"It's not, but it explains him maybe."

Ellie looks up from my laptop which she's been reading something on and says, "Did you see this other subfolder hidden in Pictures? It has all the school's information. It has the administrative handbook, security codes, emergency procedures, even an insanely detailed map. This could come in handy."

"I'll take a handy," Wheeler says.

"Again, ewww."

I look over Ellie's shoulder at the file she's talking about. She's right—it has everything you could want to know about the inner workings of Asheville High School. And to think we didn't even have to break into an architect's office to steal the original blueprints. God bless technology.

"Holy shit!" Wheeler says, leaping to his feet a couple minutes later. "You're not going to believe this one. History, 1989. Oh man."

"That's when my parents graduated," I say.

"Well, wait till you see."

My fingers fly over the screen until I come across the 1989 folder. The print is so small I have to squint:

Friday, May 19th
Senior Picnic Bird Attack

During tug-of-war on the all-purpose field, a whistle sounded and a flock of birds flew out of Johnson's Woods and descended on the picnic, flying everywhere and relieving themselves on everyone.

"Yuck," Ellie says.

"No, it's get better," Wheeler says. "Open the picture."

Thirty seconds later, all of us are laughing as hard as Wheeler. A blur of birds fills the screen, their white bird shit streaking down the kids' shirts and matting their hair. Students run around as if caught in the middle of a bombing run. But it's the guy standing in the middle of the photo with his head shit splattered as he swings at passing birds that make this the single greatest photo in the history of mankind.

Stranko.

"T-shirts," Wheeler says, borderline hyperventilating. "We need to make T-shirts."

"And rent a billboard," Adleta adds.

It's not a bad idea. What I really want to know though

is how they pulled off a prank like that. And I have a good idea who to ask. Uncle Boyd.

"So where do we go from here?" Malone soon asks. "How does this help us find the Chaos Club?"

"Because it's information. And yeah, the Chaos Club is anonymous. We know that. But what if we make them find us instead?" I say.

"I think they already did that, dude," Wheeler says.

"That's not what I mean. What's cool about the Chaos Club is you never know when they're going to strike next. That's probably why they've never been caught. They're usually good for a few pranks a year and always one at the end of the year, but what if they suddenly started doing more?"

"Why would they do that?" Adleta said.

"They wouldn't."

"So then what's your point?"

"The five of us pretend to be the Chaos Club," Malone says, sitting up. "That's what you mean, isn't it? You want us to pull pranks too."

"That's the idea."

"What will pulling pranks help?" Wheeler asks. "The goal is to find out who they are and destroy them, not do their work for them. Why make them even bigger heroes than they already are?"

Adleta gets it now too.

"Oh, you don't want us to just pull pranks—you want us to pull bad pranks, ones that would make the administration have to act. Is that it?"

"Yeah, I got the idea in Watson's class the other day when he said sometimes it's good for symbols to be torn down. I started thinking, what if we hijack the Chaos Club—their ideas, their websites, even their cards—until they finally have to show themselves? They've lived in the shadows for almost forty years. There's no way they're going to sit by and let us pretend we *are* the Chaos Club. They'll be forced to respond too, like the administration. Either way, it'll make things happen."

Everyone goes quiet thinking this over. I'll admit the plan's not foolproof—the Chaos Club could just ignore us and then we're putting ourselves at risk for no reason—but it's not an awful plan either.

"I like it," Wheeler says. "Destruction for a good cause. I'm in."

"What sort of pranks do you have in mind?" Adleta asks.

"Whatever gets their attention, especially anything dumb, elaborate, or over the top. The Chaos Club prides itself on quality. I'm sure the five of us can come up with some stupid pranks to draw them out or pranks where the administration would have to act."

Adleta says, "Count me in."

"And if we get caught?" Malone asks.

We all just look dumbly at each other.

"I don't need an answer," she says. "I'm just trying to see all the angles. But I'm in too."

"Good," I say, "because I need you to use your art skills

to make imitations of the Chaos Club business cards. Can you do that?"

"That should be easy enough. Design wise, their cards are pretty basic."

Leaving only one person—Ellie.

"I'll do it on one condition," she says. "We make it a contest. Best prank wins. That'll make it a lot more fun."

"I like it," Malone says. "A prank off."

"Great idea," I say, and Ellie grins with her whole face.

"What's the prize?" Wheeler asks.

"Bragging rights," Malone says.

"No," Ellie says, "even better, the winner gets a guaranteed yes."

"A what?" Adleta says.

"Whoever we decides wins gets to ask for something from us and we have to say yes. It'll be fun."

"I am one hundred percent in favor of this prize," Wheeler says.

"Why am I imagining your request would include some sort of nudity...or worse?" Malone says.

"Because you know me so well, Kate, duh."

"Don't worry," Ellie says to Malone. "He won't win. Girls are a lot more creative than boys."

"If there's a winner, does that mean there's a loser too?" I ask.

"Oh, you don't want to be the loser," Ellie says, twisting an invisible mustache. "There will be dire consequences for the loser."

"How do we determine who has the best prank?" Adleta says.

"Everyone gets a vote," Malone says, "but I think we'll know the winner when we see it."

"Is there a time limit?" Ellie asks.

"Well, it obviously has to be before we expose the Chaos Club," Malone says.

"And before the last day of school," Wheeler adds.

"But no outside help," I say. "I don't want this extending outside this room."

"Good idea," Malone says.

"Can we work in pairs?" Ellie asks.

"If someone wants to, then yeah," Adleta says.

"Good." Ellie smiles my way, making my stomach twinge. "So we're all in agreement on the rules?"

I run down my mental checklist and say, "Wheeler, what about a copycat website? Could we make it look just like theirs, steal all their pictures and stuff, but make the Chaos Club look ridiculous? I think that would get their attention."

"Dude, you want me to be irritating? That's right up my alley."

Exactly, it's Heist Rule #11: *Play to your crew's strengths.*

Because pranks are really nothing but heists for beginners. Same concepts, same rules, only without the federal offense aspect involved—at least hopefully without.

"What can I do?" Ellie asks.

"How about being available to anyone who may need

student or teacher info? You can get all that as an office aide, right?"

"Not just that, but the principal's schedules, keys to any place on school grounds, you name it."

"They let you at that stuff?" Malone says.

"Well, let's just say the office is a busy place," Ellie says. "So yeah, I can do that."

"And me?" Adleta says.

"You're the inside man with Stranko," I say. "I need you to stay close to him—closer than you'd normally be probably—and report back on anything you hear."

Adleta thinks it over and says, "That means I'm going to have to apologize."

"Uh, yeah."

What's shocking is that I'm not afraid of Adleta anymore. Or not as much as I used to be. I mean, yeah, he could probably throw me straight up through the ceiling into the family room, but after the Stranko Caper, I trust him.

"Okay, I'll apologize tomorrow, then start sucking up to him."

"Cool," I say. "I know you don't want to do it, but we need it. I'll make it up to you somehow."

"How about letting me cage-match Stranko?"

"I'll see what I can do."

The meeting breaks up shortly after that, and we head upstairs, Wheeler leading the way, followed by Adleta and Malone. Ellie pauses at the base of the steps.

"Nice job today, Mongoose."

My ears begin to burn.

I need to say something clever. Or suave. Or witty. Something.

I know what James Bond would do in this situation—he'd grab Ellie and plant some superspy kiss on her that makes her clothes magically fall from her body. I'm still playing at beginner level though, so Not Max goes for something a little more basic.

"Maybe we should read through the files together?"

"Great idea! This weekend?"

Ugh. Stupid reality.

"I'm grounded for at least a week for being assigned to work crew," I say. "But maybe the weekend after that?"

Ellie shakes her head. "Let's make it this Friday."

"But my parents—"

"Just be ready around seven," Ellie says. "And act normal, Mongoose. I'll take care of the rest."

CHAPTER 8

Cows greet us at school the next day.

Nine of them.

On the roof.

Somehow during the night they've been: (A) paraded? (B) airlifted? (C) thrown? onto the main building, and now: (A) lounge? (B) graze? (C) wait? while we do our daily zombie walk inside. From the edge of the building where the cows stand hangs a sign reading: *Chaos Club.*

This is what we're up against.

"Awesome," the guy next to me says.

I can't argue with that.

"Hey, you're one of those Water Tower Five idiots, right?" he says.

I can't argue with that either.

Fifty yards down the sidewalk, Mrs. B, Stranko, and Officer Hale look up at the distraught cows, probably discussing how to get them down. Mrs. B has a small smile as she assesses the situation. But Stranko looks biblically constipated as he watches, and then unconsciously, pointlessly, reaches to his hip for the cell phone that isn't there.

Heh, heh, heh.

In Watson's first-period philosophy class, we have prime seats for the cow show. Having taught since before the wheel was invented, Watson knows we're useless until the cows are rescued, so he keeps the blinds open so we can watch. Watson's at his desk, wearing sandals, baggy pants that haven't been washed since the '90s, and an untucked short-sleeved shirt with a coffee stain on the stomach. All teachers at Asheville are required to wear dress pants and a shirt with the school mascot on it, but I guess when you've taught for more than thirty years, rules don't mean that much. Talking with Watson is Jeff Benz, Watson's senior aide. Students go all Hunger Games to become Watson's aide because it means doing little more than goofing off and joking with Watson.

Everyone watches as two trucks—one hauling a long metal ramp, and the other with an attached trailer— arrive out front. The ramp is extended to the roof, and two agitated men in cowboy boots ascend the ramp.

Watson says, "Jeff, do you know what it would be called if those cows all suddenly jumped off the roof?"

"Why no, Mr. Watson," Jeff says. "What would it be called if all the cows jumped?"

"Mooicide."

Groans fills the room.

"Don't mind me," Watson says. "I'm just milking the situation for your entertainment."

For the next thirty minutes, we witness the Great Cow Rescue until the men finally coax the animals down the ramp. Once on the ground, they're led past the Zippy the Eagle statue, an Asheville High landmark that the school paper recently reported will be removed for renovation. It's a good thing too. After years of numerous neon paint jobs and even the welding of a mauled metal squirrel into his beak, Zippy's just plain trashy looking.

Ellie and Malone are in this class with me, but we've all agreed it's best to play it cool. There's no reason to give people suspicions about who's behind the hell we're hoping to unleash. But speaking of hell, Libby Heckman's in here too. She sits three rows over from Malone and has spent the year giving her a death glare. But Malone pays Libby zero attention, something that only intensifies Libby's hate-generated stare. The fact that room is still standing is a miracle.

"Mr. Watson?" Tami Cantor says. "Do you get pissed when things like this happen?"

"You're asking if I get mad cow disease?" Watson says.

"Come on, I'm being serious. Don't interruptions like this bother you?"

"Well, if you've been paying attention, Ms. Cantor, you'd realize I'm all for the tearing down of symbols and making your mark in the world."

"Sort of like that right there?"

"Exactly," Watson says pointing to the *Write Your Name in the Wet Cement of the Universe* banner over the board. "Learn it. Know it. Live it. The Chaos Club may live up to its name, but I think it's good for a system to be shaken up at times. Of course, if you repeat that, I'll deny ever having said it."

With five minutes remaining in the period, the trailer gate is closed as the last cow disappears inside. Cheers erupt in our classroom and throughout the rest of the building.

"It's been a long time since I've *herd* that much enthusiasm," Watson says to Benz, loud enough for all of us to hear. "It's hard to have a beef with their interest though."

"Okay, but cud you ask them to stop?"

Over our groans, Jess Galley says, "Have the two of you have been thinking up cow puns the entire time?"

"You are udderly correct," Watson says.

On the way to second period, Malone sidles up to me, with Ellie following closely behind. Malone has us follow her to an empty locker bay, where she pulls a black Chaos Club card from her book bag.

"How did you do this so fast?" I ask.

"It didn't take too long, not once I found the right font. And we have a great laser printer at home," she says.

"How many did you make?"

"Just this prototype for now. I wanted to make sure it was okay before I printed more."

I look around to make sure no one can see us, then examine the card more closely.

"It's perfect. Looks exactly like the real ones."

"With one small addition," Malone says.

She points to a small white ink drop in the bottom left-hand corner. It takes me holding it inches from my eyes to see what it really is: a small water tower icon with a miniscule 5 on it.

"You know, sort of an extra f-you to the Chaos Club," Malone says.

"You don't think they'll notice?"

"Who cares if the Chaos Club notices? What are they going to do, prank us again? And if Stranko sees the change, he'll first have to figure out what it means, and even if he does, it's a long shot he connects it to us."

It's flimsy logic and a risk, but I like the addition and tell Malone so.

"Cool, thanks," she says. "So run a bunch?"

"Absolutely."

"I have a late shift at the climbing center tonight, but I should be able to get these finished after that."

I'm still amazed all this is happening. I ask people to do things, and they do it. If I'd known it was this easy, I'd have started speaking up years ago.

"So have you two figured out your pranks yet?" Ellie asks.

"I have an idea percolating," Malone says. "I just don't know how to pull it off yet."

"You'll come up with something," Ellie says, then turns to me.

I look at my feet.

"I'll take that as a no. I'm not worried though. You're good at planning things like that."

"Really?"

Ellie cocks her head.

"Are you fishing for compliments, Maxwell Cobb? Okay then, yes, you're good at plotting. Remember in Mr. Hubbard's seventh grade history class how our group's army beat everyone else in that military battle game? That was all because of you. And your Rube Goldberg device in science last year that maneuvered an egg across a table and cracked it into a bowl? Or what about that extra credit assignment you wrote about *Gatsby* for English? Is that enough evidence for you?"

"All right, I'll come up with something," I say.

"Make that something good enough and all your dreams can come true," she says.

Believe me, I've given the reward of a guaranteed yes more thought than the prank itself. I'm not exactly sure what I would do with the prize, but it would definitely be a strong test of my already-questionable morality.

"And even if you don't win," Ellie says, "at least make sure you don't lose. Because remember—dire consequences."

After school, Adleta, Wheeler, and I serve our first of five work crews, and to get straight to the point—work crew sucks. It's three hours of humiliation, sweeping the halls while kids deliberately toss garbage in our paths and chipping at crusty toilet bowls with a Spackle knife. Do me a favor and remind me of this day if I ever consider full-time employment in the custodial arts.

The only positive in the experience comes after an hour and a half of slave labor, when Mr. Jessup leads the three of us down a back hallway and through a set of heavy doors into an area marked *Restricted*. Along the walls are desks stacked three high. A mountain of boxes waits for us at the end of the corridor by the loading dock.

"What are all these?" Wheeler says.

"What the food comes in each week," Jessup says. "You need to tear the tape off the bottom of each and flatten them for the recycling bin out back."

"Can we have box cutters or something?" Adleta asks.

Jessup doesn't even bother replying. He leaves us staring at the mountain of brown boxes, unsure where to start.

"This blows," Wheeler says.

"No doubt," Adleta says and kicks at the pile.

In the next ten minutes, we each suffer a dozen paper cuts, and our shirts are soon covered in streaks of blood, like we're been sprinting through thornbushes.

"Screw this, man," Wheeler says. "I can't even feel my fingers anymore. It's break time."

We follow Wheeler back down the corridor, where

he stops halfway to the door and takes out his phone, opening a map I've never seen before.

"What are you doing?" I ask.

Wheeler ignores me and uses his shoulder to shove aside a series of desks, moving them just enough to expose a small cubbyhole door in the wall.

"Bingo," Wheeler says.

"How did you know that was there?" Adleta says, coming forward and moving the desks even farther.

"Stranko's files. There's a great map that shows a lot of the older parts of this building that are blocked off or hidden from us."

"You mean, like secret passages?" I ask, now getting out my phone to see what Wheeler's talking about.

"Not that cool, no, but there are shortcuts through this building and rooms that are closed off like this one."

Wheeler drops to his knees and slides a rusty latch on the door that sounds like a cat whose tail is being stepped on. The door opens with an equally painful shrieking noise, and Wheeler crawls through, disappearing into the dark.

"What do you think?" I say to Adleta.

"I think…uh-oh," Adleta says.

I turn, and coming our way is Becca Yancey.

Becca is a junior like us and could easily be class president, but she's too busy saving the world through organizing blood drives and raising money for leukemia victims. She also wears the Zippy mascot costume at every home football and basketball game, not that it helps us win. Right now, she's carrying a green recycling bin filled to the top with plastic bottles. If the rumor's true that she's moving at the end of the school year, I'm not sure who will fill her place. Is Gandhi still alive?

"Hey, Becca," Adleta says.

"Hi, guys. Find anything good?"

"Just goofing off," Adleta says. "Work crew and all."

"Yeah, I heard about that. Funny."

"You won't, uh..." and Tim motions to the open door.

"Don't be ridiculous," she says. "You boys have fun. I have twenty more bins to hunt down and empty."

Becca heads for the loading dock, and I call Wheeler back. His dirty face appears a few seconds later.

"What's back there?" Tim says.

"Just boxes of files and old floor hockey equipment," Wheeler says. "Stupid stuff like that."

"Maybe we come back when we have more time," I say. "There might be something cool."

"Like my balls," Wheeler says.

Adleta starts laughing.

"What does that mean?" I say.

"Dude, you've never played Like My Balls? How do you survive the day? It's all I ever do. Anytime the teacher makes a statement, try adding 'like my balls.' You know how like in history, Mr. Navarro is always saying, 'History is a living breathing thing...'"

"Like my balls," I finish.

"Exactly, man. It'll change your life."

"Like my balls."

"See? You're a natural."

Since we've committed petty theft together and scrubbed toilets next to each other, I decide now's probably a safe time to ask Adleta something that's bothered me for weeks.

"Can I ask you a question? Why'd you show up at the water tower? You don't seem the Chaos Club type."

"What does that mean?"

"No offense, dude," Wheeler says, "but he's right. You're more the organized-sports guy, not the cause-trouble guy."

Adleta looks away for a few long, uncomfortable seconds.

Finally, he says, "Because I need something that's just mine."

Wheeler says, "Huh?"

Adleta leans against a box before answering.

"Everyone knows I'm good at lacrosse, right? That it's pretty much all I do. But no one knows how Stranko convinced my dad to sign me up for an athletic trainer to keep me in the best shape possible so I can play in college and go pro. Or that now I have a dietician who tells me what I can eat. Or that I haven't had a free weekend in three years because I'm always at some lacrosse camp or tournament. No one even asked my opinion. And when I tried to register for AP U.S. History this year, Dad wouldn't let me because he said the extra work would get in the way of my training. Who does that?"

Wheeler and I look at each other, trying to figure out how to respond, but Adleta's not finished.

"It's like they're forcing me into being this thing I'm not sure I want to be. Yeah, I destroy on the lacrosse field, and that's cool and I like it, but I didn't choose this life—my dad did. And you've seen my dad. It's not like I can just tell him to lay off a bit. He'd lose his shit. It's what he does best. With the water tower, I hoped I'd have at least one thing that was just mine. But even that backfired, and now my dad and Stranko are on my ass even more. Part of me just wishes I'd tear my ACL and be done with it all for good."

It's weird seeing Adleta being, well, human. And an AP class? I wouldn't have guessed that in a million years, which makes me feel like a dick.

"That sucks, man," Wheeler says. "But at least you have us now."

"Yeah, you're part of a crew that's going to take down the Chaos Club," I say. "That's a big plus."

"Like my balls," Tim says, and we all start laughing so hard it's another five minutes before we start working again.

The rest of the school week is a continuation of tortuous ragging about the water tower, followed by three hours of slaving on work crew. The worst duty by far?

Cleaning out grease traps in the kitchen. I may never eat again.

By the time Friday evening finally arrives, I should be exhausted, but the excitement of going out with Ellie has me filled with adrenaline. I do the best *angry and bored grounded kid* I can, slumping around the house with the occasional dramatic sigh while secretly readying for a date without my parents becoming suspicious. This is not as easy as it sounds. It's hard to act normal when you drop your fork three times at the dinner table because your palms are so sweaty.

At six thirty, I put on a pair of jeans and a gray hoodie. I check the mirror, then switch the hoodie for a navy-blue T-shirt.

Then back to the hoodie.

Then a different pair of jeans.

God, is this what it's like going on dates?

Am I even allowed to call this a date?

Screw it, I'm calling it a date.

I finally go with my original getup, and for my brilliant idea of the week, I don't put on shoes or socks because I have to look unprepared.

A few minutes after seven o'clock, Dad calls up to me from downstairs.

My throat's so dry I can barely get out a "Yeah?"

"You have a visitor."

I do a quick check in the mirror, combing my hair with my fingers and breath-checking into my cupped hand. Coming down the stairs, I don't just have a lump in my throat—it's an entire watermelon.

Ellie's at the front door saying, "...due Monday and we were supposed to meet after school. It's twenty percent of our final grade and—"

It's not hard to see where she's going with this, so I play along just like I did in Mrs. B's office after nabbing Stranko's phone.

"Hey, Ellie."

My parents move aside, and there, glaring at me, stands Ellie in her black-and-gold Asheville High jacket, a red backpack at her feet.

"Where the heck were you?"

My mouth drops.

"Oh man..."

"I even reminded you after school, Max. You know I'm leaving with the youth group tomorrow morning and won't be back until late Sunday. How's this supposed to get done?"

Ellie drops to a knee and begins rifling through her backpack. She's breathing funny, and Mom and Dad looked concerned, even a bit worried. Ellie's so good, I'm starting to think I actually did forget to meet her.

"What's this project, Max?" Dad says.

"It's a research project comparing Greek philosophers," I say, improvising. "We've worked on it all week in class and were going to meet at the library today after school to finish. I just forgot. Maybe we could ask Watson for an extension on Monday?"

"That won't work," Ellie says. "How many times this week did he say 'Due Monday. No excuses'? My parents are going to kill me."

"What about finishing online?" Dad asks.

"We're not allowed to use the Internet," Ellie says. "Watson wants us doing what he calls 'old school research'—books, magazines, and newspapers only."

"We'll just turn in what we have," I say. "It should at least get us a C."

Mom and Dad practically shout, "What?"

"A C stinks, Max," Ellie says. "My parents don't accept Cs. They start researching convents to ship me off to when I get a B."

"We don't accept Cs either," Mom says, almost defensively.

Ellie puts her backpack on and says, "Look, I have to go. The library closes in three hours. I just wanted to see why you didn't show up. And now I know—because you're selfish. Forget it. I'll finish by myself."

And there it is, bobbing like a ripe worm waiting for my parents to bite. Mom's brow furrows, and I see her looking at me from the corner of her eye, but Dad chomps like he hasn't eaten in days.

"Get your shoes, Max," he says. "You're not going to leave her to do all the work."

"Unless you forgot your book bag at school too," Mom says.

"No, I've got it."

"Then go get it. Hurry up."

I walk, not run, to my room and sit on my bed, trying not to laugh. Or throw up.

Because confession time—I've never had a girlfriend. Or kissed a girl.

Or even had one over to the house.

It's not that I'm a member of the all-ugly team. It's just that the girlfriend-getting opportunities have been scarce. Okay, nonexistent. Mom, ever the optimist, tries to comfort me by saying I'm a "late bloomer," which is parent-speak for, "You are going to die a sad and lonely virgin."

When I get back downstairs, Ellie says, "I really appreciate this, Mr. and Mrs. Cobb. You're saving my life."

"I wouldn't go that far, but we're happy to help," Mom says. "The library closes at ten, right?"

"Yep," Ellie says. "I'll have him back right after that."

Mom and Dad tell us to be careful, and then we're out the door and heading down the walk, halfway to freedom.

Ellie whispers, "No matter what, don't look back."

No problem there.

Once we're safely inside Ellie's car, I say, "So you didn't go with the Crybaby this time?"

"I have more bullets in my gun than that, silly."

Ellie starts the car, and some terrible boy band song blasts from the speakers. She turns the radio down but not off.

"You look dressed to rob a bank," I say.

"Maybe next time. Tonight we have a different mission to complete. Ready, Mongoose?"

"Gun it, Puma."

And with that, Ellie gives a whoop before driving us off into the night.

CHAPTER 9

Located in the old part of town, the Whippy Dip Ice Cream Emporium's been in business for more than three decades. It was also the spot of my parents' first date when they were in high school. That's a bit too creepy of a coincidence for my liking.

Because it's mid–October and not exactly ice cream weather, the Whippy Dip is deserted. Or *desserted*, as Mr. Watson would proudly say. Still, we can see four workers through the closed Place Your Order Here window. That might seem like overkill, but after the football game's over—a game that we'll no doubt lose—there'll be a tsunami of students in the parking lot.

"You know, heist films say you should work in private as much as possible. I'm pretty sure the Whippy Dip doesn't count as private," I say.

"Yeah, but it's ice cream, Mongoose. Ice cream calls for rule breaking."

Ellie hums while looking over the massive menu. Me, I have my hands jammed in my pockets, trying to avoid the million and one worst-case scenarios I've dreamed up, most of which end with either me puking or Ellie losing a limb. We both order our cones—hers with sprinkles, mine without—and I insist on paying because, dammit, I'm standing by my belief that this is a date and that's what guys on dates do.

We sit at a nearby bench, where Ellie and I both take out our laptops. She also has a spiral notebook with her and flips through a dozen or so pages already filled with meticulous notes on the files in Stranko's cloud.

"Wow, you make me feel like a slacker," I say.

"Why? How much have you read through?"

"Er, only some."

"Meaning zero. But that's okay. I've been doing it all week during second period while I'm in the office. I have a lot more time than you anyway, with you doing work crew and all."

The next fifteen minutes are as un-date-like as they can possibly be. Ellie takes notes on files, commenting when she finds something interesting, while I make lame jokes and try to look at her while keeping my head pointed toward my laptop screen. Question: Is it possible to pull an eye muscle?

"Oh, here's something," Ellie says. "Look at this."

I scoot close enough that our hips touch.

The file Ellie's talking about is named AHS PR Plan, and it's a bullet-pointed list on how to raise the school's image in the community and beyond. Most of it's standard bureaucratic nonsense, like increase the number of National Merit Finalists, offer more AP courses, a Celebrate Asheville festival, etc. But it's the final item that stands out.

"Did you see this one about the aerial shot of the student body coming up?" I ask. "Have you heard about that?"

"No, why would they want that?"

"Maybe for the website? Or yearbook? I'm not sure."

"What are you thinking?"

"I don't know, but we're looking for opportunities, right?"

After another ten minutes of eye straining and file reading, first one, then two and three cars trickle into the parking lot.

"The game must be over," Ellie says. "Maybe we should get out of here."

We pack up our stuff and leave the picnic bench. On the way to the car, I text the other three about the aerial photo, figuring maybe one of them can figure out an angle.

"So where to, Mongoose?" Ellie says.

"You're the driver, Puma."

"Well, we can either do more research or we can quit for the night."

The last thing I want to do is more reading, but Not Max certainly doesn't want to go home. Who knows when I might be out with Ellie again? If there is an *again*.

"Is there a third option?"

Ellie bites her lower lip, thinking it over.

"Do you trust me?"

Like she needs to ask.

Soon we're heading back through town, passing the bright lights of the emptying football stadium. Eventually the subdivisions give way to cornfields and—God forbid—actual nature. I have no idea where we're going and don't care. Ellie's singing along to the *Grease* soundtrack, and I join in, not embarrassed at all that I know all the words due to Mom's addiction to musicals. After ten minutes, Ellie slows and turns onto a small dirt road bordered on both sides by *Trespassers Will Be Prosecuted* signs.

"Um."

"Relax, Mongoose. The coast is clear."

We follow the road and soon enter a forest I never knew existed. We weave our way up a large hill, the dirt road now nothing but a set of beaten-down tire tracks.

"You're not taking me here to kill me, are you?"

"Don't be silly," Ellie says. "If I were going to kill you, I'd have poisoned your ice cream."

She pulls into a ditch on the side of the road by a bullet-ridden sign now warning *Trespassers Will Be Shot.*

"Ignore that one too," Ellie tells me, killing the engine. "Bullets can't stop Puma and Mongoose tonight."

I follow Ellie as she hikes up the hill through the trees. It's so dark, I can barely make out her silhouette in front of me and have to trust in the crinkling leaves to keep up. If she is about to murder me, at least I won't see it coming. Suddenly, the rustling stops, and Ellie puts her hand in mine. Warm electricity crackles up my arm. Her hand is cool but soft as she pulls me along.

"Close your eyes," she says. "It's just up ahead. No peeking."

I do as I'm told, allowing Ellie to guide me for a dozen or so steps until the ground becomes softer.

"Okay, now you can look."

I open my eyes and my mouth drops. We're standing at the edge of a field at the bottom of a large hill. On top, where a full moon is rising, stands a twenty-foot platform with a massive radar dish pointing straight into the sky like a monstrous metal spiderweb. It's something right out of a painting.

"Wanna race?" Ellie says.

Without waiting for my answer, she blazes away.

Now I understand where the name Puma came from.

Ellie's freakishly fast, disappearing up the hill and into the night before I can get my legs moving. All I can do is follow the sound of her giggling as she sprints ahead of me, a wild animal unleashed. I do my best to keep up, but it's useless. By the time I get to the top of the hill, sucking air like I've been underwater for two minutes, Ellie is leaning against the ladder, not even breathing hard.

"You should"—pant—"run track."

"And let it interfere with my international spying gig? No way."

"We're not international yet."

"Give it time, Mongoose. We're going worldwide."

Ellie starts up the ladder, and I follow slowly.

"The last time we climbed a ladder, it didn't work out so well," I say.

She smiles over her shoulder. "This time'll be better. I promise."

The metal is cold on my hands as I scale the platform and approach the radar dish. Ellie crouches at the top, waiting for me beside a mechanism made up of two massive cogs and a hand crank. The dish is inches over our heads. Ellie stands and her top half disappears through a cut-out space in the dish right above her. She works her hands up through the hole, then hoists herself onto the dish, which thrums in response.

"You coming?"

My shoulders are broader than Ellie's, so I have a harder time squeezing through the space, but soon I'm standing on shaky legs beside her. Above us, the moon is blindingly white and so close that it looks like I can touch it. We stand enjoying the view and the silence. The sky seems impossibly large from here, and I feel smaller than I've ever felt.

"Isn't it like we're the only people alive?" she says.

"And at the highest point on the planet."

"My dad says there used to be other dishes here too. One there," she says, pointing, "and another there."

"What was it all for?"

"To track satellites at first, then something with mapping the surface of the moon. Once the government sold the land, they tore down the other dishes. I guess they forgot about this one."

"How did your dad find out about this place?"

"It belongs to someone in our church. He comes here when he needs to think."

"And you?"

Ellie's fingers tighten around mine.

"I come when I *don't* want to think. When the *Slaughterhouse-Five* thing got really bad last year, I came here a lot. I was so angry at everyone—the people calling our house and hanging up, the kids at school saying I was a book burner—that I needed a place where I could just disappear."

"Has it gotten better?" I ask.

"Better enough. I've just gotten used to it, I guess. I still want the Chaos Club to pay though. They made an already-bad situation even worse. Here," she says, crouching down, "do this."

Ellie begins crab walking backward to the edge of the dish. I don't think about what I'm doing. I just follow her lead and am soon lying beside her, holding her hand, our heads on the lip of the dish, staring straight up into a thousand pinpricks of light.

"I feel like I could fall up," I say.

"Or just disappear."

"That'd be even better."

Her voice is barely above a whisper. "So do you like it?"

"It's awesome. Thanks for bringing me here."

"I'm glad to share it," she says. "I thought you could use something special. Whenever I feel lonely, this is where I come. It always makes me feel better."

"When do *you* get lonely?"

"Why does that surprise you? Of course I get lonely. And sad. And moody. I'm not always happy, Max. Who is?"

"Sorry."

"You don't need to be sorry. Everyone thinks they know how everyone else is, but they're usually wrong. People see what they want to see. It makes everything easier. If they want to think of me as the sweet, happy church girl, that's fine because I am that way too. It's just not true all the time."

Overhead, the flashing red lights of an airliner cross the sky. I should be cold, but Ellie's hand in mine and her body beside me has me warm enough to stay here all night.

"What are you thinking about?" she says.

"Watson."

"You're here thinking about a sixty-year-old guy? You're weird."

I can't help it. Out here in nature, my mind has turned to the *Write Your Name in the Wet Cement of the Universe* banner over Watson's boards and Just Max/Not Max. Normally, I wouldn't tell anyone about that, but Ellie's not just anyone.

"Oh, Just Max isn't bad," she says. "He's nice and

sweet and smart. But I'd be lying if I said I didn't like the Not Max side of you too. We wouldn't all be leading these dangerous lives if he wasn't around. Just try not to overthink this. Enjoy being here in this space."

It isn't long before a special sort of silence descends. It's a warm, comfortable quiet that puts me completely at ease. I'm not thinking about the Chaos Club, who I am, or anything. I'm just in the moment and it's perfect.

"Can we come here again sometime?" I say.

"I'll have to check my schedule. I'm pretty busy, you know."

"What with skipping youth group and all."

"And my job as a phone thief."

"And eventual toppler of governments."

We're looking at each other as we say all this, and I know this is when I'm supposed to kiss her. I've also seen enough movies to know not to ask the girl if I can kiss her. The cool guys never do. Girls like confidence, and right now, Not Max is overflowing with confidence.

I lean in and begin to close my eyes...

Oh shit.

Ellie's eyes aren't closing. In fact, they're growing wide with horror the closer I come.

Shit, shit, shit.

Now Ellie's on her feet and backing away from me, looking mortified.

"I'm sorry, Max," she says. "I mean, I like you and all but..."

"No, it's okay," I say, hoping I fall over the edge and die so I don't have to think of this moment ever again. "I just thought, uh, you know…"

"It's just we're friends, and I don't want that to mess that up. And right now I don't want anything that could distract us from our Chaos Club plans. Is that okay? I'm sorry if I made you think this was anything more than just friends. Good friends, Max."

Well, if we're good friends, then maybe you can douse me in gasoline and light me on fire so I don't have to hide in shame the next time I see you.

"I can live with just being friends," I say, one hundred percent lying. "We'd better get back. It's probably close to ten."

✛

On the return trip to town, Ellie has on the local college station down low, a slow instrumental song all echo-y that would make everything seem like a dream if this wasn't all nightmare-y. It takes all my self-control not to throw my body from the speeding car.

At quarter past ten, Ellie pulls into my driveway, and I open the door before she's even in park.

"Max, I'm sorry," she says before I can escape. "You're really a sweet guy."

No, Just Max is a sweet guy. And sweet guys don't get girls like Ellie Wick.

"It's fine," I say. "I'll see you Monday."

Unless I can find an Ebola patient to lick.

Inside the house, I head upstairs, where Mom and Dad are in their room, the lights still on. I try to creep by without being heard, but Mom has bionic ears and calls for me to come in. She's in bed reading, and Dad's in the bathroom, probably on the iPad, a habit that drives Mom crazy.

"Get your work finished?" she says.

"Yeah, sorry I'm late," I say. "We stopped at Becca Yancey's for her notes."

"I'm glad it worked out. She seems nice."

"Ellie? Yeah, she's great." Great at tearing my heart out of my chest and tossing it into a wood chipper. "I'm going to crash," I say. "It's been a long week."

"Okay, sweetie," Mom says. "Good night."

I turn, ready to escape into the safety of my room, when she says, "Oh and, Max?"

"Yeah?"

"Research project my ear," she says. "You owe us an extra day for that. Get some sleep."

Awesome. First humiliation, now time added on to my sentence. What's next? A paper cut on my eyeball?

I throw myself onto my bed and stare lifelessly at the knobs on my dresser, wondering how I could've been so stupid. That's what I get for following the lead of fictional characters in unrealistic movies. I'm not sure for how long I stay zombified, but at some point I fall asleep, and I don't move from that position until my phone buzzes at 2:37 a.m. with a text from Wheeler.

Have epic prank idea for the aerial photo. Details on the way.

CHAPTER 10

Wheeler calls it Operation Schlonger, and Ellie assigns us code names matching our jobs:

She's Right-Hand.

Adleta is H_2O.

Malone's Pornographer.

Wheeler's Architect.

And me, I'm Mole.

Generally, capers fall into one of two categories:

1. Those like the Stranko Caper, where most of the work occurs during the heist's execution.

2. And those where the majority of the work is done in planning and the actual heist is mostly hands-off.

Operation Schlonger is the second type.

The five of us have put in two weeks of prep work planning for today. As one thousand juniors and seniors leave the building at 10:00 a.m. to shoot the aerial photo, there's really nothing to do but hope it all goes according to plan.

Malone and I walk near the front of the stream of

students heading across the parking lot for the football field. All one thousand of us are wearing brand-new, district-paid-for yellow T-shirts with *Asheville High* displayed across our chests. It's a perfect fall day with a cloudless, pale-blue sky overhead and just warm enough that no jackets are needed. Ellie's ahead of us at the front of the line with Stranko and Jill Banks, the district's public relations' officer. Mrs. Banks is in a business-y skirt-and-jacket deal and always walks like she's clenching a walnut between her ass cheeks. This whole *let's share the awesomeness of Asheville with the world* stupidity is all her idea, but really it's just a way to justify her existence and paycheck. When Mrs. Banks got out of her car at school this morning, Ellie was waiting for her, ready to explain she was to be her student ambassador during the shoot.

It's Heist Rule #12: *Have an insider.*

"Should be anytime now," I say, watching as Ellie nears the gate.

"And if it doesn't work?" Malone says.

"Shh, don't jinx it."

The line suddenly stops as Mrs. Banks and Stranko get to the stadium gate and see what Adleta was assigned to do last night. It's five full minutes of standing around, the words "soaked" and "a swamp" drifting back from the front of the line. I watch Ellie the whole time, and she's watching Banks and Stranko brainstorm a solution. It's been two weeks since my disastrous failed kiss. In that time, I've done my best to avoid her, and when we have been together, she's spared me more humiliation by never mentioning it.

Ellie waits for a break in the adults talking before tapping Banks on the shoulder and pointing to the other side of the school. After brief words between Stranko and Banks, the front of the line starts marching toward the intramural fields.

"Why do you look so surprised?" I say to Malone. "Adleta said he took care of it."

"Yeah, color me skeptical."

We step out of line and take a quick jog to the fence. The football field is more a swimming pool at this point, the result of Adleta's sneaking into the stadium last night after practice and turning on the sprinkler system. Now the picture will be taken at the intramural fields, which have no bleachers or press box from where Stranko or Banks can get a bird's-eye view.

It's Heist Rule #13: *Set the rules when you can.*

Once we reach the intramural fields, the section leaders, made up of senior student government members, take over. They call the members of their assigned homeroom, and the field becomes a mass of identical gold shirts. This whole prank is Wheeler's idea, but I helped with the details and planning. One of his final jobs was to spray-paint the area in ten-yard sections like a real football field. It should make this go so much more smoothly and eliminate the chances of being discovered.

"Let's go, everyone!" Stranko shouts into a bullhorn. "We're running behind."

I swear he's glaring at me as he says it.

"I'd better get going," Malone says. "I'm over there in Becca's group."

"You know what to do?" I say.

"Yeah, I think I can keep it straight, Einstein," she says. "I already did the hard part anyway."

"So to speak," I say.

"Right, so to speak."

The press release Banks sent to the media showed a diagram of the picture the hired pilot and photographer are supposed to take: *AHS Pride*, the letters formed by students standing in meticulously prepared positions in our yellow T-shirts. When Wheeler and I went to Malone with his idea and what we needed her to do, she was less than enthusiastic.

"Ew, gross! No way."

"Come on. It'll be awesome," Wheeler said. "You're the artist. We can't do this without you."

"Something tells me you've drawn your share of those before," she said.

"Well sure, but not on this scale. It needs to stretch across the field and be broken down into forty sections, one for each homeroom. There's no way I can do that."

Malone looked at me for help, but I just smiled back. Her sigh of defeat came a lot quicker than I expected.

"Let's just say for a minute I do this," she said. "How are

you going to get them to follow these instructions? Don't you think Banks will have already sent them the design?"

"Max and I will take care of that," Wheeler said. "So that's a yes?"

Malone rolled her eyes and said, "And to think I call myself a feminist."

"Do you need help? Because I can model if you need me to."

"Sure," Malone said. "Let me borrow a microscope from one of the science labs."

"Ouch."

I have Mrs. Nally for homeroom, and our position is on the fifty-yard line, close to Banks, just like Wheeler and I planned. Jeff Benz, he of Watson's-senior-aide fame, is our StuGo, or student government, rep and charged with arranging us on the field.

"You," he says, pointing to me and showing me the diagram. "You set up on the end here. The line forms behind you."

The diagram Benz holds looks like something a sick computer would barf out. The sheet is covered with *x*'s, each representing a student's placement on the field. Malone designed the layout so each team leader only has one piece of the map, not the whole image of the full design. That way, no one knows what's being created. At least that's the hope.

StuGo reps wander from group to group, making sure the sections line up as they should. Adleta's in the front of his section, ready to intercept Stranko if there's a problem. He gives me a thumbs-up and a big *this is going to be great* smile.

Adleta's right to think that. Like I said, the hard part's finished. Hopefully, that means never having to attend StuGo meetings ever again. Officially, student government is for kids who want to plan dances and decorate the school for various stupid reasons throughout the year. But unofficially, StuGo is for padding college applications. Normally, you couldn't pay me enough to go to one of their meetings, but they were put in charge of organizing today's activity. With the group's "Everyone is welcome!" philosophy, infiltration was easy. Even easier was switching out the board-approved diagram and replacing it with Wheeler and Malone's work. It's not hard to be sneaky when every moron in the room is engaged in a hot, borderline violent debate about homecoming snacks: potato chips or pretzels? These are the heavy questions of the universe StuGo wrestles with on a weekly basis.

Now with the fake diagrams in the hands of the StuGo reps, everything is going beautifully. The juniors and seniors, just happy to be out of class, are following the barked orders, and we're all well away from where anyone can see what's really happening. All we need now is the pilot to fly overhead and shoot the picture. Simple. Just like we drew it up.

Then.

Ellie waves her arms to get my attention.

I give her a *What?* gesture with my hands.

She points violently to the far end of the intramural field, where Stranko and Banks are now walking with six beefy football players. Their destination? The thirty-foot-high scaffolding used by the marching band director during practice to make sure everyone is in lockstep with one another. Wheeler must've not seen the tower last night. I even missed it today in the daylight.

The five of us break rank from our homerooms and race to each other.

"If Stranko gets up there, we're screwed," Wheeler says.

"How much time do we have?" I ask Ellie.

"Five minutes before the plane shows up," she says.

"We were so close," Adleta says.

"I sort of wanted to see how it looked," Malone says.

"I can give you an up close and personal," Wheeler says, and Malone gives him a shove, but it's a friendly one.

"No, we're not giving up," I say. "We need to stall."

It's Heist Rule #14: *Be ready to improvise.*

"Mr. Stranko?" I say.

"What is it, Cobb? Why aren't all of you with your homerooms?"

"We just thought you should know there's something weird with the design."

"What do you mean 'weird'?"

"Isn't it supposed to say Asheville Pride or something like that?" Ellie says.

"AHS Pride, yes," Mrs. Banks says.

"Well, it doesn't," Adleta says.

"No, it does," Banks says. "I drew up the design myself. The picture is going on the front of the district website."

"No, he's right," Malone says. "We're not forming letters. There are too many long, straight lines. It's weird."

Stranko looks over to the field where one thousand students stand, many of them staring into the sky, waiting on the plane to shoot their picture. We've only stalled for a minute. Somehow we need to kill four more.

"Help us push the tower over there, and we'll see if you're right," Stranko says. "We don't have a lot of time."

If you've ever been in a tug-of-war with a semitruck, then you know what it's like trying to hold back the scaffolding tower as the varsity offensive line tries to push it forward. Hard doesn't even begin to describe what it's like fake pushing when you're really pulling. I use muscles I didn't know I had. And I use them poorly too. Because despite our stalling, the wheels on the scaffold roll closer and closer to the intramural field. We're within twenty yards of the far end of the field when Stranko orders us to stop.

"Are you sure you should climb without a helmet, sir?" Wheeler says, blocking his path. "Like when we repainted the tower?"

"Don't be a smart-ass, Wheeler," Stranko says and

wraps the bullhorn's strap over his shoulder and begins climbing. Mrs. Banks goes to follow him but stops when she realizes her skirt has no pocket for her phone. Ellie holds out her hand.

"I'll hold that for you. We'll stay down here."

"Thank you," Mrs. Banks says, returning the smile. "We should talk about you doing an internship this winter. You're just so pleasant."

"That'd be super!" Ellie says. "What you do seems so interesting!"

I have to chew a hole in my cheek to stop from laughing.

Mrs. Banks climbs after Stranko, and Malone hits Wheeler in the stomach when he tries looking up Mrs. Banks's skirt. From the field, a cheer goes up at the sight of an approaching plane from the west.

Mrs. Banks's phone rings, and Ellie looks at it before answering. I lean in so I can hear too.

"We're one minute out," a voice says. "Are you ready for the shot?"

Ellie, doing her best Mrs. Banks's voice, says, "Roger that, Brent," before hanging up.

"Brent," I say. "Like you're old friends."

"Oh, we go way back."

It had taken Ellie two days of calling local photography studios to find the name of the photographer hired to shoot the picture. Once she hunted Brent Whoever down, it was a short conversation, just long enough to make one request as Mrs. Banks—that he tether his digital camera to the school's Dropbox account. That way, any picture he shot would be immediately transmitted.

"Because I want to be able to update the website right away," Ellie-as-Banks explained.

"That won't be a problem," Brent said to her.

That poor sucker. Because technically, by "the school's Dropbox account," she really means the anonymous Dropbox account Wheeler set up.

Just as the plane starts over school property, Stranko bellows a barbaric, "No!"

We all practically give ourselves whiplash looking up. Mrs. Banks is gaping at what she sees. Stranko fumbles with his bullhorn and shouts, "Clear the field! Clear the field!"

But it's too late.

Banks's phone rings in Ellie's hand one more time.

Brent says, "*This* is what you want a picture of?"

"Take the picture," Ellie says.

"Roger that...I guess."

From the tower, Stranko shouts a final and pointless, "Clear the field!"

But from high overhead, Brent begins taking pictures on this beautiful fall day of one thousand students proudly representing the school in their gold Asheville High T-shirts, everyone strategically arranged to form the largest, most anatomically correct boner the world has ever seen.

CHAPTER 11

Monday, the first day of homecoming week, ends with an announcement ordering all students to the auditorium for a mandatory meeting. Mrs. B, Stranko, and Officer Hale are already there, standing in the middle of the stage waiting for everyone. The five of us sit together near the back, no longer worrying about the old rule about not being seen together. Screw worrying about someone, somehow, connecting us to Stranko's phone and the boner pic. We're untouchable. I mean, did you see the aerial photo? Because over a million people have viewed it on H8box, not to mention the local news and even a few worldwide outlets crediting the picture to the Chaos Club, courtesy of Wheeler adding the club's name to the picture. Yes, the Water Tower Five have gone global, just like Ellie predicted.

But even though the whole attempted-kiss debacle was almost a month ago, I still feel weird around her. How can I not? I always make sure there's at least one other Water Tower Fiver between us as a buffer. Today, I'm lucky that we're on opposite ends with Wheeler in the middle, crowing about his fake Chaos Club website that went live last night.

"Go ahead and admit it. I'm a genius, right?" he says.

"Yeah, man, it's awesome. You have a future in counterfeiting," I say.

Like Malone's Chaos Club business cards, Wheeler's version of the official website is close to an exact knock-off. He's got the same pictures, history, contact email, timeline, and even a complicated slideshow—everything that would make a visitor to the site believe they were at the actual site. But if you look extra closely, you can see Wheeler's followed Malone's lead and included on each page the small white water tower with a five in the middle. And his final addition? A mock write-up explaining how the Chaos Club tricked the student body into producing the now-viral massive erection picture.

"But do you fully appreciate the finer points I added? I mean, come on, if this doesn't piss off the Chaos Club, nothing will."

He's right about that. Included is:

1. A paragraph in the bio bragging that the club funds its pranks through fencing stolen items.

2. Pictures shot through bedroom windows of people in various stages of undress.

3. A photoshopped picture of Stranko in his underwear cavorting in the woods in the moonlight.

4. A video of a guy in a hockey mask with a voice distorter, antagonizing the Asheville cops and school administrators, ending his rant with, "The Chaos Club is unstoppable, bitches."

Like I said, it's awesome, if not highly disturbing.

"Where did you learn how to do all this?" Ellie asks Wheeler.

"H8box. It's like the best teacher in the world. You can learn anything there."

"Who's the guy in the mask?" Malone asks.

"A H8box friend. He lives in St. Louis, so no one can ever link this to him."

"And the stalking pictures?"

"Lifted from other sites. Do you like the one with Stranko?"

"I've got to give you credit on that one," Malone says. "Great photoshopping. You should work for the CIA."

"Yeah, he's going to freak," Adleta says. "The cops will probably show up."

"Don't tease me, dude," Wheeler says. "Stranko getting braced by the cops is like my greatest fantasy. But I didn't even show you the best part yet—pick a search engine, any search engine, and type in Chaos Club."

On my phone, I start with the big search engines first like Google, Bing, and Yahoo, before moving on to lesser-known ones like DuckDuckGo and Dogpile. On each, Wheeler's Chaos Club site is the top return.

"How did you do that?" Malone says.

"Trade secret," Wheeler says. "So say it, everyone, I'm a…"

"Genius, Wheeler," we all say. "You're a genius."

"Now just imagine what you could do if you tried in school," Malone adds.

"Okay, let's not get ahead of ourselves."

As the remaining students trickle in and find a seat, Mrs. B taps the microphone and waits for quiet before starting.

"I hope all of you have had a good start to homecoming week. A special thanks to StuGo for decorating the halls."

When we all entered the building today, the halls were filled with balloons, streamers, and posters. They barely survived the morning, and by the end of lunch, all of it was down. Now the hall floors resemble Times Square after New Year's Eve.

"And speaking of StuGo and decorations, I can't wait to see what they do with the gym for the dance this Saturday. I hope to see everyone there."

If Mrs. B's truly hoping for my attendance, she's going to be disappointed. There's zero chance of me asking anyone to the dance. One rejection a semester is my limit, thank you very much.

"Now," Mrs. B says, "I'm sure most of you have noticed that our beloved Zippy the Eagle statue has been taken away for a makeover. I don't know about you, but I will miss seeing him out there each morning. The good news is that this year marks the seventy-fifth anniversary of this school district. An end-of-the-year celebration marking this occasion is in the planning stages, and I'm happy to say that is when Zippy will make his return. The board office is hoping for student input, so anyone interested in joining the planning committee should come see me."

I look down at Ellie, who's already waiting for me.

"I'm on it," she says.

It's Heist Rule #15: *Gather as much info as you can.*

Mrs. B thanks us, tells us to keep working hard, then hands the mic to Stranko, who swaggers his way to the front of the stage.

"I'm going to keep this short," Stranko says. "I've brought Officer Hale here so you understand just how serious we are about this topic. At the beginning of the year, we made the rules clear to you, but recent actions have necessitated changes. I'm specifically referring to last week's photo incident."

Snickering fills the auditorium.

"Quiet!" Stranko barks. "Some of you may find what happened funny, but trust me, we will find the perpetrators. And when we do, they will be severely punished. Severely. Punished."

Stranko punctuates the air with a finger, and Hale does the same. Monkey see, monkey do.

"So first," Stranko says, "anyone caught vandalizing the school or disrupting school activities will face expulsion.

Also, anyone with knowledge of vandalism, even if they didn't take part, will be punished as well."

Groans fill the theater.

"Also, in the past, we've been lax about students using the sporting fields whenever they wanted. But as of today, the fields are off-limits once school practices or games are over."

More groans.

"And finally, any student caught on school grounds after eight o'clock who isn't a part of a school function or activity will face suspension. This is a zero-tolerance policy. We are not fooling around."

Behind Stranko, Mrs. B stands quietly. You figure Stranko had to be the one who strong-armed her into this new policy. Because can you say overkill?

"That's all for now," Stranko says. "We'll be emailing this information to your parents this evening, and—"

Before I know what's happening, Wheeler's standing on his seat, his hand high.

"Excuse me, Vice Principal Stranko?"

The entire auditorium turns our way. Malone tries to pull Wheeler down, but he shakes her off.

"What?" Stranko snaps.

Wheeler says, "I think I speak for everyone here when I say how appalled I was by this prank. When I heard on the news how much money the school spent for that pornographic photo, I went from being limp on my couch to standing erect. I was stiff with embarrassment for the entire town. Once those delinquents in the Chaos Club are caught, I hope you're extremely hard-on them."

Wheeler smiles, looking as sweet and innocent as a child…a child who just threw out three boner euphemisms in ten seconds. Stranko's chest heaves like he wants to launch himself across forty rows at Wheeler. Instead, in a moment of what must be Herculean restraint, Stranko says a steely, "Oh, they will be punished severely. You can guarantee that."

We're all released a few minutes later, and as we head up the aisle, Malone says to Wheeler, "Not smart. Why not just come out and confess that we did it?"

"Oh, come on. What's he going to do? Expel us?" Wheeler says.

"Uh, yeah, that's what he just said," Adleta says.

"He did?" Wheeler says. "I must not have been paying attention."

Ellie says to me, "Well, we wanted to write our names in the universe's wet cement."

"It'll be fine," I say.

"Exactly. We knew we'd have to take risks to destroy the Chaos Club. We're not going to let some silly rules stand in our way."

As the five of us stand in the lobby, Malone's nemesis, Libby Heckman, and one of her hangers-on, Sara Yu, emerge from the auditorium. Libby's carrying a half-finished charcoal drawing that, in all honesty, looks exactly like her, almost as if it's a photograph. As they pass, Libby says to Sara, "Don't you wish some people would just do everyone a favor and die?"

"Especially certain people," Sara says.

Both girls start laughing their bitchy heads off, and something inside me just sort of snaps.

I say to the two of them, "And if some people aren't careful, someone might falsify evidence proving they're in the Chaos Club and give it to Stranko."

Both girls straighten like they've just straddled an electric fence. They turn the corner, and Libby does a quick glance over her should at me. Her eyes are full of fear. Then the girls are out of sight, hopefully running for their lives. Wheeler, Adleta, and I start laughing, but Malone wheels around on me.

"Don't do that again," she says.

"Huh?" I say.

"I don't need you or anyone else fighting my battles for me, Max. It makes me look weak, which is what they want. It's embarrassing."

"I wasn't fighting your battles for you. It just sort of came out."

"Well, try to keep yourself in check. You're only making it worse. I've got it taken care of."

"Taken care of how?"

Suddenly, Malone's anger is gone, and she's rising in front of me, growing somehow larger, her eyes full of fire.

"Well, there's a contest going on, isn't there?"

And when I hear the laugh that she and Ellie share as they walk away, I'm the one feeling fear. But for Libby.

"You guys want to do something?" Wheeler says.

"Like what?" I say.

"I don't know, something. Does it matter?"

"I would but I can't," Adleta says. "Lacrosse conditioning and all."

"You should just quit," Wheeler says.

"Yeah, like that's going to happen."

Adleta leaves us, and I tell Wheeler I know where we can go, thus independently putting an end to Mom's *I don't want you hanging out with that Wheeler boy* rule. We're halfway down the hall on our way to freedom when we pass Mr. Watson. He's like a rock in the middle of a stream, standing still as a river of students floods past him.

"Ah, Mr. Cobb," he says. "Can I talk with you a moment? Relax, you're not in trouble."

Wheeler tells me he'll wait, and Watson and I step into the doorway of his classroom.

"I just wanted to tell you I've noticed a marked difference in you these last couple weeks," Watson says. "And I mean that in a good way."

"Um, thanks," I say.

"There's no need to thank me. I've just noticed how you've been carrying yourself differently of late, like you've grown up somehow. I see it in class, how you participate more. And in the halls, where you're talking with more people. I'm not sure what happened to you, but I think it's a nice change."

"I didn't think teachers paid attention to things like that."

"Let me fill you in on a little secret, Max. Teachers are a lot more aware of things than we let on. Seeing you these last couple of weeks, I'm proud of you."

I can't help but smile.

"That's all I wanted," Watson says. "Go have fun with your friend."

Five minutes later, Wheeler and I are pulling out of the parking lot in his cruddy Chevy Concours, a car mostly held together by duct tape and gum. But at least Wheeler has his own car and isn't stuck having to borrow the mom mobile. Wheeler hauls ass off school property like we're trying to outrun a nuclear blast, the music pumping so loudly through blown speakers my ears are close to bleeding. Within fifteen minutes, we're outside of town, pulling off the road onto a bumpy trail that marks the start of Boyd's property. I have Wheeler park in front of a trailer with a splintered front door and windows covered in thick plastic sheets.

"Your uncle lives in that shit hole?"

"He's not my real uncle, but no, he mostly lives in the barn."

We get out of the car and head down the dirt path leading away from the trailer. Weeds grow high on both sides of us, and the faded red barn looms up ahead. The only bright spot, literally, is a fifteen-foot-high metal sculpture resembling a shiny, upside-down pyramid with mannequin arms and legs sticking out in all directions.

"So he's a serial killer?" Wheeler asks.

"If he is, we're safe."

Boyd's barn is a junkman's dream. You name it, it's somewhere inside. Old kitchen appliances, rusted tools, torn furniture, computer keyboards and towers, black-and-white TVs, and rusty farming equipment fill makeshift aisles. The floor is concrete but barely recognizable for all the rope, pieces of sheet metal, and lawn equipment covering it. Everything in the barn goes to his sculptures, which, despite how he lives, sell for outrageous amounts of money. Whatever he does with the money, he apparently doesn't spend it creating a comfortable living environment.

Music blasts from the back, where Boyd stands with a beer in his hand, staring at Asheville High's very own Zippy the Eagle statue. Here, away from home, Zippy looks smaller, even fragile, despite standing six feet high with a wingspan covering ten feet. Boyd's so fully focused on the statue that he doesn't notice us until we're only a few feet away. When he finally sees us, he comes over offering a hand.

"So, wait, you're the one doing the restoration?"

"Yeah, cool, right?" he says. "Mrs. B helped me set it up."

"Is this what she was talking about when you came to get me at the school that night?"

"Yep, it's for the big celebration in May. I have until then to get it looking brand-new."

"How long is that going to take?"

"I don't know. A month? Two? That's what's nice about dealing with people who don't know anything about what you really do—you tell them you need it now to get started, and then you can sit on your ass a lot and work when you want to."

Wheeler clears his throat dramatically, and I introduce him to Boyd.

"You like AC/DC?" Wheeler says, pointing to the speakers playing "Dirty Deeds Done Dirt Cheap."

"Shit, yeah. When I was eight my dad took me to see them on the Highway to Hell Tour."

"Oh my God! With Bon Scott?"

"Absolutely. My life was never the same again."

"How many times have you seen them?"

"Fourteen."

"Oh my God."

I've made a grievous error. I've just introduced Wheeler to himself twenty years down the road. I'm never going to get him out of here.

"Wheeler's aiming for the lowest GPA in our class," I say.

Boyd toasts Wheeler with his beer.

"I didn't hit bottom," Boyd says, "that would be John

Mantooth—no, seriously, that's his name—who's been in jail the last twelve years, but I was close. And look at me now, living the dream. My own boss, a beer when I want it, no old lady dragging me down. I couldn't have planned it any better if I'd tried. So is this a social call or business?"

Isn't it annoying how adults can sense whenever you want something?

I say, "Do you remember a bird attack happening at your senior picnic?"

"Oh man," Boyd half shouts. "The bird-shit picnic! That was the highlight of senior year."

"How did they make the birds crap on cue like that?" Wheeler asks. "I mean, how do you command a flock of birds to do anything?"

Boyd goes to his minifridge and pulls out another beer.

"Ah, one of the few things I learned in school. Is Mr. Huntley still there teaching psych? He explained it all to us on the final day. The trick, he said, was conditioning."

Wheeler and I both make a face.

"You haven't had psych yet? Oh man, you have to take it. It's a total mind screw. Conditioning is used to train someone—or in this case, birds. Huntley said he figured someone went out to the intramural fields for months, spread birdseed, then blew a whistle. Eventually, the birds in the woods understood that the whistle meant food was available. So when the senior picnic came, someone blew that whistle and—presto!—birds doing what birds do, raining down shit."

Wheeler says, "Man, that took some serious commitment."

"Oh, they were serious about it all right. It doesn't sound like the group now does nearly anything as elaborate. Cows on the roof? Seen it. Painting the water tower? Bush league, man. But the Chaos Club then, they were proud of that tradition."

"Wheeler's the one who set up the student body boner pic," I say.

Boyd toasts our way. "See, that's what I'm talking about—creativity and dedication. That's what goes into an epic prank. But do you know the most impressive thing? I'll bet if you asked people at my next reunion what they remember from high school, they'll struggle to name their teachers or what classes they took, but they'll know every last detail from those pranks. That's what called creating a legacy."

"Stranko's probably never forgot it," I say.

"Well, the thing you wouldn't know is that for part of high school, Stranko was actually pretty cool to hang out with. He was a joker—not on the level of me or your dad, but funny, good to be in class with because he kept things light. He was an athletic beast too, especially at lacrosse. And, man, the girls loved him, probably because he was one of the few guys who would actually bust a move at the school dances. That guy could really get down. I was jealous as hell. Because if you guys haven't figured it out yet, girls love a guy who will dance."

"Wait a minute," Wheeler says. "Are you sure we're

talking about the same Dwayne Stranko? Tall, bald, looks like Sloth from *The Goonies*?"

"That's the one," Boyd says. "He had hair then, of course, but yeah, he was a good guy."

"Well, that's not the Dwayne Stranko we know," I say.

"You can blame his parents for that. They were never what you'd call friendly people—you sure as hell didn't want to go over to the Stranko house—but they mostly let Dwayne do his thing. Then at the end of our sophomore year, he got busted with some guys trespassing at the city pool, drinking beer and doing stupid stuff—throwing chairs in the deep end, raiding the concession stand, you get the idea. Supposedly when the cops showed up, Stranko was standing naked on the high dive serenading everyone with 'Bohemian Rhapsody.'"

"Not an image I needed," Wheeler says.

"No doubt," Boyd says. "After that night, Dwayne disappeared for the entire summer. When we got back to school in the fall, he was different—buzzed hair, sitting up straight in class, paying attention and never joking. Some people thought he'd been sent to military camp. But his mom and dad didn't have a lot of money, so I doubt that. My guess is his parents shut him down completely, molded him into exactly what they wanted."

"Someone obedient," I say.

"Right, and when parents try to do that to a kid, they usually win, unless the kid is really strong. Whatever happened to Stranko, he wouldn't talk about it. I do know the lacrosse coach benched him for the first half of the season our junior year though, which hurt his scholarship chances. Stranko became super serious then and only got worse from there. By our senior year, man, the guy was unbearable. It was bad enough that he was so uptight, but it got to the point where he demanded it from everyone else. Flash forward twenty years, and I can only imagine how awful he is now that he has power. He wasn't always that way though. Not that it excuses his being an asshole."

"Which he is," Wheeler says.

There's more talk about Stranko and some talk about the Chaos Club, but not much. Mostly it's Boyd drinking beer and showing us around the barn, telling us how he obtained certain junky items. We leave after twenty minutes, and on our way back to town, there's no gushing from Wheeler about how cool Boyd and the barn are like I assumed there would be. In fact, Wheeler's not talking at all. Instead, he has the radio on and doesn't even bother changing the channel when commercials come on, like usual.

Outside my house, I say, "Maybe we should skip the rest of the week, save ourselves the pain of more homecoming torture."

Wheeler cracks a weak smile and says, "I'll see you in the morning, man."

He pulls away, and I'm left wondering: (A) what's eating him, and (B) if I'd really ever cut school.

I decide (A) I don't know, and (B) probably not.

Four days later, I'm happy as hell I'm not a school cutter, because if I were, I'd have missed out on what's easily the most memorable pep rally in Asheville history.

CHAPTER 12

Friday is the big homecoming game—a guaranteed loss—so class periods are condensed to forty-five minutes, allowing for two hours to celebrate school spirit, which by my calculation is only felt by six percent of the student body. We're all herded into the gym, where I end up sitting in the top row of the bleachers with Wheeler and Malone. Adleta has some role in the pep rally, but he didn't go into specifics. And Ellie, I'm not exactly sure where she is. Probably off kissing some guy who isn't me.

"Any hits on the website?" I ask Wheeler.

He doesn't answer because he's staring off across the gym, his eyes unfocused.

"Hey, man. You alive?"

"Yeah, sorry. What's up?"

I ask about the website again.

He pushes a few buttons on his phone and says, "Ninety-eight hits since we went live. That'll go up once word gets out. We've gotten eight suggestions for future pranks though. We have some seriously screwed-up people in this school."

"Coming from you, that's saying something," Malone says.

"I know, right?"

"What type of suggestions?" I ask.

"Lots of fecal-related pranks," Wheeler says. "'Shit in the cafeteria,' 'Shit in a library book,' 'Fill Stranko's office with cow shit,' stuff like that."

"The future is going to be a dark place," Malone says.

"Like I said," Wheeler says.

"What about Stranko's phone?" I ask.

"He's not calling it anymore, but the cloud's still active," Wheeler says. "I told you he wouldn't change the password. Adults are stupid that way."

"Has he added anything lately?"

"Nothing worth mentioning, but I can tell he's accessing it by the Date Modified column."

"What's he reading?" Malone asks.

"Mostly old prank reports from the nineties. I have this image of him drunk at his kitchen table in the middle of the night, reading over the files like a detective who can't let a cold case die."

"That's sort of sad," I say.

"If by sad you mean hilarious, then yeah."

Ellie's one of the last students to enter the gym and pauses in the doorway, surveying the junior section. Malone stands and gives her a wave, and soon, Ellie's plopping down next to me. Next time, remind me to show up last so I can control where I sit.

"Where were you?" Malone asks.

"Talking with Mrs. B," Ellie says. "I'm now officially on the Celebrate Asheville Committee."

"So like instead of the Chaos Club, you're in the Brownnose Club?" Wheeler says.

"No, it's really kind of a cool idea. The plan is to make the event an all-day thing, with bands and rides and stuff. 'A celebration of Asheville' is how Mrs. Barber put it. They're hoping to make it annual event."

"When is it?" I say.

"They're scheduling it for the Saturday after school's out for the summer. So it's a long way off."

"That's a lot of committee meetings," Malone says.

"It's okay. I like that kind of stuff."

The cheerleaders enter the gym, and Wheeler and Malone start debating whether cheerleaders are demeaning to women. Go ahead and guess which side of that argument Wheeler's on. Ellie and I sit awkwardly, neither of us talking and fully aware we're not.

Eventually, Ellie says, "So how long are you going to stay weird around me?"

"What? I'm not being weird around you," I say in a clearly weird way.

"You know exactly what I'm talking about, Maxwell Cobb."

"I don't—"

"Girls aren't dumb, Max. You won't talk to me; you won't sit by me; you barely even look at me. And I know why, and I want you to stop. We're friends, and friends don't act like this toward each other."

I pick at a piece of lint on my pants. "Okay," I say. "Sorry."

"You don't need to be sorry. I get it. My main goal right now is taking down the Chaos Club. After we take them down, we'll see."

My heart hiccups.

"*We'll see?* What does that mean?"

"It means what you think it means. Now stop being a stupid boy and act normal."

Message received loud and clear. Not Max can definitely work with *we'll see.*

With the gym finally filled, the pep rally gets started, with Watson's aide, Jeff Benz, and Chloe Seymour, one of the hottest girls on the planet, playing emcees. They're trying to get everyone excited, but because they're reading from a preapproved script, they sound robotic. The seniors show the most enthusiasm, with energy levels decreasing by class until you get to the freshmen, who are so quiet they may be unconscious.

Wheeler might as well be sitting with the frosh because he's back to his staring act again. If I didn't know him like I did, I'd think he's tripping on something. What snaps Wheeler back to reality is when Chloe overenthusiastically tells us to welcome the Asheville dance team. They enter from the side door with Malone's nemesis, Libby Heckman, leading the way to center court. Then Wheeler's on his feet, whooping and hollering until finally Ellie can't take it anymore.

"Stop it."

"What? They're awesome. I love the dance team," he says.

"You love how their outfits are short and tight," Malone says.

"Right. Like I said, they're awesome."

The dance team stands at attention, hands on hips, asses out, chests forward, all with the same dumb duck face, waiting for their music to start. Trying to make the best impression I can with Ellie, I fake noninterest. I fail. Then the music explodes from the speakers, and I hear what song they're dancing to—The J. Geils Band's "Centerfold."

"Oh no," I half whisper to Ellie.

"What?" she says.

"Listen."

Not only is "Centerfold" the best '80s song ever, but it also just happens to be about a guy who realizes a girl in his homeroom is naked in a dirty magazine. So yeah, the Malone picture from last year. The dance team wiggles and thrusts and basically raises the temperature in the gym by twenty degrees. Once the chorus hits, they really vamp it up, grinding their hips and tossing their heads back ecstatically when the line is sung about the girl being the centerfold.

Two seats down, Malone isn't moving, but she's no dummy. If there's any doubt that the song's been chosen for her, proof comes halfway into the performance when the girls break from the floor and head into different sections of the stands. Libby prances up the aisle toward us, stopping a few rows away. When the chorus hits again, she points with the beat at Malone.

I'll give her credit—Malone doesn't take her eyes off Libby. She just stares back defiantly, her breathing steady. What I want to do is jump from my seat and flip Libby off with both hands. But Malone's made it clear she doesn't want me to stick up for her. And, man, I get that, I really do. But it isn't easy to just sit here. Luckily, the song is short. It just feels like forever. I can't imagine how long it was for Malone.

"Forget her," Ellie says to Malone once the song ends and the girls return to the floor to thunderous applause. "Libby's a total see you next Tuesday."

Malone doesn't move. But it's not like she's stunned and embarrassed into lifelessness. From her eyes, I can tell something's going through her head.

"Seriously, Kate. She's trash."

Malone gives Ellie a thin smile. "No, I'm fine. That was actually sort of clever."

A few seconds later though, I see Malone run her forearm across her eyes.

Chloe and Benz soon return to the floor to read the accomplishments of our fall sports teams. It's a pretty damn short list. One of the girls' cross-country team's runners came in eighth at the state meet, but beyond that, our fall teams have done as sucky as they usually have. It's only our boys' lacrosse team that ever has any success, but that's a spring sport, leaving the first three-quarters of the year an athletic wasteland.

Next on the agenda, the cheerleaders bounce spastically

to the center of the gym in their black-and-yellow outfits. Joined by Becca Yancey in her Zippy the Golden Eagle costume, the cheerleaders flip and flop around, doing a lot of "We're number one!" to a mostly disinterested crowd. They try again to raise some reaction from us by yipping a cheer about how awesome Asheville is. All of it makes me regret not falling to my death from the water tower. But then the five cheerleaders in the front row pick up the poster boards waiting for them on the floor. The girls point the cards toward the audience so everyone sees the single word on each one.

Holy shit.

Ellie, Wheeler, Malone, and I all look at each other bug-eyed while the rest of the student section starts laughing and clapping hysterically. The cheerleaders have no idea what they're holding. From their smiles, they clearly think they've finally injected a megadose of school spirit into our veins with their magical cards. But they're wrong. The squad goes into a call and response thing, holding up a card and shouting what they think the cards say.

"Asheville!"

"High!"

"Golden!"

"Eagles!"

"Rock!"

But what the cards really say, and what the students yell back is:

"The!"

"Chaos!"

"Club!"

"Is!"

"Coming!"

The entire student body leaps to its feet, actually showing some school spirit for once, even if it's in support of what amounts to a terrorist organization.

"Is this one of you?" Malone asks.

We all shake our heads.

"Well, whoever did it, it's impressive."

I say, "We should watch for anyone acting weird."

"In a crowd of two thousand going berserk?" Wheeler says.

"Do your best."

On the floor, the cheerleaders keep shoving the cards forward at the stands. In return, the students shout back:

"The!"

"Chaos!"

"Club!"

"Is!"

"Coming!"

It becomes a chant, something you'd hear rising from a crowd of overly enthusiastic political protesters. I try to watch any student behaving oddly, but I can't take my eyes off Stranko, waiting for the moment he realizes what's happening.

And then he does.

He covers the gym floor in a blur and rips the cards from the cheerleaders' hands to a wave of boos. Then Stranko gives Benz and Chloe a *move it along* motion with his finger. The confused cheerleaders walk off the floor, a couple of them looking on the verge of tears. An equally puzzled Benz and Chloe stammer through the first couple of lines from their script and announce that's it time for a tug-of-war competition between senior football players and members of the lacrosse team.

"Really? A dick-measuring contest?" Malone says.

Ellie starts giggling. "Now that'd be a good pep rally."

Some heavy metal song Boyd would no doubt recognize erupts from the gym speakers, and the guys from the football and lacrosse teams sprint into the gym from a side door like professional wrestlers entering the ring. No surprise, Stranko has the lacrosse guys all in identical black-and-gold lacrosse jerseys. Following them out is the assistant coach, Tim's dad.

A rope with a red ribbon tied around the middle is laid evenly across center court, and out comes a table with a Gatorade cooler and a plastic bowl of powdered white chalk so the guys can better grip the rope. Most of the dopes do the LeBron James chalk toss, flinging it into the air where it floats like white smoke.

"There's Tim," Wheeler says, pointing down to Adleta. He's chugging Gatorade with the others, who pound it down like it'll help them 'roid-out in a few minutes. Some of them even have three cups. I'm convinced that in twenty years, they're going to discover that energy drinks cause leprosy or blindness. When that happens, professional sports will be really interesting to watch.

The two teams move to opposite sides of the rope, with the three-hundred-pound Hugo King, the football team's left offensive tackle and only hope of a football scholarship, anchoring one side, and Drew "Sully" Sullivan anchoring the undersized lacrosse team. I'm not sure whose idea this was, but it doesn't take a professional sports analyst to see the lacrosse team's going to lose. And I don't just mean lose but *get their arms ripped from their torsos* lose.

After way too much arranging and rearranging of positions by guys on both sides, which in the case of the lacrosse players is sort of like straightening the deck chairs on the *Titanic*, Benz announces we're ready to start.

"The first team to pull the ribbon past the black tape markers on either side wins," he says. "Let's countdown from five."

"Can the football players count backward?" Wheeler asks.

"Shh, this is exciting," Ellie says.

The crowd counts down, and before they hit one, both sides are leaning back on their heels, their faces red and strained, trying to yank the other team out of their shoes. After a full minute of no give on either side, I realize I'm wrong about the lacrosse team, and I quickly see why. They've rooted their legs to the floor, hoping the football team will tire themselves out. The football team tugs at the rope, pulling only with their arms and not their entire bodies. It's the perfect display of the immovable object versus the unstoppable force.

"Who's going to win?" Ellie asks.

"Who cares? If we're lucky, they stay this way forever," Malone says.

But they don't. It's not that one team suddenly overpowers the other. It's because almost simultaneously, guys on both sides drop the rope like it's gone electric. A few jocks get caught up in the quick release and hit the floor. Others double over, some grabbing their knees, some with their hands out but heads down, like they're trying to ward off some approaching enemy.

"What's happening?" Wheeler says.

From the floor, Hugo King answers by grabbing his stomach, shaking his head hard, then puking all over the gym floor.

"Oh yuck!" Ellie yells.

Then other guys involuntarily follow Hugo's lead, painting the gym with their watery guts. Their mouths are geysers, erupting orange-colored Gatorade into the air and onto the floor. They slosh around in the puke, clutching their stomachs, pointlessly trying to stop the never-ending torrent. It's a galactic pukefest, a history-making vomitpalooza.

The student section breaks for the gym doors, pushing past teachers who are fighting to get out themselves. Because we're up top, the four of us can do nothing but watch the chaos and wait for the stench to envelop us and disintegrate our faces.

"Everyone, remain calm," Mrs. B says, standing closer to the puke party than I'd ever go. "It's going to be all right."

Yeah, tell that to the guys who can't stop vomiting.

Stranko and Mr. Adleta stand on the edge of the team, watching in horror as the guys stumble about, their shirts, pants, and shoes drenched in vomit.

"Poor Tim," Ellie says, pointing.

Like the others, Adleta's covered in puke from the first one, two, or three barfings, but now, he has a hand over his mouth, his cheeks puffy as he tries to stop himself from spewing again. He turns his head—looking, looking, looking—his cheeks growing bigger, like a professional trumpet player—and then he begins staggering away from the team.

Right at Stranko and his dad.

And then I get it.

But it's the coaches who really get it.

Stranko sees what's coming and even puts up two hands, like that can stop the inevitable, but the fire hose stream of orange puke hits him square in face, filling his mouth and eyes. Then, like a sprinkler, Tim turns and pukes again, this time into his dad's open mouth. Adleta drops to the floor, writhing around with his arms wrapped around his middle while Stranko and Mr. Adleta slough handfuls of vomit from their mouths.

"Did Tim...?" Ellie says.

"I think so," I say.

"How?"

"I don't know. But he did say he wanted something all his own."

"Well, it looks like he got it."

"I'm impressed," Wheeler says.

"I'm nauseated," Malone finishes.

Students continue rushing away from the toxic air of the gym and into the fresh air of the hall. Adleta's still in the fetal position on the floor, but he's turned away from his dad and Stranko and faces us as if he knew all along exactly where we were sitting. He's far away, and his face is an orange-painted mess, but he gives us a look that is impossible to misinterpret.

It's victory.

CHAPTER 13

In the two weeks following the pep rally pukeathon, three weird things happen.

The first occurs that night at the homecoming game, which, no surprise, we lose. I don't have to be in the locker room to know the guys blame the loss on their mystery illness, a convenient excuse they can thank Adleta for. As for how Adleta pulled it off, he group texted us after school with the answer: ipecac.

If you don't know, ipecac is syrup that causes you to throw up. Some girls have been known to drink it to simplify their eating disorders, so you have to be over eighteen to buy ipecac in a store. Online though, everyone is an adult with a few clicks of "Yes, I am over 18," so it wasn't hard for Adleta to get enough bottles to not only induce vomiting in twenty guys but also to speed up the process considerably.

In the packed nurse's office, Stranko, Mrs. B, and Officer Hale interviewed the victims and dealt with angry parents, but beyond a lot of embarrassment and tired stomach muscles, everyone was fine. Not fine enough *not* to lose the homecoming game 49–6, but fine enough not to die.

But here's the thing—the whole prank unnerved me. It's not just that I can still smell the vomit as if microscopic, vile-smelling puke particles have permanently embedded themselves in my nostrils; it's because, at its core, the prank was just plain mean.

Don't get me wrong: Was the prank creative?

Yes.

Was anyone hurt?

Not really.

And did the prank do exactly what we wanted it to, which is make the Chaos Club look like assholes willing to injure people?

Yes.

So then why does Adleta's prank make me uncomfortable?

Probably because when I think of the guys who were the victims...well, aren't they feeling the same hatred and curl-up-and-die embarrassment I felt after the water tower? Is that something I really want to be responsible for? Is it possible to be Not Max without becoming heartless? I don't know. Or maybe, just maybe, I'm being a baby about the whole thing.

Goddamn empathy.

Still, it isn't my guilty conscience that's the first weird thing that happens—it's the theft of the school's Zippy the Golden Eagle mascot costume.

According to the school newspaper's website, Becca Yancey wore the costume during the homecoming game, flapping around like a dope as usual, then changed in the locker room before halftime so she could walk onto the field with the other popular kids/politicians-in-the-making who were nominated to homecoming court. When Becca went back to the locker room before the start of the third quarter, Zippy had flown the coop, as Mr. Watson might say. Becca's impassioned plea during the morning announcements asking for Zippy's return had me feeling so bad I considered initiating a Buy a New Zippy Kickstarter campaign, but one project a year is my limit.

The second weird thing that occurs isn't a single event but a string of weirdness from Wheeler that lasts an entire week. Not only is Dave late to Weird Science every day, but he also leaves five minutes before the end of the period. Hansen never even asks for an arrival or dismissal pass. Wheeler just comes and goes as he pleases. He's also absent from lunch, which he'll freely tell you is his favorite class. Even when I text him about what's going on, I get no response. He's become Mr. Mystery.

On Friday, after a whole week of this bizarre behavior, Mrs. Hansen leaves a reminder on her classroom door to get our jackets and meet her on the football field for the Great Balloon Launch. Last week, the odds on Wheeler actually showing up for class after being given permission to leave the building were somewhere around 100 to 1, but today, Wheeler's at the fifty-yard line with other students in our class, watching as Hansen, in her a white lab coat and aviator goggles, inflates a massive twenty-foot weather balloon with an air compressor. Painted on the balloon is the lopsided smiley face we added yesterday. This experiment has been two weeks in the making, and in that time, we've studied air currents, weather patterns, GPS tracking, and even Federal Aviation Administration guidelines. Fun, fun.

I stand beside Wheeler, who's wearing a shirt with a picture of a woman holding a beaver covered in soap bubbles in one hand and, in the other hand, a razor blade. Her thought balloon reads, "My husband makes the strangest requests."

"Subtle," I say.

"Awesome, right?"

While Mrs. Hansen inflates the balloon, two students grip the metal ring at its base so the balloon doesn't prematurely go off.

(Side note: prematurely going off is one of my biggest fears.)

Mrs. Hansen says, "And what are we filling Larry with, everyone?"

"Helium," Wheeler says.

We all gawk at Wheeler, who's just volunteered his first correct answer in two and a half years of high school.

"But why not hydrogen, Dave?" Hansen says. "Wouldn't that work just as well for Larry?"

"Because the reading last night said hydrogen's too volatile. The *Hindenburg* was filled with hydrogen."

"It was, Dave, and there's no need to kill Larry before he's fulfilled his destiny. His death is coming soon enough."

"Why is he named Larry?" someone asks.

"After my soon-to-be ex-husband," Mrs. Hansen says. "Sending him into space has long been a dream of mine."

If all goes according to plan, Larry will rise into the air carrying a small camera mounted inside an orange protective case to record the flight. At around ninety thousand feet, Larry—poor, corpulent, unsuspecting Larry—will burst from the atmospheric pressure, sending the case plummeting to the earth until its parachute engages. Hansen plans on tracking the GPS signal inside the camera after school, and on Monday we'll watch the footage. It's awesomeness like this that is precisely why everyone signs up for Weird Science.

"This is safe for birds, right?" Becca asks.

"Unless there's a pterodactyl up there big enough to swallow this, then yes, Becca, no birds will be harmed."

"But what will happen to Larry after? Are you going to recycle him?"

Hansen starts to answer, but Wheeler does it for her.

"Weren't you listening yesterday? She'll bring the balloon back Monday so we can inspect the remains. Sheesh."

Whoever kidnapped Wheeler and replaced him with this Wheeler-bot will pay dearly.

After double-checking that the camera and GPS are working and after another review session of FAA regulations and the earth's atmosphere just to drive home that this is an educational experiment, we do an enthusiastic countdown. At zero, Larry the Balloon lifts into the early November sky at more than thirty miles per hour with the orange case dangling from its base. It's a holy moment with no one speaking as Larry grows smaller and smaller before finally disappearing into the clouds.

"Godspeed, John Glenn," Mrs. Hansen says. "Does anyone know that allusion?"

"It's what they said to John Glenn as he lifted off into space. It was in the extra credit reading," Wheeler says.

"Okay, man," I say, grabbing his arm. "Who are you and what did you do with Dave Wheeler?"

"Dude, I like astronauts. Sue me. Haven't you ever seen *The Right Stuff*?"

On the way back to building, Wheeler's beside Hansen, asking questions and behaving like, well, a real student. The bell rings as we hit the inside of the building, but instead of going to lunch, Wheeler peels off toward the media center. I watch through the window as he takes a seat in the back and opens up an Algebra I book. He doesn't even notice me until I sit down across from him.

"What in the hell is going on with you?" I say.

"What do you mean?"

"I mean this," I say, poking at the math book. "You've never opened a textbook in your life."

"That's not true. I used to look at my health book all the time last year."

"Because of the vagina diagram."

"Man, that was a great picture."

"It was, yeah, but come on. You know what I'm talking about."

Wheeler puts down his pencil and digs into his backpack. Shockingly, there are other textbooks in there. And folders. Honest-to-God folders. From one of them, he pulls a sheet of paper and hands it to me. It's his school transcript, filled with line after line of Ds and Fs for both freshman and sophomore year. By the time he graduates, projected to be by his thirtieth birthday, Wheeler's transcript will be a meme used to scare children into studying harder.

"Do you see it?" Wheeler asks.

I don't.

"Look at my class rank."

At the bottom of the page in the class-rank box, 508/509 is printed.

"Who's dead last?" I ask.

"Joe Vogelsang."

Ah, him. A year ago, Joe drank an entire bottle of Crown Royal when his parents were out of town, then took their car for a joyride. One ignored red light and two paralyzed people later, Joe's now awaiting trial.

"I can't beat him," Wheeler says. "He's still a student here and not doing any of his work, so I can't beat him for the lowest rank. At least until he's convicted and officially removed from the school roster."

"I still don't get it."

"Number two's good enough for me, man," Wheeler says. "I proved I can be the worst—at least the worst of the nonfelons—so now it's time for the dramatic turnaround. Let's see how good at this I can be. Who knows, maybe my brothers were onto something with the whole studying thing. Besides, you heard Malone the other day. Imagine what I could do if I really tried. None of this is that hard. I just have to do it. And seriously, who wants to end up living in a stupid barn like your uncle? I mean, yeah, he has money and stuff, but the guy's pretty much a loser. No offense."

I give him a *none taken* wave of the hand. "So you're now Nerdy Wheeler?"

"Instead of Screwup Wheeler, yeah. Why not try something new, right? But, man, let me tell you, it sucks. I have all these credits to make up, and I'm in guidance all of third period now doing courses online, and I have permission to be here working during lunch, but it's so much, dude. The good news is my mom's so thrilled that she says if I pass all my classes this semester, she'll help me get a new car."

"And get rid of the Wheelermobile?"

"All things must come to an end, dude. Besides, if I pull this off, I'm a shoo-in for Most Changed in the yearbook next year."

If ever there was an *I'll believe it when I see it* moment, this is it. But I don't tell Wheeler that. Mostly I'm impressed. It's sort of what I'm doing with Not Max. So, I say, good for us.

Well, good for us until Stranko walks into the media

center. He comes through the doors and gives the room a quick once-over. When he sees us, his head jerks to a stop, then he comes our way. Not that I blame him. Wheeler, even Nerdy Wheeler, unsupervised anywhere is definitely cause for concern.

"What's going on here?" Stranko asks.

"Just getting my homework done," Wheeler says.

"Homework? Right."

"No, seriously. Look."

Wheeler pushes his book and a page of algebra problems toward Stranko, who smirks as he looks it over.

"Good luck with that. At this point, you'd have better luck putting out a house fire with a cup of water."

"Thank you for your support, sir."

Stranko scowls, which only grows in intensity when he notices Wheeler's beaver shirt.

"And would you care to explain your shirt to me?"

"This?" Wheeler says, pointing to the woman. "Well, as far as I can tell, the family owns a petting zoo or maybe they live in the woods, I don't know, but for some reason, her husband wants the beaver shaved. Maybe it has fleas or something."

Stranko's eyes go full-on coin slot.

"Is that right?"

"Well, sure," Wheeler says. "Why? Do you have a different interpretation?"

Stranko's lip twitches.

"You need to turn that shirt inside out," he says. "Then

I never want to see it in the school again. Do we understand each other?"

"Absolutely, sir. Thank you for your continued concern
about my well-being and education."

Wheeler sits there, staring up at Stranko, who's not
moving.

"I said turn the shirt inside out," Stranko says.

"You mean right here? Now?"

"That's what I said."

Wheeler shrugs, then mouths *perv* at me as he stands
up. He takes his shirt off, deliberately fumbling with it
longer than he has to before turning it inside out. When
he finally gets the shirt back on, he gives Stranko a
Happy? look.

"Never again," Stranko says, then leaves without
responding.

"Jerk," I say.

"Who cares? He'll get his."

"Wait, are you saying the New Studious Wheeler
didn't completely kill off Old Devious Wheeler?"

"Dude, this is just an upgrade, not a brand-new install.
The old me isn't going anywhere."

Which is a scary thought indeed.

The final and weirdest thing to happen that week occurs
on Thursday evening while I'm dangerously flirting
with an aneurism by studying precalc. My phone pings

announcing a text, and I have to read the message twice to understand what I'm being asked to do.

Ellie: Tremblay's Pet Shop. Buy 200 goldfish. Meet at the window outside Room 103 in an hour.

Me: ?

Ellie: Hurry, Mongoose.

What choice do I have? It's Heist Rule #16: *Be ready when your team needs you.*

I use the excuse that I forgot I needed a copy of *Macbeth* for English tomorrow to escape the house. Tremblay's Pet Shop is in Freehold, one town over, and it takes me twenty minutes to get there. When I arrive, it's 8:55 p.m., and a guy so old looking I worry he might turn to dust right in front of me is locking up.

"I need two hundred goldfish," I say.

He lets out a sigh that, considering his age, he probably shouldn't. When you're close to 150 years old, you should conserve as many of your remaining breaths as possible.

"Piranhas?" he says.

"No, goldfish."

"I mean, do you have a piranha? Is that what the fish are for?"

"Oh, duh, yeah. Exactly."

It takes Tremblay a good ten minutes to scoop out two hundred goldfish from the massive tank in back. Honestly, it's more like two hundred give or take twenty. I seriously doubt whatever Ellie needs the goldfish for is dependent on exact numbers. The total comes to just under forty dollars, and I leave the store hauling a box with ten clear plastic bags filled with seriously freaked-out goldfish.

On the way back to school, I use Stranko's school map on my phone to find out exactly who Room 103 belongs to. It's Mrs. Roberts's art room, located in the back of the building. Twenty minutes later, I'm giving myself a hernia as I lug what's essentially a box of water to the correct window. Already there, waiting in the darkness and holding their own boxes, are Wheeler and Adleta.

"Goldfish too?" Adleta asks.

"From Tremblay's," I say.

"I had to go to the PetSmart in Athens."

"I was all the way over in Bakersfield," Wheeler says. "We should demand gas money."

"No sign of Ellie?" I ask.

"Ellie?" Adleta says. "My text was from Kate."

"I got one from both of them, telling me to move my ass," Wheeler says.

The window blind suddenly goes up, and standing there are both Ellie and Malone, dressed all in black and wearing ski caps. Malone opens the window, and Ellie leans out, saying, "Come on, there's not a lot of time."

"What's going on?" I ask.

"I'll explain later. Hurry."

We begin handing bag after bag of goldfish through the window to Ellie and Malone. With each bag we pass through, the girls disappear into the dark art room. I can't see where they're going, but I can hear water running inside. After I hand Ellie my final bag, she starts to close the window.

"Wait a minute," I say. "At least give us some clue."

Ellie and Kate break into grins, and Malone says, "Operation Aquatic Art is under way."

CHAPTER 14

I have to wait until morning to see the final product. I show up to school early, but even then I have to fight my way through dozens of students already packed into Mrs. Roberts's art room, where everyone is staring at the ten-foot-tall glass display case used to show off award-winning art. But it's not the art that has their attention— it's the six hundred goldfish swimming among the pottery and now-blurry charcoal drawings. Hanging from a paper clip chain attached to the case is one of Malone's Chaos Club cards.

Both Malone and Ellie stand on chairs in the back of the room, and on my way, I kick a garden hose connected to the faucet on one of Roberts's many paint-splattered sinks. I pull up a chair between the girls, both of whom are struggling not to smile.

"How'd you even get in here?" I whisper.

"We hid in the storage room until Mrs. Roberts left," Malone said. "After that, the room was ours."

"You guys waited here until we showed up at nine? That's insane."

"But worth it, right?"

There's no denying that. The glass case is a massive

pulsing orange cloud. In a day or two, it'll be murky with fish crap, but for now—

"It's a work of art," Ellie says.

"Shoot, I had to make up for the hours I spent on Wheeler's boner diagram," Malone says. "That whole thing left me with a bad taste in my mouth."

"That's what she said," I say.

"Funny guy."

When Adleta and Wheeler enter the room, Adleta bulldozes a path for them to the front of the crowd. After seeing what Ellie and Malone have accomplished, they come our way.

Wow, Adleta mouths to the girls.

Wheeler holds a thumbs-up close to his chest.

Soon, all five of us are on chairs, watching the revolving door of students enter and leave the room. Even teachers show up to see the school's newest aquarium.

"Is that caulking?" Adleta asks.

"Yeah," says Malone. "I ran strips around the edge of the case and where the doors normally open. I'm not sure how secure it is though. If it gives out—"

"We'll have a goldfish holocaust," Wheeler finishes.

"Why didn't you take the art out first?" I ask. "Didn't you have a piece in there?"

"Two, actually," Malone says, "but to create, you must destroy."

"That's not the only reason," Ellie says, and she and Malone start laughing.

"What's so funny?" Adleta asks.

"Just wait," Malone says, then looks to the doorway.

Oh no.

It's Libby. It only takes her three steps into the room before she's shouting, "Oh my God!" and shoving her way to the display case. When she gets a closer look, she goes full-on hysterical, pounding at the glass so hard we're all probably seconds away from a goldfish tidal wave. Luckily for all of us, Mrs. Roberts steps out from the crowd and gently guides Libby into the hall. I'm not sure if it's to calm her down or protect the rest of us from a Libby rampage.

"Oh man," Malone says. "Libby's charcoal self-portrait for the Scholastics Competition was in there. That's a shame. And she was sure to get a Gold Key for it too. Maybe even a scholarship."

"Wow, bummer," Ellie deadpans.

Then they both start giggling, trying—and failing—to control their volume.

Wheeler and Adleta join in too, but I don't. I can't. I won't. Of course, like an idiot, I say, "Man, that has to suck if you're Libby."

Malone's eyes darken. "Are you purposely trying to sound like an asshole or are you actually showing sympathy for Libby Heckman?"

"No, but—"

"Good, because I'd hate to think you feel sorry for her. That would mean you've forgotten what she put me through last year. And what she did at the pep rally last week. Girls commit suicide over things like that, Max. Maybe some girls you know have actually even considered it."

"I just meant—"

"So you don't get to try to make me feel bad about this, you got it? You wanted us to pull a prank in the name of the Chaos Club, and that's what I did. If I chose Libby as my target, that's my decision, not yours."

"But—"

Malone drops off the chair and walks through the jam-packed students still in the room.

Wheeler gives me a *yeeesh* look.

Adleta's not even looking at me.

And Ellie says, "I'd think you of all people would be a little more supportive."

"I'm just saying maybe that may have been a little much. You saw Libby, right? And that's the drawing she's been working on for weeks. It's completely ruined."

"So what? Maybe try to see it from Kate's point of view next time and not just your own. I have to get to my locker before class."

"Smooth, dude," Wheeler says.

I couldn't have said it better myself.

For the rest of the day, I feel like shit, which is only compounded by Malone ignoring my apology texts. But am I wrong? Making a bunch of guys puke and destroying a girl's art—how does it help us get back at the Chaos Club? What was business before is now personal, and I don't like it. Or maybe I'm overreacting. Stranger things have happened. It's really an ethics question, so I do the only thing I can think of: I stop by Watson's room on the way out of the building.

"What can I do for you, Max?" Watson asks. He's at his desk in the back of the room with his feet up, an *Existential Dread Is My Copilot* coffee cup resting on a pile of today's pop quizzes.

"I have a philosophy question," I say.

"Then you came to the right place. Fire away."

"Is revenge ethical?"

Watson raises his eyebrows.

"Now that is an excellent question. Maybe it should be this week's Big Questions of Existence topic."

"I'd rather hear what you have to say on it."

"Well, not to be evasive, but it doesn't matter what I think. What matters is what you think. All questions of ethics are like that. The answer depends on what you believe in—your religion, if you have one; your upbringing; your environment. You have to set your own parameters for what's acceptable. If you don't, someone else will do it for you."

"I should've known better than to come here looking for a straight answer."

Watson laughs and says, "I'm not one to give answers.

I'm more interested in giving you the tools to come up with the answers yourself."

"And in this case?"

"That means thinking about what you believe in and why—the why is the important part—then making decisions based on that. It's the only honest way to do things."

"You're like the illegitimate child of Yoda and Socrates," I say.

"That might just be the best compliment I've ever received," Watson says. "However, I will say that revenge and justice aren't the same thing. Most people make the mistake of confusing the two."

I wish I could report the clouds parting and a rainbow of understanding shining down on me, but no, two weeks later, I'm as confused as I was before. I do know that I hate having people mad at me though, and Malone's cold-shouldering me gets to be too much to take, so one night, I drive to the Asheville Climbing Center, where she works. Just the sight of those walls with their tiny handholds is enough to make my stomach do somersaults. I find Malone at the base of the expert wall with a group of college-y-looking guys in a semicircle in front of her. Kate's wearing black soccer shorts and an employee shirt with the sleeves cut off. She looks absolutely badass.

"I can't," she's saying to one of the guys. "I'm not allowed to climb during work hours."

He says, "Come on, I'll even make it easier for you. I put up ten bucks and you put up nothing. Just race me."

"Like I said—"

He snorts and says to the guy next to him, "I knew it was all talk. No girl's that good."

If he's trying to push Malone's buttons, he's picked the right one. Without a word, she clips onto the wall and motions for a coworker, another girl who looks like she could snap me in half. Once the guy clips in, he and Malone stand waiting at the base of the wall.

"Want a head start?" he says.

Malone ignores him and asks the worker for a quick countdown.

At zero, Malone is gone, a spider monkey climbing the wall. Her legs and arms flash this way and that as she rockets toward the ceiling. It takes her less than twenty seconds to climb fifty feet, and when she reaches the top, she clangs the cowbell at the ceiling's base. Then Malone pushes off the wall and drops down, rappelling past the poor bastard who isn't even three-quarters of the way up.

As she unclips, she tells the guys, "Have your friend give Mia my ten bucks when he gets down. Whenever that is."

The girl who spotted Malone gives her a high five and says, "You're so hot."

"Thanks, Mia," Malone says. "I'll see you later."

I follow Malone as she walks to another area of the building. She's not even breathing heavy.

"That was amazing," I say.

"I shouldn't have let them get to me like that. But whatever," she says. "So why are you here? Looking to lecture me again?"

"No, I wanted to apologize. I shouldn't have said anything about Libby."

"But you still think I shouldn't have done that to her?"

"Honestly?"

"Of course."

"I don't know."

I tell her about what Watson said about revenge and justice and how I feel like we're confusing the two in our pursuit of exposing the Chaos Club.

"So what if we are?" Malone says. "That's not your problem. If Adleta wants to puke on Stranko and his dad, and I want Libby dead for what she did to me, then that's on our consciences, not yours. I totally wish I could just forget what she did to me, let it go and pretend like it's no big deal, but I can't."

"I get it," I say. "I just wanted to say I was sorry. I was an idiot. I'll mind my business next time."

Malone softens, and her eyes drop for a second while she works something out.

"Well, since you didn't mind your business, I'll be guilty of it too," she says. "Ellie told me about you two at the radar dish."

My cheeks get so hot, my head may burst into flames.

"Don't get embarrassed," she says. "I totally get

it. Ellie's cute and cool. You'd be crazy not to try to kiss her."

I don't say anything because: (A) I don't know how to respond, and (B) I'm hoping if I focus hard enough, I'll teleport to another planet.

"But, look, here's the thing—and I feel like a bitch saying this, but you're a good guy—I think you need to be careful around Ellie."

"What?"

"It's just…look, I like Ellie, I really do. She's really nice, like scary nice, but I've heard things about her, Max. Like maybe she's not as nice as she makes herself out to be."

"What have you heard?"

"Rumors mostly."

"About what?"

"That she lies, Max. All the time. I admit I haven't witnessed that, but I don't know, I can see it somehow. She's so good at acting. We've seen that firsthand. I just don't want to see you get hurt."

"I don't think you have anything to worry about. She blew me off."

"Maybe that's for the best."

Getting rejected is "for the best"?

Yeah right.

At home, I do two things:

First, I delete the naked picture of Malone from my

phone. It's something I should've done months ago. But before you give me the Good Guy Award, know that my finger hovered over the Delete Photo button for a good two minutes. Still, I did push it.

Dammit.

Second, I google *Chaos Club*, and it takes digging through three pages of links to Wheeler's fake site to get to the real one. On the real Chaos Club site, I hope to find a denial of the pranks we've pulled in their name, but there's nothing. The only change I can see from the beginning of the year is a picture of the cows on the roof. They don't even bother mentioning the water tower prank, almost like it wasn't a big deal to them.

Question: If we're going to all this trouble to get back at a club who doesn't care what we're doing, aren't we being laughed at all over again?

Later that week, Ellie catches me on my way to lunch.

"You need to get on board," Ellie says. She's doing that bouncing-on-her-toes thing she does when she's excited. "I would've thought you'd be first to come up with a prank. Now you're almost last."

"I will eventually."

"What's stopping you?"

Fair question. Mostly, I haven't thought of a prank yet, but a good part of it is the whole guilt thing.

"I'll come up with something soon," I say.

"Okay, but in the meantime…"

Ellie pulls her phone out and moves in close.

Would it be creepy of me if I sniffed her hair?

"I need your help," she says. "But you can't tell anyone." She unlocks her phone and shows me the picture on her wallpaper.

"Oh my God," I say. "Stealing isn't very Christian-like, Ellie Wick."

"Neither is what I'm going to do with it," she says.

"What's the plan?"

"I think it's time the school got an image makeover. I can give you the details when there aren't so many ears around, but it's a two-person job. Are you in?"

I hesitate just one second, but it's one second too long.

"What's wrong?" Ellie says. Then her brow furrows. "Wait, you're not thinking about quitting, are you?"

"Huh? No."

"You are, aren't you? It's because of Tim's and Kate's pranks, right?"

Man, I swear sometimes girls have ESP or something.

"You can't quit, Max. We need you. I need you."

I certainly like the sound of that.

She says, "You may not like the last two pranks, but remember how you felt after the water tower? That's why we're doing this."

"You say that, but it's become personal."

"But it *is* personal, Max. How can it not be? The Chaos Club embarrassed us and has gotten me twice now. People are still slipping Hitler pictures into my locker. The Chaos Club needs to pay for what they've done. It's almost like none of this is real to you because it was a couple months ago."

"It's still real," I say but wonder if maybe she's right. I can't remember the last time someone called out, "Water Tower Five!" to me in the hall. And I'm sure not getting Hitler pictures in my locker.

"I'm worried the others are losing interest too," she says. "It's like every club here in the school. Have you ever noticed they all sort of die off in the winter, once kids have gone long enough to put it on their college applications? But I think with us it'd be too bad if we gave up. We have something awesome here."

"Yeah, we should go into business."

"One step at a time, Mongoose. So come on, will you help me?"

Guilty conscience versus time with Ellie?

No contest.

"I'm in," I say.

"You don't sound fully committed."

"I'll get there. It's a good idea you have."

"Wrong," Ellie says. "It's a great idea."

"Right, a great idea. Let's do it."

"Game on!"

Ellie claps hard once and looks so happy I think she might kiss me. Call it horny-teenage-wishful-thinking.

"It's going to take me a bit to figure out exactly how I want to do this, but I'll let you know," Ellie says. "Thanks a ton, Max."

I figure I'll just fake it until I feel it. It's worked so far. Besides, it's Heist Rule #17: *Commit one hundred percent.*

But it turns out I don't need to fake it at all. Commitment suddenly isn't an issue.

Not after I get to school the next morning.

Like most kids, once I get off the bus and enter the school, I go directly to my locker to get my books for the day. But today that's easier said than done because Stranko's standing at my locker bay in front of a line of yellow caution tape. A large group of students laugh and talk excitedly as I weave my way to the front to see what's going on. It takes a few seconds to understand what I'm looking at. It's like the Blob has swallowed one of the lockers. But not just any locker—it's my locker. Yellowish, spongy dough, sticky and reeking of yeast, is bursting from the locker, spilling from the air vents, and dripping onto the floor.

"That your locker, Cobb?" Stranko says.

I'm speechless.

"I should've guessed."

Mr. Jessup arrives and tiptoes to my locker, approaching it from the side. He wedges his hand into where he thinks the combination lock is and pulls away a handful of mucus-like dough. Then Jessup inserts a key into the middle of the combination dial and flattens himself against the lockers, backing away as far as he can and still reach the latch.

When Jessup lifts the latch, the door bursts open. My folders and books and black hoodie slowly erupt from my locker in a mass of smothering dough, oozing onto the floor like beige lava. The final item to seep out is a dough-filled bucket along with dozens of black Chaos Club cards. Even from ten feet away, I can see none of them have the small water tower graphic on them.

"How many other lockers are there like this?" Stranko says to Mr. Jessup.

"Four," he says.

You can probably guess whose lockers those are.

CHAPTER 15

Ellie names it Operation Sex, Drugs, and Suicide.

My code name is Weegee, "after the famous crime scene photographer, duh," Ellie says.

Her code name is Meryl, after actress Meryl Streep.

"I'm not sure she ever played a role like this," I say.

"Because she couldn't handle a role like this."

Ellie and I stand on the high school football field on the eighth and final night of our photo shoot. I haven't seen any of the other Water Tower Fivers since winter break started a week ago. That's not by design but simply the result of busy lives. Schoolwork, sports, jobs, family responsibilities, and whatnot get in the way of what we'd all really like to do, which is work on destroying the Chaos Club. But no, Wheeler's at the local tutoring center full time now, Malone's busy anchoring people at the rock wall, and Adleta is in Orlando for a lacrosse tournament. That leaves Ellie and me to pull her prank, to which I say—excellent.

"Make sure you have the scoreboard in the background," Ellie says, lying down on the fifty-yard line.

"The scene of the notorious Hitler-moustache prank," I say.

"Exactly."

I stand over Ellie and dump out a garbage bag. Condom wrappers, Bud Light cans, and an empty Maker's Mark bottle spill onto the frozen field. I arrange them artfully around Ellie, the evidence of a wild night I'm certain neither of us has ever really had.

"Where did you get the alcohol?" I ask, shooting another picture.

"Out of my neighbor's recycling bin. He has a real problem."

"Like we're ones to judge."

"Exactly," Ellie says. "Guilty of trespassing and possession of stolen goods. We're headed for eternal damnation."

I move to another angle and get low to the ground. Each camera flash is like a lightning strike.

"That should do it," I say. "Unless you have any others we need to take."

"No, we're good. That's the last one. No point in pushing our luck."

Back in Ellie's car, she changes her outfit in the backseat, threatening to decapitate me if I sneak a look. I take my chances anyway. Even with the heater going full blast, it takes a couple minutes for the car to warm up.

Ellie says, "So what about your prank?"

"What about it?"

"Have you thought of one yet?"

"I'm working on it."

"You don't seem at all interested in the guaranteed yes. I would've thought you'd jump all over that."

"I'm going to do something. I promise."

"If you're not careful, you'll run out of time."

"Schools not out until May."

"It'll come faster than you expect."

"Like my balls. Unfortunately."

Ellie's laugh is a sunshine-y sound I've come to depend on in the last week. It's one of the few things giving me a break from my perpetual pissy-ness from the dough-in-the-locker prank. (Yeast, water, and dough in a bucket overnight, in case you were wondering.) Worse was that Stranko had the nerve to imply we'd played the prank on ourselves. Ellie's crying at the suggestion put an end to that line of thought quickly, but it made me even madder than I already was.

We pull into my driveway shortly before ten o'clock. Except for our Christmas tree lit in the family room window, the house is dark. I don't want to go in yet. The more time I've spent with Ellie, the more comfortable I've gotten with her. And the more comfortable I've gotten with her, the more I joke-flirt with her in a not-so-subtle-yet-safe way.

"Maybe we should celebrate the end of our photo shoot with a kiss," I say.

"Oh, you think, huh?"

"I'm pretty sure it's bad luck not to."

"We'll just have to risk it."

You can't blame a guy for trying.

"What did I tell you about *us*?" Ellie asks.

"You said after."

"*Maybe* after, yeah. We have a lot to do still."

"But are my chances getting better?"

"Oh, absolutely. With each passing moment."

"Then I'll be strong and soldier on."

I go to get out of the car when Ellie says, "I do need one small favor on Monday."

"What's that?"

"A favor? It's a small act of kindness. I thought you were smarter than that."

"Tell me."

"I want to see his look when it goes live. Can you make that happen?"

"How in the hell am I supposed to do that?"

"You? Maxwell Cobb? The mastermind behind the Stranko Caper? I think you can come up with something."

Ellie does that bat-her-eyelashes thing that the female species has perfected through thousands of years of evolution. Like all males, I'm defenseless against it.

When I think later about what Ellie wants, I realize the difficulty isn't in the execution but in having the balls to do it. I will because Ellie's the asker, but I keep thinking of a quote I once heard about how there's a fine line between courage and stupidity. In this case, it's a very, very fine line.

The rest of the week is spent suffering through exam prep and wondering just what sort of moron schedules semester exams for the three days following winter break. The only answer I can come up with is a moron who loves to ruin kids' vacations. In this case, Stranko. He takes exams überserious, even sending out an email to every high school parent about how all classroom doors will be locked when the bell rings and how tardy students will receive zeroes. So imagine Stranko's irritation when Monday comes and students and teachers are milling in the halls, unable to enter any of the classrooms because none of the doors will open. Zero. Not a single one.

We're all loitering in the halls, watching teachers pointlessly enter and reenter keys in their locks while Stranko pushes his way through the crowds, yelling at Mr. Jessup over the walkie-talkie to "get these damn doors open."

"Wheeler?" Malone says to Ellie and me outside Watson's room.

"No chance," I say.

By some miracle of the universe—or, in reality, a combination of make-up work, extra credit, and much pleading by his mom and guidance counselor on the defendant's behalf—Wheeler's pulled his grades to within striking distance of passing. The looming reality couldn't be more mathematically simple: Pass the exams, pass the classes. Fail the exams, fail the classes.

"Maybe Tim?" Ellie asks.

"Not me either," Tim says, coming up behind us. "I've made my entry in the competition. Unlike some people."

"Mine's coming," Ellie says. "Sooner than you think, actually."

"What about you?" Adleta says to me.

"Someday."

That's when my phone buzzes.

And Ellie's.

And Tim's.

And Malone's.

And everyone else's around us until the entire hall is a sea of miscellaneous chimes, rings, and tones signaling arriving texts.

We all receive the same message:

Courtesy of the (Genuine) Chaos Club.

"Wow," Malone says. "As much as I hate them, I have to admit that's impressive."

Word soon spreads that during the night, the Chaos Club took every door off its hinges and reinstalled it at another classroom. It's takes the team of Mrs. B, Stranko, and Mr. Jessup the better part of a half hour to unlock every room with master keys.

How am I supposed to think of a prank that competes with that?

After Watson's exam, which is easier than I expected, I say to Ellie, "Do you still need me to do it?"

"Absolutely. Why wouldn't I?"

"Well, with the Chaos Club thing, I thought maybe you might want to have all the attention to yourself."

"Are you kidding me? This is the best time. We'll totally steal their spotlight," she says. "Why do you have that look on your face?"

"Stranko, he'll kill me."

"Oh, foo. You don't need to worry about him. Just be confident. It works every time," she says with her best angelic voice and praying hands under her chin. "If you want me to, I'll put in a special word with the big guy."

"That's good because I may be seeing Him sooner than expected."

Mrs. Stephen's precalc exam is next, and by the time I'm finished, I feel like I've spent the last hour and a half tumbling and crashing inside an industrial-sized dryer. I'm pretty sure the Pythagorean theorem and reciprocal identities were invented solely to make teenagers' lives horrible. How else can you explain a teacher saying things like, "To find the zeros of the logarithmic function, one would exponentiate the left and right sides of the equation"?

The daily schedule for exam week at Asheville High makes almost as much sense as having the exams immediately after winter break. We get out ninety minutes early each day, but only after suffering through two, two-hour exams and a mandatory one-hour study session with our homeroom teacher. I'm five minutes into this study session when I get permission from Mr. Ewing to go see Stranko.

It's time to die young.

I want to take my time getting to Stranko's office, but unfortunately, I'm on a tight timetable. I make a quick stop in the bathroom outside the main office and turn on my phone's video camera app before sliding it into the pocket of the shirt I've worn specifically for this purpose. As Ellie requested, I reach Stranko's door at 11:42 a.m. His expression sours at the sight of me.

"Can I come in?" I say.

Stranko sighs and puts down the lacrosse magazine he's reading instead of doing his real job, whatever that is.

"Sit."

Shockingly, Stranko's office doesn't have black walls decorated with instruments of torture. Instead, there's a desk, a bookshelf with actual books (and not just ones for coloring), a framed college degree on the wall (probably from an online university), and a minifridge (likely filled with human heads). The most shocking item is a picture on his desk of an older couple who are probably his parents or the scientists who genetically engineered him at the Asshole Farm. My only seating option is a straight-backed, wooden chair created solely for discomfort. The moment I sit, my ass starts aching.

"What do you want, Cobb?" Stranko said. "I'm sort of busy here."

Uh-huh.

"Sir, I just came to say that over break, I did a lot of thinking and realized I need to make some changes in my life. With the new semester starting soon, I wanted to apologize for my behavior over the first part of the school year. I promise that second semester will be much less chaotic."

And that, friends, is some Olympic-level bullshit. I look at the clock over Stranko's head. 11:43—two minutes to go.

"Well, let's hope you're right about next semester," Stranko says. "You could use some maturing."

I have to hold down the middle finger struggling to show itself.

"Yeah, I could definitely grow up some."

Stranko stares, trying to figure out if I'm being a smart-ass, and then sighs, leaning back in his chair. He has to be exhausted from the morning's events with the doors. What he doesn't know is that his day's seconds away from getting worse.

"Look, Cobb, I'm not stupid," he says. "I know what the students here think about me. That comes with the job. And part of that's my fault because I'm not touchy-feely like Mrs. Barber, and I'll never be. I'm intense and I can be a yeller—I know that. But do you think I enjoy being a hard-ass all the time? Believe me, it's not fun. But it's the job. What I do here, keeping all of you in line, helps Asheville be what it is, which is a damn fine place. I love this school. But once you let discipline slip, quality slips. That's something my dad always used to say."

I glance at the picture on the end table, taking a closer

look at Stranko's father. Although it's just him and his wife smiling on a couch, the man's eyes are hard.

"You probably could loosen up just a little," I say, sort of joking.

Stranko half smiles—or maybe half un-frowns is more accurate.

"Agreed. And you could meet me in the middle by tightening up some."

"I'll do my best."

It's possible there's a real human in Stranko somewhere— the joking, dancing, young Stranko just biding his time until he can make a triumphant return. Wouldn't that be nice? The thought makes me not scared of him for the first time in my life. It's not a feeling that lasts long.

"Actually, while you're here, let me show you something," Stranko says and removes a cell phone from his pocket and places it in front of me. "This is my new phone. I had to get this one because I lost my old one. In fact, interestingly enough, it disappeared on the day of your little stunt in the cafeteria with the trophy. Do you remember that?"

I swallow my terror.

"Is there anything you want to tell me about that day?"

I can barely get words out.

"What do you mean?"

Stranko leans so close and speaks so quietly that if anyone else were in the room, they couldn't hear him.

"Don't bullshit me, Cobb. I don't think it's any

coincidence that my phone went missing at the same time you idiots were chasing each other around the cafeteria. I'm going to figure out what happened, and when I do, I'm going to rain hell on whomever was involved. If you have any information that could help, this is your chance to let me know."

I don't piss myself, but, man, I could.

"I don't know anything," I say.

Stranko doesn't move.

"Of course you don't, Cobb. Of course you don't."

A knock at the door saves me.

Mrs. Engen, Stranko's secretary, hurries in and whispers something I can't make out. Not that I need to hear her. I sit up and reposition myself to capture everything. Stranko performs a few clicks on his computer and goes from serious to concerned to infuriated all in a matter of seconds.

"You, get out."

"What's wrong?" I say.

Stranko doesn't answer, doesn't even tell me to leave again because he's fully focused on the pictures Ellie's uploaded onto our fake Chaos Club site. They've been there since this morning, but the program Wheeler pirated for Ellie only sent the mass email and text to the staff and student body two minutes ago.

"Dammit!"

Stranko pounds the desk so hard, he's lucky his hand doesn't go all the way through. I remain frozen, so the camera catches everything. Stranko's eyes strain like they might come out of his head. It's frighteningly awesome.

"Dammit! Dammit! Dammit!"

I practically hit the ceiling at the outburst.

"What are you still doing here?" he shouts. "Get the hell out!"

I leave so fast there's a vapor trail.

In each office I pass, guidance counselors, secretaries, and even the school psychologist are staring at their computers. In the classrooms, I walk by kids who have their phones out, not even trying to hide their laughter.

I'm happy for Ellie. Her idea was brilliant, and I'm sure some part of her wishes everyone knew that she's the one who's pulled this off. Because even though she's in every picture, no one can tell it's her. Why? Because she's wearing the Zippy the Golden Eagle mascot costume she stole during the homecoming game.

Among the pictures we took:

1. Zippy spray-painting a naked woman on the side of a vacant building downtown.

2. Zippy with an ax poised over a neighborhood dog's neck.

3. Zippy pretending to take a leak on the school sign.

4. Zippy hunched over, ready to snort a long line of white power through his massive beak.

5. Zippy passed out on the football field surrounded by beer cans and condoms.

6. And the final image—Zippy standing on a bucket with a noose around his neck.

Oh, and prominently displayed in each picture on Zippy's feathery chest? A Chaos Club card.

After school, I head in the direction of Ellie's homeroom and spot her in the hall coming my way, unable to hold back her excitement.

"Did you get it? Please tell me you got it."

I tap the phone in my pocket.

Ellie throws her arms around me and kisses my cheek hard in the middle of the crowded hall. The tent I pitch could house a circus.

"Can I see it?" she says, referring, unfortunately, to the video.

"Let's wait until we get to your car. Too many people around."

"Come on then!"

Ellie pulls at my hand, dragging me toward the exit. Her excitement is contagious, and soon, I'm rushing through the halls with her. We're closing in on the front lobby by the main office, when coming toward us is the last person in the world I want to see: Stranko. I slow a little, thinking maybe we should duck into a classroom, but Ellie's tugs at my arm.

"Relax," she says. "Act natural."

I grip Ellie's hand tight as Stranko approaches. We don't need to worry though. Stranko goes right past us like we're not there. He's on a mission, and from the tight set of his jaw, it's one to seek and destroy. And I know Stranko's target because he was muttering the name under his breath as he passed.

"We have to follow him," I say.

"Why? Do you think he found out who did the doors?"

"I'm not sure, but we can't let him get away."

"Why?"

"Because he's about to bust Wheeler."

CHAPTER 16

Being right sucks.

Ellie and I watch from behind a locker as Stranko goes into Mr. Fleiger's room and escorts a stone-faced Wheeler to his office with Mr. Fleiger following.

"What do you think he did?" Ellie says.

The possibilities:

a. Wheeler got caught planning a prank.
b. Wheeler got caught pulling a prank.
c. Wheeler got caught cheating.
d. Wheeler got caught with Stranko's phone.
e. All of the above.

Everyone knows when you don't know the answer you're supposed to choose *C*, but in this case, I fear it's *D*.

"We need to let the others know," I say. "If this is all about to go to hell, they need to be prepared, maybe even leave the country."

Heist Rule #18: *Protect your crew.*

Ellie sends a text to Adleta and Malone, and we take up surveillance in the lobby, sitting on a ratty couch across from the receptionist's desk. While we wait, Mrs. Wheeler comes through the front doors and heads straight for Stranko's office. It's not two minutes before Adleta and Malone show up, walking and talking together as they approach. No chance this scene would have happened a year ago. Funny how that happens.

"Anything yet?" Adleta asks.

"They're still in there," I say. "Wheeler's mom just showed up."

"But we don't know why?" Malone says.

"No, but it can't be good."

We all stare pointlessly at the office for a few seconds, as if the answer will suddenly appear on the glass.

"By the way, nice prank, Ellie," Malone says. "Suicidal Zippy should be the cover of the yearbook."

Adleta says, "People in my homeroom were going crazy. Even Mrs. Bross was laughing."

"Thanks, guys. Max deserves some of the credit too. He took the pictures."

I scowl and wave off the recognition.

"What's wrong with you?" Malone says.

"This isn't going to end well."

"Seriously? You're such a Debbie Downer. You don't know why they're in there. For all you know, Wheeler called Fleiger an asshole."

"No, Stranko's onto us."

I tell them about going to film Stranko in his office and his asking me what I know about his missing phone.

"And you denied it, right?" Malone says.

"Of course."

"Then that's all you need to do."

"That's not the point. He suspects us. We need to be careful."

It's another ten minutes before Stranko's door opens and Wheeler and his mom come out. Wheeler struts like he doesn't care about whatever just happened, but his mom looks just the opposite, even pointing an angry finger back toward Stranko's office.

"Man, she's pissed," Adleta says.

"No Stranko though. That's a good sign for us," Ellie says.

I give Wheeler a low whistle that draws his attention.

"Any bets?" Adleta says.

"I'll go with cheating," Malone says.

She's probably right. But considering all the work he's been doing lately to turn things around, the thought makes me feel like the world's worst friend.

"Hey, guys," Wheeler says.

"*Hey, guys?* That's it?" Malone says. "What happened?"

"Fleiger accused me of cheating, and I called him a dick."

Malone looks at us with I-told-you-so eyes.

"So why does he think you cheated?" Ellie says.

"Because I got a B on his stupid exam."

"He knows that already?"

"Yeah, it was a Scantron test."

Ah, the Scantron, the lazy teacher's test format. So easy a chimp can grade it.

"The thing is, I didn't cheat," Wheeler says. "I studied my ass off for that exam. It's not my fault that for review, Fleiger read off every question straight from the test. I just wrote them all down."

"Did you tell him that?" Ellis asks.

"Yeah, and all he could say is there was no way I could do that well after screwing around all semester. Finally, I just lost it."

"And called him a dick," Malone says.

"A shriveled dick, but yeah."

"So what happened in the office?"

"Mom took my side, of course. She knows how much I've been studying. By the end of the meeting, she wanted to call both of them dicks too."

"You mean shriveled dicks," Adleta says.

"The thing is I don't blame Fleiger for accusing me. It's not like I have the cleanest record. But Stranko really pushed that I was cheating and even called Mrs. Nally to grade my first-period exam and let me know how I did. He's really after me. Now I have to take a different exam from Fleiger tomorrow. You just know he's going to make it impossibly hard so I fail."

"How's that fair?" Malone says.

"Stranko called it a 'compromise.' I think he was just trying to get my mom out of the office before she put him through the wall."

"You'll do great," Ellie says. "I know you will. I can help you study if you want."

"I'll be fine, but thanks."

"What about calling him a dick? Did Stranko hit you with verbal assault?"

"Another week of work crew," Wheeler says, making a whoop-de-doo motion with his finger. "Okay, I'd better go. Mom's waiting for me."

He gets a few steps away before turning back.

"What sucks is I did study. It's not like I'm dumb. I have good DNA. My brothers prove that. I guess it's going to take people a while to catch up with this new version of me."

Now I feel even guiltier for having doubted him. Am I really any better than Fleiger and Stranko?

"See?" Malone says. "There was nothing to worry about."

"I'm not so sure," I say.

"Why's that?"

"Because I know Wheeler. Stranko had better watch his back."

The rest of exam week goes quietly, and on his retake, Wheeler earns a C-, giving him his first no-F report card since seventh grade. The achievement is celebrated in the Wheeler household like he's just cured cancer. In my house, the Bs and Cs filling my report card are met with a resigned "We know you can do better, Max" from my parents.

The first few weeks of the new semester are quiet—so

quiet, in fact, that I'm lulled into a sense of normalcy. Classes are tolerable, and we even get a snowstorm on a Friday, giving us a three-day weekend. Life overall is good, so of course, something has to come along and screw it up.

It's a freezing Wednesday during third period, and I'm zoned out at my desk in Navarro's class watching *Dances with Wolves*, the social studies department's idea of a unit on Native Americans, when my phone vibrates in my pocket.

Ellie: Get up here now.

By *here,* Ellie means the main office where she's still an aide. Claiming it's an emergency, I ask Mr. Allen if I can use the bathroom. I then hurry through the hall, taking the steps two at a time as I head for the office. As I pass the girls' bathroom just off the lobby, the door opens and Ellie pulls me inside.

"What are you doing?"

"Relax, no one's in here," she says. "Something big is going on. A couple men in suits looking all official came in earlier. They said something to Mrs. Engen, and she turned so pale I thought she might pass out. All the aides were told to go to the library for the rest of the period. I doubled back and came in here. Stranko came out and offered to shake hands, but they wouldn't take it. They're all up in his office right now."

"Who are they?"

"I'm not sure, but they weren't very friendly looking."

"I don't get it," I say. "What does this have to do with me?"

"I'll show you."

Ellie checks the hall to make sure it's safe, and we step out, giving us a clear shot of the lobby.

"That," Ellie says, and I look to where she's pointing.

Oh.

Taped above the office door on the glass frame is one of our replica Chaos Club cards.

"Wheeler," I say.

"That's what I'm thinking."

"This can't be good."

"Where are you going?" Ellie asks.

"To find out what Wheeler did."

Two minutes later, I find Wheeler in the foreign language lab. He's at a computer with headphones on, repeating into a microphone what the animated Spanish-speaking mouse on the screen is saying. Wheeler's so focused it takes a second to get his attention.

"What did you do?" I say once he joins me in the hall.

"Huh?"

"You know what I'm talking about. Men in suits came into Stranko's office. Ellie saw the Chaos Club card you put up."

An evil, satisfied smile slowly creeps across Wheeler's face.

"Oh man, it worked."

"What the hell did you do, Dave?"

"Nothing big. I just sent a couple emails from Stranko's account."

"Didn't he deactivate it by now?"

"Yeah, but I can still use his email by logging into his office computer. This building is basically deserted if you get here early enough."

I'm afraid to ask, but I have to.

"What were the messages?"

"Just some private thoughts Stranko shared with the White House. It turns out he really doesn't agree with a lot of the president's policies. Apparently, he's angry enough to make some very specific threats."

"So those guys—"

"Are probably Secret Service," Wheeler finishes, and once he starts laughing, he can't stop. "Did they take him out in handcuffs? Please tell me they did."

"It's not funny, Wheeler. He could end up in jail. I'm no fan of Stranko's, but he's never going to stop looking for us now. Don't you get that? You didn't take care of anything. You've just pissed him off for eternity."

"He'll get over it."

"You've committed a federal crime, Wheeler."

"Oh, just stop. Nothing's going to happen."

"You don't know that."

"No, but I do know I'm not done with Stranko yet."

"What's next? Framing him for murder?"

He only answers with raised eyebrows.

I walk back to Navarro's room, expecting the Secret

Service to drop out of the ceiling to waterboard me in the janitor's closet. The two granola bars and can of Red Bull I downed after second period crash in my stomach like a tidal wave reaching land.

I'd talked myself into being okay with Adleta's and Malone's pranks, justifying what they did by believing the lie that their victims deserved the revenge, but Wheeler's crosses a line I can't ignore. Potential federal prosecution will do that to a guy.

Back in Navarro's room, I send a text to all the other members of the Water Tower Five.

Meet in the theater before lunch.

The rest of the crew is already at the front of the stage when I walk in an hour later. I can hear them even from the back of the theater, and they're making no effort to hide their conversation.

"Oh man," Adleta's saying. "Practice is going to suck tonight."

"Sorry about that," Wheeler says.

"No, it's worth it. I only wish we could've heard those Secret Service guys grilling him. I hope they did a full body-cavity search."

"They looked so serious," Ellie says. "I'll bet Stranko had to change his boxers afterward."

"Yeah, I wish I could've been a fly on the wall in that meeting," Malone says.

Wheeler sees me coming and says, "Max is pissed at me though."

Malone says to me, "You're worried he'll get caught?"

"Partially that, yeah."

"Dude," Wheeler says, "I told you I was careful. I used Stranko's computer, and it's not like the Secret Service can trace his phone. I already told you, the phone's been deactivated and the battery died a long time ago."

"And if you do get caught somehow?"

Wheeler puts his hands up in a *so what* manner.

"I'm a minor. What can they really do?"

I'm no vocabulary wizard, but I think the appropriate word here is *naive*.

"You said 'partially,'" Malone says. "What else are you mad about?"

Wheeler says, "Yeah, why did you summon us here, King Max?"

They're all waiting for my answer, and I'm worried they're ready to revolt. I need to tread lightly. Because the thing is, I still want to take down the Chaos Club, and to do that, I need their help. At the same time, the pranks bother me, but they already know that.

So how do I handle the situation?

By following Heist Rule #19: *Lead with confidence and people will follow.*

"Look, what we've pulled off this year so far has been amazing," I say. "No, strike that—*your* pranks have been amazing. I haven't even pulled mine yet. So I can't really sit here and give you crap for who your pranks are against, especially since they're all damn impressive."

Everyone seems to straighten a little at this.

"At this point though, I think we need to rethink our strategy. Nothing we've done has helped us expose the Chaos Club. And my locker still smells like a bakery. So I don't think more pranks are going to do anything."

"What's the plan then?" Wheeler asks.

"Give me a few days to think that over," I say. "But no more pranks for now, okay?"

This is the moment it could all go to hell. I've basically just given an order. In the movies, the heist crew leader is always dealing with adults, not teenagers. And it's not like there was ever a vote making me the group Leader with a capital *L*. The four all stare at me, and I brace myself for the assault of laughter that's about to begin.

Then Ellie says, "Okay."

Adleta says, "Cool."

And Wheeler says, "Whatever you say, boss."

It takes longer than I'm comfortable with, but Malone finally says, "Got it."

And just like that, I'm a freaking genius.

"Wait a second," Wheeler says. "Is this all a setup so you don't have to pull a prank?"

"No, that wouldn't be a fair. You did your prank. I'll do mine."

"Promise?" Malone says.

"Promise."

February hits a week later, and let's be honest, February sucks. It's freezing cold, perpetually dark, and everyone walks around like their brains have gone cold and dark too. February defenders—of which there can't be many—argue it's not the worst month because it's so short. But if your most redeeming quality is that you're not around very long, you might as well not be around at all. And don't get me started on that stupid spelling. Eliminate that dumb *R* and maybe we can talk.

Maybe it's because of February's high suck factor, but for the life of me, I can't figure out how to continue the investigation into the Chaos Club. I suppose we could go with Adleta's initial idea of beating his way through the entire student body until someone confesses, but that's probably our last resort. The others have even stopped asking me what we're going to do. Ellie pushed the hardest, asking on a daily basis, and then eventually, even she gave up.

Then an envelope.

Like the one I received inviting me to the water tower, this envelope is taped to the inside of my locker at the end of the school day. My pulse pounds in my ears as I tear it open and pull out a folded white sheet of paper.

The picture is grainy and shot from far away, but it's clear enough that you can tell that it's me on the football field with a camera. I stand over Ellie, who, thankfully, is safely hidden inside the Zippy the Golden Eagle mascot costume.

Written on the back of the picture:

Meet at Ryder Park Baseball
Field 4 tonight at 10.
Tell anyone, we turn you in.
Don't show up, we turn you in.
Do anything stupid, we turn you in.

CHAOS CLUB

CHAPTER 17

I go because of the threat.

I go because I'm pissed.

I go because I'm scared.

I go because it's our first real lead.

I go because what choice do I really have?

But mostly, I go because that's what a leader does.

I don't tell the other four. I'm not sure if the Chaos Club knows their identities, but since they shot that picture at the football field, they must know Ellie's involved, and I want to protect her at all costs.

Does that mean it's (one-sided) love?

In the time between receiving the note and lying to my parents by saying I'm going to the library to work on—you guessed it—a group project, a hundred questions have come to me:

Who took the picture?

Why not just turn me in?

Why do they want to meet?

Is this another setup?

All good questions I'd like answers to, but not the one I'm really concerned with:

Who in the group snitched?

Because either someone in the group ratted us out, or we've fallen victim to the one uncontrollable variable in every plan—randomness. You can plan a heist down to the last second, practice it until you dream it in your sleep, and double then triple check that every battery is charged, every schedule is running on time, and every person is in their exact position, and still be tripped up by a random act of the universe—the power going out, a dropped tool, a sudden sneeze, or, worst of all, a stranger accidentally wandering onto the scene.

Is that what happened here? Did someone walking by the football stadium on that December night see us and shoot the pictures? Then, realizing later what he or she had witnessed, contact the Chaos Club?

I consider calling Boyd because he'd know what to do. Most likely, he'd get to the park early, hide somewhere where no one would ever see him, then come out when the Chaos Club arrived, helping me overpower them and ending their reign of terror. Clearly I've watched too many movies. But because the note specifically said not to tell anyone, I don't call Boyd. And this is too important to screw up. Besides, Boyd might tell my parents. Like I need more trouble in my life.

So I'm alone as I get to the vacant Ryder ball fields shortly before ten. The fields are near the school but aren't on school property, so I won't be in violation of Stranko's zero-tolerance trespassing rule. The infield of field four is concrete hard, and the rain and snow of the last few months have leveled the pitcher's mound. For a clear view in all directions, I wait at second base and pray no one's parachuting in, bringing death from above. My head's on a swivel, and I'm questioning every life choice I've ever made. I mean, agreeing to meet my sworn enemy? Alone? In the dark? How crazy does someone have to be?

Completely crazy.

It's a few minutes after ten when I hear feet scraping on the hard dirt of the adjacent ball field. I squint hard into the darkness, and two figures emerge around the visitor's side dugout, stepping onto the field, and...

They're wearing masks.

And not like hockey masks or cute little bunny masks with a rubber band across the back, but full-fledged demon masks that cover their entire heads. Both stop dead when they see me, standing silent in the moonlight and looking creepy as hell.

Maybe this wasn't such a good idea after all.

Their loose-fitting clothes make determining their exact sex difficult, but the person on the left is clearly bigger and at least a foot taller. If I had to guess, I'd say one guy, one girl. They start toward me in confident strides, and it's only my clenched butt cheeks that stop me from shitting myself. At ten feet away, the bigger one pulls a small box from his pocket and holds it up to his mouth.

When he speaks, his voice is obnoxiously distorted, like he's a kidnapper making a ransom call.

"Give me your phone."

Yep, a guy.

"What?" I say.

He holds out a hand.

"Give me your phone."

"Why?"

"To make sure you're not recording us."

Huh. I should've thought of that.

I hand him my phone, and he pushes a few buttons. The smaller one leans in and whispers something that has the big one nodding.

"I'm turning off your phone-finder app too. I don't want anyone to know where we're taking you."

"Whoa, wait a second. I'm not going anywhere."

The small one takes the distorter and holds it up.

"We're not going to hurt you."

A girl.

"Where are we going?"

"Someplace private."

"More private than this?"

The guy reaches into his jacket and pulls out a mask identical to the one they're wearing, except this one has duct tape over the eyes.

"Put this on," the girl says.

I may be dumb enough to come here, but I'm not dumb enough to put myself completely at their mercy.

"I'm out of here," I say.

"We're not going to hurt you," she says.

"There's no way I'm putting that mask on."

The guy grabs for the distorter and holds it up.

"If you leave, Stranko gets the picture tonight. How long do you think it'll be before he figures out who's in the mascot costume? Now put the mask on."

Again, do I have a choice?

I can't see anything with the mask on, and the small slits at the nostrils and mouth have me suffocating. I'm led by the arm across the hard infield and off the diamond completely. We're on grass for a bit, and the girl says, "Be careful. Don't slip. There's a step down here."

Ah, kindhearted kidnappers, the best kind.

Then we're walking on concrete, and I hear the chirp of a car door unlocking.

"No, it's okay," the girl says when I slow down. "You'll be fine."

A door opens, and I'm guided down so I don't bang my head on the car. I can't tell what the car's make is, but I know it's small because my knees hit the passenger seat in front of me. When my two captors get in, only a few feet separate us.

"Drive around a bit," the guy says. "I don't want him knowing where we are." Then to me, "If you peek, Stranko gets the picture."

The radio comes on, and we start driving. At first, I do a good job keeping track of our location. I've lived in Asheville my whole life, so I know these roads. But the turns become so constant that eventually I lose any sense of direction. When we finally come to a stop after twenty minutes of driving, we might as well be in China.

"This way," the girl says once we're outside the car. "It's not very far, but we need you to be quiet."

"Why?"

"Because we told you to be," the guy says.

I'm guessing we're walking across another empty parking lot. Of course, for all I know, it's a dead-end road, someone's driveway—or a walkway to an open vat of hydrofluoric acid.

"Just a little farther," she says. "We're heading inside."

"To a murder shed?" I say, only half joking.

Neither reply. If I live through this, I need to stop being such a smart-ass.

We walk on what's probably a sidewalk for a few seconds, then without any sort of transition, the night sounds fall away and the air warms up as we step inside some structure. My guards are on either side of me, and I'm led a dozen or so steps before the door we just entered closes with a click. Whatever sort of building we're in, there can't be many people around. The only sound is the constant drone of a heating system. After another minute of walking, I'm led inside what has to be a small room. There's no noise in here, and I sense that the walls aren't too far out of reach. But it's the unmistakable smell of wet paint that has me most confused. Even with the mask on, it's overwhelming, like somehow I'm in the backroom of a paint store.

"Sit here," the girl says.

"Can I take off my mask? I'm dying."

"Actually, we need to tie your hands behind your back now. We don't want you taking off your mask before it's time."

"What does that mean?"

"It means put your hands behind your back. We don't have all night," Mr. Attitude says.

Having come this far, I do as I'm told. Thankfully, the rope isn't so tight it cuts off circulation.

"Do you know why you're here?" the guy asks.

I should be scared, but I'm not. Probably because I realize that underneath the tough-guy act, he's really just another dumb high school kid like me.

"You're the one who brought me here. Why don't you tell me why?" I say.

"Don't be stupid. We want to know why you're trying to get us in trouble."

"What do you mean *trouble*?"

"Stop the shit, man. You know what we're talking about. The fake website—"

"The aerial photo—"

"The pep rally—"

"The goldfish—"

"Zippy—"

"And siccing the Secret Service on Stranko," the guy says. "That trouble."

Well, it's nice to know our work hasn't gone unnoticed.

"You're the ones who started it by getting us busted at the water tower," I say. "Then you went and stuffed our lockers with dough."

There's a long enough pause that I'm guessing the guy and girl are communicating without speaking. Maybe with semaphore.

The girl says, "We didn't pull those pranks."

"Yeah right."

"We didn't."

If my fingers weren't laced, I'd be making fists.

"Why lie to me? Do you still think I'm secretly recording this or something? Like I'm going to run to Stranko if you tell the truth? You have my phone, remember? Besides, it's not me you need to worry about. It's him."

Another pause, and then the girl has the distorter.

"You're swinging at ghosts," she says.

"Not anymore."

"What do you mean?"

"Have we set you up at all lately? No. We've given up."

"I wish we could believe that."

I'm trying to get a clue as to who these people are—some hint in what they say or even how they say it that'll lead me to their identities. But there's nothing.

"If you don't believe me that I've quit, then why am I

here? If you want to threaten me, fine, but I'll just tell you the same thing again—I'm not hunting you anymore, so you don't have to worry."

"We're not threatening you," the girl says.

"No, you've already done that."

"That was just to get you to show up."

"Then what do you want with me?"

"We're here to make you an offer."

Even through the voice distorter, I can pick up the girl's tone. She sounds almost worried, like she's the one tied to the chair.

"What's the offer?" I say.

"We'll forgive what you've done if you accept a position in the Chaos Club. There's only a few months left in the year, but it would be a good setup for next year. We need someone to carry the torch for us, and you've been chosen."

There's a pause, and then the guy says through the distorter, "We're told a midyear invitation like this has never happened before. You should feel honored."

I have a hard time finding words. Of all the scenarios I played out in my head before coming here, I never imagined this one. Me, in the Chaos Club?

"Who told you to do this?" I ask.

The guy says, "What do you mean *who*?"

"You said you were told this has never happened before. Who's in charge? Is there some sort of, I don't know, alumni panel or something?"

This time the pause is longer than I'm comfortable with. I imagine the two trying to figure out how to respond to the *gotcha* I've just nailed them with.

The girl finally says, "We can fill you in on the specifics later. But, Max, this is your chance to be a part of something special. I mean *really* special. We're planning something everyone in the town will witness live. Nothing's even been done like this before—"

"That's enough," the guy says.

I decide to push my edge.

"How did you find out about me?"

"We got an anonymous email with the picture attached."

"Anonymous?"

"Completely."

"Why would someone do that?"

No answer.

"We don't have all night," the guy says. "What's your answer?"

"What happens if I say no?"

"You don't want to do that."

"But what happens?"

"There will be ramifications."

The girl is on the distorter again. "Join us and we'll tell you everything. Isn't that what you want?"

In a way, yes.

Why did they choose us for the water tower prank?

How do they pull off their pranks unnoticed?

Who's their leader?

What's their next prank?

With just a quick yes, I can know the answer to all this and more.

Plus, becoming a member of the Chaos Club is as close to a professional heist crew as I'm likely to get.

It's just too great an offer to turn down.

But.

"Go screw yourselves," I say.

"You're not serious?" the guy says.

"I already have a crew, and we're taking you assholes down. You'll regret ever messing with us."

"We told you—"

"Max," the girl says, this time without the distorter. "You need to reconsider."

"Or you'll give Stranko the picture?"

"Worse."

Her voice is soft and serious. I could still change my mind, I guess. A big part of me still wants answers. But no. They're just trying to scare me, to blackmail me into joining them, like they blackmailed me into coming here. So hell no.

"I'm out."

The girl sighs, and both of them start moving past me for the door.

"You started this, remember that," the guy says.

"What's that supposed to mean?"

The doors opens, and I say, "Aren't you going to untie me?"

"The ropes aren't too tight," the guys says. "You'll figure it out."

"But how will I get home?"

Then the girl whispers in my ear, "Good luck, Max."

I don't recognize the voice. Or maybe I do. When the door closes, I'm alone, and suddenly all my macho bullshit is gone. I jerk at the ropes trying to free my hands and find that the guy was right. The ropes are loose but not *that* loose.

My feet aren't tied, so I stand up but quickly bang into a table or desk or something. I fall back into the seat and work the ropes, my breathing coming faster. It takes a good minute to get one hand out. After that, the other's out in seconds. My hands tear the mask off my head, and I use my sleeve to wipe the sweat off my face. It's only then that I open my eyes.

Oh no.

I'm in the school.

In Stranko's office.

Which has been painted neon pink.

The entire office—the walls, his desk, the ceiling, the chair I'm sitting on, even the state lacrosse trophy—all of it's neon pink.

I barely have time to process everything when someone's putting a key in the door, and suddenly I've broken the most important heist rule of all—I got caught.

CHAPTER 18

Of course Stranko has me arrested.

Handcuffs, police car, fingerprints, mugshot...all of it.

And yeah, Hale's car isn't an official cop car since he isn't a real cop, but it has the mesh-wire guard and no latches on the inside of the back door. Hale even proudly tells me there's no point in trying to call anyone because of the cell phone jammer he's installed, so it might as well be a cop car. Or a potential rapist's car, the creep.

Being arrested is just as humiliating as you might imagine, possibly even more so. The real cops don't put me in a jail cell, thank God, but I'm locked in a room that's probably used for interrogating real criminals. I almost wish I were in a cell because iron bars would make it harder for Mom and Dad to murder me, which they're going to do.

I guess this is what happens when you try to write your name in the wet cement of the universe. It hardens, trapping you in place, then begins downpouring shit on you.

Not Max can kiss my ass.

Through the door's window, I can see Stranko's still here at a desk with Hale, the two of them relaying the story to a cop who's hunting and pecking her way through my arrest report.

An hour earlier, when Stranko opened his office door and saw me, he held up a hand before I could say anything. His was eerily calm as he surveyed the room, then eventually, he stepped into the hall and called Hale. In the five minutes we waited, the only thing Stranko said in my presence was a quiet, "God, I'm not going to miss this."

Stranko's the least of my worries though, because my small window gives me a perfect view of Mom and Dad's arrival. They look worried as they listen to Hale and Stranko explaining what happened, but they're not fooling me. They have to be rage-filled, homicidal maniacs faking concern to ensure the police will release me. And once that happens, the bloodbath will begin. This room offers nowhere to hide, so I'm stuck sitting here like the penned-up convict I am. Dad, unshaven and looking like he's just taken a hammer blow to the forehead, shakes both Hale's and Stranko's hands. I didn't think it was possible to feel worse than I already do, but seeing Dad's embarrassment does it.

I have fifteen seconds until Mom and Dad get here. That's fifteen seconds left to live. What should I do with those fifteen seconds?

Bang my head on the chair until I'm unconscious?

Punch myself in the groin to generate some tears?

Get a running start at the door so that when it opens,

I can smash past my parents and race into the night to live a life on the lam?

But it's too late. The door opens, and my parents appear in the doorway. They're both slump shouldered and—oh man—what's that look they're giving me?

Rage?

Embarrassment?

No, worse.

Disappointment. Sad-eyed, slow-moving, tired-voiced disappointment.

I'd prefer rage.

"Let's go home, Max," Mom says.

That's it. Not a "What were you thinking?" or "Do you know how much trouble you're in?" Just Mom's, "Let's go home, Max."

Dad doesn't say anything. In fact, he's not even looking at me.

"I'm sorry," I say.

Nothing back from either of them. I can actually feel myself growing smaller.

"I said I'm sorry."

Without looking at me, Mom says, "We heard you."

I keep my eyes to the floor on my way out so I won't have to see Stranko. I expect at least some talking once we get outside, but no, Mom and Dad just walk to the car, with me trailing behind. Even when we're inside, away from the ears of anyone who might hear them laying into me, the silence continues. We drive home with no talking, no radio, no nothing. I'd prefer shout-ing instead of this terrible nothingness. If parents receive a *How to Effectively Punish Your Children* pamphlet, this has to be in the "Only for Professionals" section because, man, it's brutal.

At home, the silent treatment mercifully ends with Mom saying, "Come sit down, Max."

When they use your name it's just the worst. The formality, the seriousness. That's when you know you're in atom bomb–sized trouble. Mom and Dad sit on the couch, and I'm across from them in the La-Z-Boy, exhausted and sorry, self-conscious and worried, all at the same time.

"Tell us everything," Mom says.

Dad's staring at the space where my chair touches the carpet.

"From the beginning," he says.

I knew this was coming, but with it here now, I'm still not sure what to say. I mean, I know the whole story, but telling it all to them can only end in Ellie, Wheeler, Malone, and Adleta getting in serious trouble. But isn't there a point where that doesn't matter? Where the truth is more important than protecting your friends?

I don't know the answer to that.

I do know, however, that I've failed my parents. So I decide on the fly that I can't fail Ellie, Wheeler, Malone, and Adleta too. I have to protect my crew. Because what good would it do to involve them? How would explaining the other four's role in this help my parents understand the arrest of their criminal son?

So here's what I tell Mom and Dad about:

The water tower.

Today's letter.

And my kidnapping and offer to join.

What I don't tell them about:

Anything implicating the other four.

I do explain their part in the water tower, but beyond that, I leave Ellie, Wheeler, Malone, and Adleta out of it. I don't even tell my parents about the fake website because the pictures on it are from pranks the other four did. So yes, I lie. And I feel bad for doing it, but it's necessary.

"Is there anything else?" Mom says.

"No."

"Why didn't we hear about the water tower from the school when it happened?" Dad says.

The question's a right hook to the jaw I didn't see coming. Dad's staring directly at me, giving me no chance to work up a lie.

"Boyd came and got me," I say.

Dad sighs and Mom's eyes narrow. She's *this* close to growling.

Uh, sorry, Uncle Boyd.

My parents exchange silent words with a long look, then Mom says, "We'll pick this up again in the morning, after your father and I have had a chance to talk."

"Okay," I say, getting up. "I'm really sorry."

Neither of them says anything back.

I'm halfway up the stairs when Dad says, "Max, leave your laptop and phone outside your door."

Um.

Now I understand what it means to break out in a cold sweat.

"Did you hear me, Max?"

"Yes, sir."

I walk upstairs thinking about my browser history. And my text messages. Usually I'm pretty good at erasing my web adventures, but I can't remember the last time I cleared my history. If Mom asks me, "Max, why did you do a search for 'naughty teachers in glasses'?" I may die of embarrassment. But considering the alternatives, that may not be a bad thing.

I make myself a ghost for the rest of the weekend. When I do venture downstairs, Mom and Dad keep to basics, like asking me to pass the mustard or to turn the TV down. I'm told I'm grounded for an indefinite amount of time. My guess is until I'm forty-six. They also break the news that I'm to be charged with trespassing and criminal mischief, which could put me in jail for up to sixty days, along with a $5,000 fine. I could be prison bound by the spring.

On Sunday night, while all of us are in the family

room, the doorbell rings. I automatically rise from the couch, but Dad stops me.

"You stay," he says.

He opens the door, and I hear Ellie's voice.

"Hi, Mr. Cobb. Is Max here?"

Dad's normally a big Ellie fan, but not tonight. He blocks the door so she can't see or come inside.

"He's not allowed to see anyone right now, Ellie, but I'll tell him you stopped by."

"Is everything okay?"

"Everything's fine. He's not allowed visitors."

"Because I've texted him and called a bunch of times but haven't heard back."

Ellie's confused and upset—bonus for me?—and suddenly I'm pissed at Mom and Dad for sending her away to worry even more. I stand up and start for the door.

"Max, sit down," Mom says.

I keep going.

"Maxwell Connor Cobb."

I clear the corner, and Ellie and I see each other, but Dad blocks me from getting closer.

"I'm okay," I tell Ellie.

"What happened?" she asks.

"I'm just in some trouble. I'll talk to you soon."

"Okay, I guess."

Dad tells her to be safe driving home before closing the door.

"You should probably get up to bed," Dad says to me. "We have an early day tomorrow."

In the morning, I learn something new—school districts have lawyers. In the case of Asheville, the lawyer is Mr. Huelle—rhymes with mule—and he's about as friendly and personable as his name. He's in a full suit and sits sour faced beside Mrs. B at the end of a long table in the high school conference room on Monday morning. Also present are Stranko and Hale, who take seats on Mrs. B's side. Assuming my parents are on my side, which is debatable, I'm outnumbered three to four.

"Jim, Beth, it's nice to see the two of you. I just wish we were all meeting under different circumstances," Mrs. B says.

"You and us both, Mrs. Barber," Dad says.

Mrs. Barber. I guess no matter how old you get, there are just some people you can't force yourself to call by their first name.

"Well, Max, we're here today to discuss what happened the other night and what to do about it," Mrs. B says. "Mr. Stranko has already filled me in on what he saw, but I'd like to hear your version of the events, please."

Déjà vu all over again.

My right knee bounces spastically underneath the table as I repeat the story I told my parents, about finding the note in my locker and what happened after meeting the Chaos Club at the baseball field. My eyes are glued to the table as I talk, not because I can't look at Mrs. B but because the three goons sitting beside her are as intimidating as hell.

"I know I shouldn't have gone, especially after what happened at the beginning of the year, but I felt like I had to."

"Why?"

"Because I hoped it would give me some clues as to who's in the Chaos Club."

"And did it?"

"It's a boy and a girl," I said. "I know that."

"Anything else?"

I shake my head.

Stranko whispers something to Hale while Barber taps her pen on the folder in front of her.

"So your story is that members of the Chaos Club invited you to meet, then blindfolded and transported you here to the school, where they put you in Mr. Stranko's office so that if you turned them down, you'd get in trouble."

I see where this is going, but it's too late.

"My question is—why would they do that?" she says.

"Do what?"

"Why would they set you up to get in trouble a second time? What would their motivation be? Why not just invite you? What's the purpose in vandalizing Mr.

Stranko's office and getting you in trouble for turning them down?"

There's no safe answer. I can't tell them that the Chaos Club blackmailed me into coming with threats of showing the picture of me at the football stadium because it proves I was working with Ellie. And once that gets out, the other three would eventually fall too. I just hope the Chaos Club didn't keep their promise of sending Stranko the picture.

"Max?" Mrs. B says, bringing me back.

Everyone is looking at me, waiting for my answer. Nothing to do but give the standard response every guilty teenager is programmed to give when they know they're busted.

"I don't know," I say.

"Did you do anything to upset them?" Mrs. B says.

I shake my head.

"Do you have the note?" Stranko asks.

I do, but it's too incriminating.

"I lost it."

"Convenient," he says, then opens the folder in front of him and removes a piece of paper, looking at it for a few seconds before sliding it over to me. It's the picture of Ellie and me at the football field. The corners of my vision gray, then blacken as the room begins to collapse in on me.

"Who's this in the picture with you?"

"It's no one," I say.

"No one?"

There's only one option here: make up something absurd.

"I filled the costume with newspaper to fill it out. I did everything by myself."

"Newspaper?"

"Yes, sir."

"Where did you get the mascot costume? It's been missing for months."

"Um, I found it?"

"Of course you did," Stranko says. "So then who took the picture?"

"The Chaos Club."

"Right," Stranko says. He has a smug, condescending smile I'd love to punch off his face.

I refuse to look at Mom and Dad because I'm sure I can't take the looks of disappointment they're giving me.

"Jim, Beth, do you have anything you'd like to add?" Mrs. B says.

"Just that we'll obviously pay for any damages," Mom says.

"Thank you for that. Now if it's okay with you, I'd like to talk this over with my administrative team before moving forward. Could you give us a few minutes, please?"

We move to the chairs right outside the conference room and wait without talking. First period doesn't start for twenty-five minutes, but already the halls are starting to fill. The three of us sit outside the office for five excruciating minutes.

I hate all of it.

I hate the quiet.

I hate the looks the secretaries and guidance counselors give me as they pass.

I hate that I'm being talked about by people I can't hear.

When the office door opens and Mr. Watson enters with a coffee cup in his hand, I have a new hate to add to my list:

I hate that my favorite teacher is seeing me like this.

Watson slows as he passes, saying, "Max, Jim, Beth," before stopping outside the conference room. He gives a light knock, then enters without being invited inside.

"He still remembers us," Dad says to Mom.

"I always liked him."

They both sound somewhat happy in the memory. Time to take advantage of that.

"Mr. Watson's really cool," I say.

And we're back to the silent treatment.

Mr. Watson isn't inside long, three minutes tops, before reappearing.

"They're ready for you," he says. "Max, you hang in there."

Hopefully, I'll never have to face a jury in real life, because if walking back into court to hear the verdict is anything like walking back into that conference room, I'll just have to off myself in my cell. I sit between Mom and Dad and swallow down my bile.

Dad puts both hands on the table, but Mom slides

one of hers into mine underneath. It's the most attention she's shown me in days.

Mrs. B says, "Max, I want you to know I don't think you're a bad kid. I've been in this job for almost forty years and can say that I've seen my share of trouble kids, and you're not one of them."

This is promising.

"However…"

Uh-oh.

"I do think you're on a dangerous path and that if you're not careful, you could end up in some real trouble. After discussing matters, I've decided that the school district will ask the police to drop the charges in regard to the vandalism in Mr. Stranko's office. Considering your side of the story, Mr. Huelle doesn't think there's enough evidence to prove you're responsible. I tend to agree with him, as does Officer Hale."

Yes!

"However—"

Dammit.

"I also think you're lying to us. Not outright, but you're definitely not telling the whole story. I'm pretty sure your parents agree."

Out of the corners of my eyes, I see both Mom and Dad nod.

"At best, Max, you're guilty of showing exceptionally bad judgment for the third time this year and, at worst, of outright vandalism. With your lack of forthrightness and any clear evidence to support your story, you've left me no other choice than to follow school policy, which was explained in the recent assembly."

Under the table, Mom squeezes my hand tight enough to grind my bones to dust. Next to me, Dad is catatonic, and I'm holding my breath.

"You are to be suspended ten days. I could expel you for what you've done, but I don't think that's fitting here. Your teachers will send work home, but it will be at their discretion whether they accept the assignments for full credit. You can also contact them through email if you have questions."

I'm trying not to cry, but it's hard.

"Max, I understand this has to be difficult for you, but I'm hoping this sets you back on the path we all want you on. You should know that Mr. Watson came in here this morning and offered a spirited defense against your punishment, but in the end, we decided that this is best."

"I'm not lying," I choke out. "The Chaos Club brought me here."

No one responds. All that happens is Mrs. B explains how my make-up work will be available after school at the front desk. After that, we're told we can go.

There's no shaking of hands.

No thank-yous or sorrys.

No last-second reprieve by Mrs. B.

Only a triumphant Stranko smirking asshole-ishly at me.

But then again, Stranko's going back to his My Little Pony office, and I'm headed home on a ten-day forced hell-vacation, so who's the real asshole here?

On second thought, don't answer that.

CHAPTER 19

The ground rules for my suspension as laid out by my parents:

1. No phone, no Internet, and no visitors.

2. No leaving the house.

3. During the day, Mom or Dad will call the house at random times to make sure I'm there.

4. Once Mom brings my homework, I'm to finish it immediately.

5. Bedtime is nine o'clock.

So basically, prison. But better than what I feared, which was that I'd be placed into one of those mountain-survival programs where you're supposed to learn to respect your parents but only end up being sodomized with a tree branch by a crazed counselor. Unfortunately, like any inmate, the jailers don't believe me when I say I was set up. I come to this realization on the third full day of my suspension, when I apologize for the thousandth time and add, "It was stupid of me to trust them."

"Trust who?" Mom asks.

"The Chaos Club."

My parents roll their eyes.

"You still think I'm making that up?"

"We don't know, Max," Dad says. "But you lied by not telling us about the water tower, so who's to say you're not lying here?"

"I'm not lying!"

Mom gives an *if you say so* look that just kills me. Warden Dad's not finished though, and it's obvious from the edge in his voice that he's been holding in a lot of anger.

"You know, Max, if your story's true, then you should have come to us. Of course we would have been mad, but at least then we would have understood your going to the water tower. Hell, if I were your age, I would've gone. But no, you didn't tell us. In fact, you made it worse by involving Boyd in your lie. Then, as if you hadn't caused enough trouble, you make another dumb decision, and we have to suffer the embarrassment of picking you up at the police station, where I have to apologize—apologize!—to Dwayne Stranko for your ridiculous behavior. So I'm sorry if we're a little skeptical of your story. You're not the most credible person right now. You've changed this year, and I'm not sure it's for the better. Maybe instead of repeating over and over again that you were set up, you should make better use of your time by reflecting on what you've done and who you want to be."

Astonishingly, I take Dad's advice.

For the next couple days, I think about what I've done. I think about who I am.

I think about who I want to be.

Here are my choices as I see them:

I could just live out the rest of the year, the rest of high school, hell, even the rest of my life playing it as safe as I have for my first sixteen years. Basically, I could Just Max it. It's certainly the cautious, *not get arrested* way to go. But Just Max also has no confidence, no friends, and lives his life through movie characters. What good is that?

Or I could go the Not Max route. In the months since letting him surface, Not Max has spoken out, taken risks, and acquired a circle of real friends. Of course, Not Max's impulsiveness also got him arrested, twice if you count the water tower. And Not Max's parents don't trust him anymore, and I sure don't want that happening again.

So the question is, Just Max or Not Max?

Caution or impulsiveness?

Safety or action?

Silence or noise?

The hell if I know. But I do know what would happen in a heist film—the mastermind would go to his mentor for advice. In *The Italian Job*, Mark Wahlberg goes to Donald Southerland. In *Parker*, Jason Stratham goes to Nick Nolte. In *Ocean's Eleven*, George Clooney goes to Elliott Gould. I don't have a mentor—I've been flying-by-the-seat-of-my-pantsing it if you haven't noticed—but I do know someone who fits the characteristics of a mentor, or at least can fill in on short notice. That is, if he's speaking to me anymore.

"If your mom finds out I was here, she's going to murder me, you know that, right?" Boyd says.

We're pulling out of my driveway in Boyd's truck. He has a Red Bull between his legs and a half-eaten turkey sandwich balanced on one knee. I waited until Dad made his daily noontime phone check-in to make sure I'm in the house (Bonus Heist Rule: *Don't be predictable*) before calling Boyd to pick me up. He came without even asking why.

"I know she will. You're definitely on Mom's shit list right now. I'm sorry about that. I didn't have any choice. I talked myself into a corner I couldn't get out of."

"Yeah, I've been there. Don't worry about it. So how much time do we have?"

"Thirty minutes maybe," I say. "Mom makes the afternoon call but never until around two. Sometimes she doesn't call at all."

"Or she might be calling right now," Boyd says.

"There's nothing I can do about that if she is."

"You lead a dangerous life, man."

"You don't know the half of it."

"So then tell me."

I fill Boyd in on what's happened since he first rescued me at the school after the water tower. The story takes ten minutes, during which time Boyd finishes his lunch. I end with what I'm struggling with, Dad suggesting I figure out who I want to be. When I finish, Boyd checks the rearview mirror and then does a U-turn in the middle of the road.

"I thought we were going to the barn," I say.

"Change of plans, man. Field trip time."

We head toward downtown Asheville, which is made up of a dozen small stores that are inexplicably still in business, two places I don't want to ever return to—the police station and the Whippy Dip—and what turns out to be our destination: the town's administrative building. We pull into the building's parking lot, and Boyd takes a spot in the back, away from the other cars but with a clear view of the front entrance.

"Do you know why your mom doesn't like me?" Boyd says.

"Because you drink a lot?"

"No, it's—"

"Because Dad always comes back from your barn smelling like he's smoked a dozen cigarettes?"

"No, I—"

"Because of that time you and Dad were escorted by the police to the Las Vegas city limits and told not to return?"

"Okay, stop," Boyd says. "Those are all good reasons that definitely play into why she doesn't like me, but the main reason is because of that."

Boyd points to the front of the administrative building, specifically to an archway outside the main entrance.
From where we sit, the arch seems to grow out of the
earth naturally, like some sort of metal weed pushing
through the concrete. Four orange-and-green metal poles
twisted together rise fifteen feet into the air before arcing
down to the other side of the walkway. It's your basic
arch—nothing more, nothing less.

"One of yours?" I ask.

"So, twenty years ago, your mom and dad were
already living their grown-up lives—married with real
jobs, thinking about having kids, and living in a house a
lot smaller than the one you're in now. I was doing the
struggling-artist thing full time at that point, a lot like
I am now but with a lot more struggling. I borrowed
money from them a couple times, something I didn't want
to do but had to. Anyway, the city council announced a
contest for local artists to design a sculpture that would
go right there. The contest was obviously a big opportunity, not only because of the money but also because
of the exposure. So I worked on my idea for a couple
weeks and came up with something that sort of looked
like the pieces I make now. I showed your parents the
idea, and your dad liked it, but your mom, man, she hated
it. I mean, really hated it. She told me that if I was going
to live as an artist, I needed to do something a lot more
commercial, because the city council would make their
decision based on what the whole town would like. At

first I hated the idea, but you know your mom—she kept talking about how this could really launch my career, and eventually she just wore me down and I gave in. I ditched my original idea and presented a new, more commercial concept to the city council. And as you guessed, yeah, that's the one they chose. The final's right there in front of you."

We both look at Boyd's archway for a few seconds without saying anything. A man and woman in business attire walk under it on their way to the front entrance without giving the arch a second glance.

"I don't get it," I say. "Why would Mom hate you because of that? You won the contest."

"Because," Boyd says lighting a cigarette and pointing it at the building, "that arch is a piece of shit. It's boring and common and not me. It did nothing for my career except force me to take the long way through town for the rest of my life so I don't have to see it. And your mom knows it's terrible too and feels guilty about it. Your dad's told me as much. Shit, just sitting here looking at it makes me want to go sledgehammer happy. I snuck in when it first went up and removed the placard with my name on it, but everyone in this town still knows it's mine. I hate that. What's worse is I can pretend it's not mine, but I know it is, and I sold myself out for the opportunity."

"I'm not sure I see how that story relates to my problem."

"Give it some time. You'll figure it out."

"Thanks a lot," I deadpan.

"Sorry, man," Boyd says. "But if you're expecting me to tell you what to do, I'm not going to do that."

I think about Boyd's story on the way back to the house and am no closer to an answer than I was when he picked me up. Still, I thank him as I get out of the truck.

"I think you're wrong though," I say before closing the door. "Mom's a lot more practical than you think. Guilt isn't why she doesn't like you."

"You're probably right," Boyd says and laughs. "Your dad's still not allowed back in Vegas."

Inside the house, the first thing I do is check the phone for messages. No calls. So instead of having to come up with a reasonable answer for why I wasn't here, I'm free to spend my brain power working out Boyd's story and which path I'm going to choose.

Three days of headache-inducing thought later, I have my answer.

When I return to school after my ten-day suspension, there's no hiding in the auditorium or nurse's office like back in September. Instead, I walk the halls steely eyed, ignoring the whispers of "He's the one" and "He's back." Crowds part for me as if they know to stay out of my way, as if people know the decision I've come to thanks to Boyd. The decision? Simple. Quit trying to be the version of Max that will sell and start being the one I actually like.

I'm at my locker before first period, trying to remember my combination, when I hear Ellie say, "There he is!"

I look up to see the other members of the Water Tower Five heading my way. Ellie's the first one to me, practically laying out a group of freshmen in her rush to hug me. If I had known this would be her reaction, I would've gotten arrested years ago.

"Welcome back, dude," Wheeler says, clapping me on the shoulder.

"Yeah," Adleta says. "How was the vacation?"

"It sucked."

"Because you missed us?" Ellie says.

"Oh, absolutely."

"Good answer!"

"We're all happy you're back, Max," Malone says.

"Yeah, dude, the conquering hero returns," Wheeler says.

"Hero?"

"Yeah, you're a legend in this place—the Guy Who Trashed Stranko's Office. They'll probably erect a golden statue of you now that you're back."

"You're kidding, right?"

Malone says, "He's not exaggerating as much as you'd think."

"But I didn't paint his office. The Chaos Club did."

"But no one else knows that," Adleta says. "And don't correct them either. You've got a rep now."

"Yeah, as a vandal."

"No," Wheeler says. "As the badass who trashed the place, then sat waiting for Stranko to show up so he'd know you did it."

"But that's not what happened."

"Who cares? What's important is that it's what everyone thinks happened. It's called controlling the message."

"Yeah, Dave's diabolical," Ellie says, giving Wheeler a shove. "He's got a promising future running political campaigns."

"Well, it wasn't like Stranko was allowed to tell what really happened."

"Oh, he tried," Adleta says. "At practice he mentioned it a few times, saying you started crying when he caught you, but the guys really didn't believe him. I made sure of that."

"You didn't have to do that," I say.

"No, we did," Wheeler says. "You didn't rat us out and you could have to save your ass. That's huge."

"Yeah, thanks, man," Adleta says.

"I knew you wouldn't tell," Ellie says. "I just knew it."

"So are you grounded forever?" Malone asks.

"Pretty much," I say. "And we're paying for the damages to the office, but the school decided not to press charges."

"Excellent," Wheeler says.

For the next couple minutes, everyone brings me up to speed on what I've missed since I've been gone. It turns out, not much.

Adleta's in lacrosse mode full time.

Malone's time is split working at the climbing center and finishing pieces for an upcoming art show.

Ellie's busy planning with the Asheville Celebration Committee.

And Wheeler's been studying, which is a sentence that has never been uttered in the history of the planet.

"Oh, and you missed prom," Ellie says.

"Did you go?"

"No, none of us went."

"Then I don't care that I missed it," I say.

"I'll tell you what," Ellie says to me, "if neither of us has a date next year, we'll go together. How's that for a welcome-back present?"

Like I need to answer that.

"So, not to get all serious, but what's next?" Malone says. "We're finished with the Chaos Club, right? Because we all really dodged a bullet there."

"Yeah," Adleta says. "I mean, my dad's a big enough jerk. If I got arrested, he'd beat my ass into the next century."

"I hate to admit it," Wheeler says, "but I agree. I'm actually doing good in school for once. The last thing I need is to screw that up."

All opinions I wasn't expecting. Not that they're wrong. Giving up on exposing the Chaos Club would be the smart move. It would be the safe move. But it's also too much a Just Max move.

"I'm not giving up," I say.

"After what happened? Why would you keep going?" Malone asks. "None of us blame you if you want to quit."

"Yeah, dude," Wheeler says. "You were *this* close to getting expelled."

"And going to jail," Adleta says.

"But I didn't get expelled," I say. "And I'm not going to let the Chaos Club get away with what they did to me. That's twice now. I won't let it happen again."

There's a moment of tense silence, and Malone says, "What if we lay low the rest of the year, let things calm down, and start up next year when things aren't so crazy? That way we're not quitting; we're just postponing our plans."

"Yeah, like when we have a rainout in lacrosse," Adleta says.

"No," I say. "Once this year's over, they're gone. The Chaos Club will remain, sure, but with different people. Our issue is with this year's members, not next year's. And I'm going to make sure there is no Chaos Club next year. I'm going to destroy them."

Malone squints like I'm somehow out of focus. "I've got to admit it, Max, I'm impressed."

"Yeah, me too," Adleta says.

"Why?" I say.

"Because you're acting like none of this is bothering you," Malone says. "I thought you'd want out. But here you are, and you're being—God, this is weird to say—cool."

Does this means I made the right decision? Because I feel like I have. I won't go all *and the moral of the story is* with you, but here's the important part: in the choice between Not Max and Just Max, I choose…neither. I'm not going to define myself by such simple terms any longer. And I'm sure as hell not going to let anyone else do it for me either. My friends, including Boyd, have shown me the consequences of letting that happen. If I've learned anything over the past six months, it's that I'm capable of stunning feats of greatness and amazing moments of stupidity. That's who I am, and it's time to embrace that. No one else is going to talk me into redesigning my statue. That means no more separating Just Max and Not Max. From here on out, I'm simply Max Cobb.

Max Cobb, mastermind, to be exact.

(Okay, so maybe I did just go all *and the moral of the story is*. Sorry.)

"Look," I say, "I told you guys this when we started, that if any of you wanted out, you could quit. But I'm not quitting."

"Me either," Ellie says.

Which makes me smile.

"We can get these guys," I tell everyone. "I'm certain of it."

"That all sounds good, Max," Malone says, "but we're really no closer now to discovering who's in the Chaos Club than we were six months ago. What makes you so confident you can do that now?"

Which makes me smile even more.

"Because," I say, "I've figured out where and when the Chaos Club is going to strike next."

CHAPTER 20

"Hey, you're Max Cobb, right?" the guy says.

He and his friend are big enough and old enough that they're probably super-seniors—kids who didn't have enough credits to graduate on time and are stuck in high school until they either pass their required classes or turn fifty, whichever comes first. It's three weeks after I've returned to school, and the Water Tower Fivers are all at the same table in the cafeteria. I'm done worrying that the Chaos Club will suspect we're working together. What are they going to do, get me arrested again?

"Yeah," I tell the guys. "That's me."

"Is it true you destroyed Stranko's office?"

It's a question I've been asked a lot since returning. And in true Rule #2 fashion—*Be cool*—I give them my standard reply.

"My lawyer says I can't talk about it, sorry," but I add a wink, letting them know what's really up.

"Cool, man, cool," the guy says, and both of them hold out fists for me to bump.

"You're like a rock star," Wheeler says once they're gone.

"Yeah, I heard you called Tami Cantor 'Kami' on purpose today in Watson's class," Adleta says.

"I couldn't resist," I say.

"Like I said, a rock star," Wheeler says.

"Yeah," Ellie says, "a rock star who's on permanent lockdown."

"Thanks for that reminder."

I've become like one of those American hikers who accidentally crosses the border into some third-world country and is imprisoned indefinitely. Whenever I ask Mom or Dad how much longer my incarceration will last, I get the same reply: "We'll let you know." Mostly I stay in my room doing homework and watching Adleta's lacrosse games on the school website.

"Tim's the real rock star," I say. "What are you guys? Four and oh?"

"Five and oh," Adleta says. "Not that I'm paying attention."

"No way, feel free to brag," Ellie says. "You're amazing out there."

Amazing is probably the right word for it. So far, Adleta leads the league in every offensive category. It's pretty cool having a friend who's so completely dominant in something. I mean, yeah, Wheeler's dominant as a suburban terrorist, but Adleta's dominant in something that won't end with him in a supermax prison.

"And now you're a Vine star too," Wheeler says.

"What?" Adleta asks.

"You haven't seen this?" Malone says and opens the app on her phone.

The six-second video, sensitively titled "All Backbone or No Backbone?" shows Adleta standing stone-faced while his dad and Stranko simultaneously yell at him on the sideline.

"I don't know how you sat through that without going nuclear on them," Wheeler says.

"By being a master of looking like I'm paying attention when really I'm a million miles away," Adleta says.

"That's sad," Ellie says, patting his arm.

"No, I'm fine."

But I know Tim better than that now.

"That's bullshit," I say. "You shouldn't put up with that."

"Oh? And what do you suggest?" Adleta says.

"I don't know, but if puking on them didn't get their attention, maybe something else will. You're crazy to let them get away with that."

I return to my pizza but can feel Adleta looking at me.

"Does anyone else find it ironic that Max just used the word *crazy*?" Malone asks.

The rest of the table starts laughing. So we're back to this again.

"I'm not crazy," I say. "For the thousandth time, I heard what the girl said. 'We're planning something everyone in the town will witness live.' The town hasn't had anything like that until now. The Asheville Celebration will bring out everyone. That's the plan, right, Ellie?"

"That's how they talk at the planning sessions," she says.

"And we know the Chaos Club always pulls an end-of-the-year prank," I say. "What better place than the celebration they know everyone will be at?"

I should probably thank my parents for a lot of forced reflection time during my suspension and also the Chaos Club for breaking Heist Rule #20: *Explain things on a need-to-know basis.*

"What if it's a red herring?" Wheeler says.

"Exactly," Malone says. "Maybe they said it on purpose, so you'd think they were going to prank the celebration but really they're planning something else. Have you thought about that?"

"Of course I have, but there's not much we can do about it. This is the first real lead we've had. We have to follow it."

Ellie, who's agreed with me from the start, says, "Let's just assume for a second that Max is right, because he could be. What do you think we should do about it?"

That's the question, isn't it? Because it's one thing to know where the Chaos Club is going to strike next, but it's a whole different thing to know how to use it to our advantage. The good news is that I have time to plan because the Asheville Celebration isn't until school's out, which helps because this calls for careful planning and execution.

"Look, I'll come up with something," I say. "Are you guys in when I do?"

"Sure," Malone says, and the others agree. "If you're right," she adds.

"And if you come up with something," Adleta says.

"Those are big ifs," Wheeler says. "Huge ones."

"Like my balls," I say.

⊕

On a clear Saturday afternoon, five weeks after my arrest, Mom calls me into the kitchen where she's making a chicken potpie while listening to the *Wicked* soundtrack. It's beautiful outside, and all the windows in the house are open for the first time in months.

"I'm letting you know," she says.

"Huh?"

"I'm letting you know."

"Letting me know what?"

Mom raises her eyebrows and gives me a *Really?* look. Then I get it.

"Just try not to get arrested, okay?" Mom says. "What? Too soon?"

I receive congratulatory texts from everyone when I announce my ungrounding, but only Wheeler's free that night. We decide to meet up at Adleta's lacrosse game.

Behind Adleta's continuing dominance, the Golden Eagles are undefeated in division play and have only lost a single game, a 6–5 heartbreaker to Reynoldsburg when Adleta took a concussion shot to the head and was forced to sit out the second half. Wheeler and I are in the third row of the packed stands, surrounded by lacrosse parents. Wheeler's wearing his Future of the Left T-shirt that reads "You Need Satan More Than He Needs You" and has a biology textbook open on his lap. It's even right-side up.

"Miss the days of not caring?" I ask.

"Absolutely, dude. There's just so much work to do. I have an essay for Cronin right now that's giving me migraines. If I knew how much work it took to, you know, not fail, I'm not sure I would have ever started trying to pass."

"You're like one of those people who gets brainwashed by a religious cult."

"Yeah, but without the togas and free love. It sucks, man."

At halftime, Asheville is up 5–3 against Trenton, our biggest rival. Stranko's diaper must be full because he's tearing into the team right in front of us. Adleta's getting the brunt of the reaming despite having three of our goals. Tim's dad is right beside Stranko, jabbing his finger at his son while Stranko rails.

"What assholes," Wheeler says.

A parental unit seated directly in front of us turns around, frowning.

"Sorry," Wheeler says. "But they are assholes."

Both give disapproving shakes of their heads in that way all adults seem to have mastered, and the dad's frown grows even frownier when he sees Wheeler's shirt.

"Satan's no laughing matter, son," the dad says.

"Yeah, an invisible being tempting us to do evil so he can torture our souls forever. Nothing funny or ridiculous about that."

The dad glares at Wheeler but turns around without saying anything.

"Oh, and speaking of evil," Wheeler says and from his pocket pulls out a sandwich bag containing Stranko's phone. I snatch the bag away and shove it deep into my pocket before anyone can see it.

"It's ready to go, a new phone number and everything."

"Is his phone number in the contacts?"

"Like you asked."

"Under what name?"

"Mike Oxbig."

"Huh?"

"Say it out loud."

I do and start laughing.

"Are you going to tell me what it's for?" Wheeler says.

"Not yet," I say.

Because I really don't know—at least not entirely. But I have an idea marinating in my brain, and Stranko's phone plays a small role. Or maybe that's just Wheeler's friend Satan setting me up for the big beat down.

We're eight minutes into the second half when the Asheville defense breaks down and a Trenton middie fires a shot, bringing the score to 5–4. Stranko immediately shouts for a time-out. Adleta's the last to join the huddle because he was on the opposite side of the field, twenty yards from the play. His dad grabs him by the arm and shoves him into the circle of players. Stranko's yelling so loud, people in Alaska can hear him.

"You guys think you can take it easy and still win this game? Because you won't. You want to be champions, you have to play like champions. What you're doing out there is a disgrace. You should be up ten goals at this point, but no. Your sorry asses are up one. It's pathetic. If you don't put it into high gear, you're going to find your season over." Then Stranko points at Adleta. "You especially. You're playing like a loser right now."

Adleta visibly stiffens.

"Oh, do you have something to say?" Stranko asks. "I'd love to hear your thoughts."

"I think we're playing hard out there," Adleta says. "Trenton's better than you think."

Stranko is actually too stunned to talk, so Mr. Adleta does it for him.

"You keep quiet," he growls.

"Why? I just said—"

"Shut your mouth."

Adleta cocks his head.

"Or what?"

Both Adletas are locked in on one another. Everyone in the stands is quiet and staring at the showdown. Stranko actually puts a hand between them.

He says, "Okay now—"

"You don't deserve to be out there," Mr. Adleta tells

Tim. "Champions play for blood. You're playing like you're stupid. Is that it? Are you stupid? Because you sure as hell—"

And then it happens—Tim drops his stick and starts across the field.

Mr. Adleta pushes past players to chase after Tim, but Stranko grabs his arm. At midfield, one of the refs holds up a hand to say something to Tim, but he keeps walking, crossing the entire field, passing in front of Trenton's bench, then out the gate and into the parking lot. There's not a closed mouth in the entire stadium.

"Holy shit," Wheeler says.

Holy shit is right.

When the game resumes, the team's play is chaotic. Asheville gives up two quick goals and loses the lead. Stranko calls another time-out. This time though, he doesn't raise his voice. He keeps looking toward the parking lot with a dazed, humble look, like he's expecting Adleta to return. In fact, Stranko doesn't shout once the rest of the game, not even with one minute remaining when it's clear Asheville's going to lose. It's like Adleta's exit has lobotomized him. When the clock runs out, Asheville's lost by only one, but somehow it feels like they've lost by a lot more.

Later that night, a single cryptic text arrives from Adleta.

Thx.

I don't understand Tim's message until later in the week

when the Malone-Libby powder keg finally detonates in Watson's room.

Thursday's Big Question of Existence is "Does everything happen for a reason?" The class is evenly split on the question, but I'm firmly entrenched on the no side. As much as I'd like to believe there's some master plan, I can't buy into the idea that some set of galactic directions manipulates my life. And if the universe is really letting, say, little kids get sick and die "for a reason," then I say screw you, universe.

The only drawback to having this stance today is that Libby Heckman agrees and is at the desk next to me. You'd think the goldfish incident would've deflated her some, maybe even scared her off of Malone, but no, especially not today, with Malone on the other side of the argument.

"I don't fully buy into determinism," Malone says, "but I can't just accept free will either. There's a side of me that wants to believe I'm a part of something bigger. I guess it makes me feel less alone."

Lots of people on both sides agree with this.

Libby, not so much.

She raises her hand and says, "I think people like to believe everything happens for a reason so they don't have to take responsibility for themselves."

"Care to elaborate?" Mr. Watson says.

"Well, if you believe everything happens for a reason, then you're admitting you don't have any control over what you do. And that means you never have to regret anything."

Fair point.

Unfortunately, Libby doesn't stop there.

"And if you don't have to regret anything, then it's not your fault if you ruin your life. Is that why you like to believe it all happens for a reason, Kate? So you don't have to regret a decision that ruins your life?"

All eyes turn to Malone. She's never taken Libby's bait, no matter how bad it's gotten. Today's different though.

"If you have something to say, Libby, go ahead and say it. I won't stop you."

Libby has daggers in her smile. She leans forward on her desk and says, "There's nothing to say that everyone doesn't already know about you being a slut, Kate. I'm just telling it like it is."

"Which is just a way to justify being mean to people, but that's your right," Malone says. "Here's the thing though, Libby—I sort of agree with you. Not about me being a slut, but about how it feels to regret something. Probably not in the way you mean though."

Libby chuffs in a *Well?* way, like she's impatient, but she shifts just a tiny bit in her seat. There's no way she was expecting Kate to defend herself.

"Looking back on it," Malone says, "yeah, I regret sending Troy that picture of me. But not because it makes me a slut like you tell people. I regret it because I did it for his approval, and as a feminist, I shouldn't need any boy's approval to feel confident. I definitely won't be doing that again."

Libby chuffs some more. She's so good at it that she had to be a steam engine in a past life.

"But what I really regret is wasting my time worrying so much about you. I don't think about my mom or my friends as much as I've thought about you. I even catch myself having arguments with you in my head. That's just sad on my part. Who wants to live that way? I'm better than that. So in order to let all this go once and for all, I need to apologize."

"For what?"

"Well, for two things: One, for getting in the way of you and Troy. I honestly thought you two were finished, but apparently you weren't. You and I were friends in art, and I should have asked you what the situation was before agreeing to go out with him. It did nothing but cause problems, and girls shouldn't treat each other like that."

"Whatever," Libby snorts.

"And two, I apologize for your drawing. I feel bad for what happened to it in the display case, because that piece was really excellent and I destroyed it. You shouldn't have had to suffer that sort of humiliation. Believe me, I know."

"*You're* the one who did that?" Libby gapes at Malone, who's looking back at her with just the slightest of smiles.

"You're in so much trouble," Libby says, tears pooling in her eyes.

"Probably."

"I'm going to get you expelled."

"Okay."

"You think your life was ruined before, it's over now!"

"Maybe."

"I'm serious!"

Malone still hasn't really moved, but now she put her hands out in an *oh well* way.

"You are such a bitch!" Libby shouts.

No one in the room makes a sound.

Malone sighs and says, "You know, Libby, maybe if you didn't act this way, you and Troy wouldn't have the problems you do. Maybe then he wouldn't have broken up with you and come running to me in the first place."

There's a collective inhale as everyone gasps at Malone's surgically focused insult. Libby stands frozen, gaping, then beautifully and 150 percent awesomely lets out a howler-monkey scream, a sort of primal wail that only our cavemen ancestors could have understood. Tears geyser from her eyes, and she shrieks before sprinting down the aisle and out Watson's door, her sobs fading the farther she gets down the hall.

For a long moment, no one moves or breathes. Then Tina Manetti, Libby's friend, raises her hand.

"Can I go check on her?"

"Of course," Watson says.

Malone says, "I'm sorry for the interruption, Mr. Watson. I didn't want that to happen here."

Watson, who has been behind his podium the entire time, says, "You know, in my years of teaching, I've learned that sometimes you just have to let things play out. It's all over, so let's get back to our discussion."

Of course, we don't get squat done the rest of the period. Watson could begin juggling flaming bowling balls and all we'd be able to think about was Libby's epic destruction. When the bell rings, both Ellie and I rush over to Malone, who doesn't say anything until we're in the hall.

"God, that was awful," Malone says.

"Awful?" I say. "More like amazing."

"Good for you, Kate," Ellie says.

"I tried to be nice," she says.

"What made you do that?" I ask. "Libby's said stuff like that before."

Malone stares at me for a good long couple of seconds. "Do you really want to know?"

It's such an odd thing to ask, I don't know how to respond. Why would I have asked if I didn't want an answer?

"You're the reason," Malone says.

"I don't get it."

Malone frowns like she regrets bringing it up but knows she can't go back.

"It's just that watching how you've handled yourself these last couple of weeks got me thinking. A lot of people, after getting arrested like that, would've done their best to remain invisible the rest of the year. But you didn't do that. If anything, you've put yourself out there even more, like you're not going to let one thing sink you. I figured if you could do that, I could do it too. So I did. And I feel a whole lot better."

When Malone finishes, there are tears pooling in her eyes.

"That's why Tim finally walked off the field the other night," Ellie says. "You didn't know that?"

I shake my head, but now I understand his mystery text. The whole thing is so flattering, I'm not sure what the right response is.

"I'm…honored, I guess," I say.

"Yeah, well, don't go getting a big head," Malone says. "If you tell anyone I almost cried in front of you, I'll kick your ass. I'm not kidding, Max."

Deal.

Nothing is more motivating than knowing people are watching you and—dare I say it—getting inspired by you. This shocking revelation is what gives me the extra push I need to really focus on a plan to take down the Chaos Club. And as if I need any additional motivation, Ellie stops by my locker this afternoon and whispers, "Think of what you could do with a guaranteed yes, Max. The sky's the limit."

I simplify the Chaos Club problem by breaking it down to two questions:

1. What do I want to happen?

2. How do I make that happen?

Then I spend the weekend doing what I enjoy best—watching my favorite caper films, some of them twice, and filling an entire notebook with ideas. Most of the ideas are inventive but unrealistic. Others are realistic but dull. A dozen are incredibly stupid. And one makes me literally jump off my bed and stare down at my notebook, not believing the idea that just came to me.

It's crazy.

It's epic.

It's flat-out brilliant.

And I just happen to have the crew to make it work.

Before I tell the others my plan, I have to fully commit. Because if I think too much about this, Just Max may reappear and talk me into chickening out. So as soon as I get to school on Monday, I head straight for Stranko's office, where he's talking with the new lacrosse team captain, Jason Bruno.

"What is it, Cobb?" Stranko says.

"Do you have a minute?"

. Stranko tells Bruno they'll talk before practice. With Adleta's quitting, the team's in a death spiral, having lost by four on Saturday to a vastly inferior Athens team. Still, it's hard to look at Stranko and not remember his sad shock and confusion when Tim walked off the field last week.

"Remember back in September when you said we're to come to you if we know something?" I say.

Stranko says a long, "Yeah."

"Well, I know something about the Chaos Club."

Stranko straightens in his chair.

"What about them?"

"I think I know what they're going to do for their end-of-the-year prank. And I think I have a way to catch them."

"Do you now? Then tell me."

There's something in his voice—is it skepticism?—that causes me to stumble a bit.

"Well, I, uh, just know they always pull a prank at the end of the year, and with the Asheville Celebration coming up, I was thinking that would be the perfect time for them to strike."

"And you're telling me this why?"

Because you're going to be out there guarding the grounds if I warn you or not. This way I can control what you do. Otherwise, you're a wild card, and I can't have that.

"Because you're the vice principal, and you've been after them for years. I thought you might want to stop them from ruining the celebration."

Stranko doesn't blink for a good ten seconds.

"You don't ever stop, do you, Cobb?"

"Huh?"

"Even after trashing my office, getting arrested, and spending ten days out of school, you're still playing this game. Let me make it simple for you: your reputation is zero with me. If I had it my way, you'd have been expelled weeks ago."

"But I really think they're going to hit the celebration."

"Right, and I'm betting that next you'll tell me some idea you have for catching the Chaos Club, maybe even give me a role in your plan. Is that right?"

He wants me to say yes, so I do.

"Uh-huh," he says, "and then, when the time comes to execute your plan, something happens. Maybe you have me in one place while your friends vandalize a different area or you trick me into busting the wrong people while you attack someplace else. Am I close?"

"No, I—"

"I'll save you the trouble, Cobb. You can't fool me. I know who you are and what you are, and if your club comes within a mile of the Asheville Celebration, I will make it my life's goal to have you in jail. Do you understand?"

"But I—"

"Now get out of here and tell your friends you failed."

I hotfoot it out the door and head for the bathroom, where I take a newly purchased burner phone from my backpack. Then I send a single text to Stranko's old phone, which is currently packaged in a bubble-wrapped envelope addressed to Stranko's home. Accompanying the phone is a letter from a Good Samaritan explaining how she discovered Stranko's address in the contacts file after finding the phone in a booth at McDonald's where "two loud and rude teenagers had been sitting."

The whole thing almost makes me feel bad for the guy. Almost.

CHAPTER 21

Ellie calls it Operation Eagle Eye and gives each member of the Water Tower Five code names related to our roles.

Adleta is Sluggo.

Malone is da Vinci.

Wheeler is Captain Calamity.

Ellie is Puma.

And I was hoping for Mongoose, but once Wheeler hears the plan, he renames me Master Baiter.

I blame Sun Tzu for that. If you're not up on your early-fifth-century BC military strategists, Sun Tzu was a general whose *The Art of War* is still studied today. In my search for a way to set up the Chaos Club, I ran across this Sun Tzu quote: "Hold out baits to entice the enemy. Feign disorder, and crush him." Using that idea as the template, I arranged Operation Eagle Eye into three parts: Bait, Wait, and Punish.

Catchy, yeah?

Well, except for the whole Master Baiter thing.

At this point in a heist film, you'd be treated to a planning montage where each crew member works on his or her individual assignment.

You'd see:

Adleta rejoining the lacrosse team after a lecture from his dad and Stranko and suffering through a forced apology to the team.

Malone working long nights in Boyd's barn, her clothes and body smeared with plaster as she creates her masterpiece.

Ellie producing a short documentary about Zippy, still currently under renovation and scheduled to make its long-awaited return at the upcoming Asheville Celebration.

Wheeler hijacking the school's sound system to announce during seventh period, "This is Captain Calamity, and I have a message for the Chaos Club. You are put on notice that I, Captain Calamity, will expose your identities at Saturday's celebration. Your reign of terror ends there. Show up if you dare."

And finally, me sending Stranko texts he's come to believe are from a high-ranking member of the Chaos Club about an end-of-the-year prank. How did I trick Stranko into believing this? With a deft hand like any master baiter would.

The last day of school comes way too fast, and with most of my brain power going toward planning our assault on the Chaos Club, I'm going to have to come up with good explanations for my terrifyingly bad performance on my precalc final and the C- I received on my Weird Science project. (Solar Oven S'mores—don't ask.) But right now, I have more important things on my mind. Because unlike most kids who are attending parties where they're drinking warm beer from red plastic cups, settling yearlong arguments with either a hug or a fistfight, and writing lies in each other's yearbooks ("I loved being in the same English class together!"), at 8:30 p.m., I'm hiding in the tree line on the edge of the parking lot with Puma. She's dressed in black spandex workout pants and a long-sleeved, tight black Under Armour shirt like our first night at the water tower. And yes, it's as distracting now as it was then.

Setup for the Asheville Celebration began two days ago, and carnival rides and booths fill the front lawn. Erected on the walkway to the school is a fifteen-foot-high curtained barrier concealing the Zippy statue that arrived this morning. A large stage has been constructed in front of the school's entrance, with a large white screen behind it that will show Ellie's documentary tomorrow. And there, sitting in lawn chairs on the stage like the Royal Guard of Assville, are Stranko and Hale.

"What are you smiling about?" I say.

"This," Ellie says. "All of this is awesome. How often in life are we going to get to do something like this?"

"Probably not very much."

"But we are now. That's why I'm smiling. Even if this doesn't work, this has been an awesome year. I've loved having a project for all of us to work on. It almost makes everything that's happened worth it."

I couldn't have said it better myself.

"Ready?" I say.

"Absolutely."

I take out my phone.

Me: Where r u???

We watch through the trees as Stranko takes his phone from his pocket.

Stranko: ?

Me: I'm in the tunnel. Hurry up.

Stranko: ?

I've texted about the tunnel to Stranko's phone more than a dozen times in the last week, but whenever he's asked for more information, I haven't answered. Now it's finally time to give him what he wants.

Me: Duh.

And with that, I attach a picture I've had waiting for just this moment.

Stranko stands up and shows the text and picture to Hale, who rises to join him. But Stranko shakes his head, and Hale sits back down. No way Stranko's going to leave the statue unguarded. When he descends the stage stairs and disappears into the building, I send a text to Adleta.

On his way.

Adleta doesn't reply, but he's not supposed to. Leading up to this night, Adleta's job was to keep close tabs on Stranko, and the only way he could do that was to be a part of the team again. It's only because of his sacrificial apology to Stranko and the team that he knew tonight's practice schedule and, therefore, Stranko's whereabouts. It also gave Adleta a reason to be in the school well after hours—something we needed from him.

"I'm sort of bummed I'm going to miss this," I say.

"We won't," Ellie says.

Before I can ask what she means, her phone vibrates.

FaceTime Request from Tim

She clicks Accept, and suddenly we're in the loading dock, looking at the small open door and tunnel that Wheeler, Adleta, and I explored during work crew. Adleta crouches among the boxes on the opposite wall, hidden and waiting for Stranko.

"Wow, I should've thought of this," I say.

"That's why we're a great team."

I gnaw at a fingernail waiting for Stranko to appear on Ellie's screen. But what if Stranko misunderstands the photo? Or he knows where the tunnel is but doesn't go? Or shows up with someone else? Not that he would. If Stranko is going to bust the Chaos Club, he's going to do it by himself. Which is unfortunate for him. If I'm not mistaken, I think the correct term is *hubris*. Wouldn't the Asheville High English Department be proud of me?

Adleta's wedged back in the boxes, so for minutes

we can only see the tunnel entrance, but then Stranko's jeaned ass fills the screen.

"There he is," Ellie whispers.

Stranko has no idea he's only a few feet from Adleta. He stands staring at the open door without moving for so long I think maybe the phone's frozen. Then he takes one slow step forward and another, like an animal warily approaching unexpected food in the forest.

"He's thinking about it," Ellie says.

Stranko takes one more step, then bends over for a better look at the tunnel. He's probably wishing he had a flashlight with him right now. He inches ahead, then kneels in front of the tunnel, his head almost inside.

"Come on," I say. "Get in there."

But Stranko doesn't enter. He just kneels there, listening hard, probably hoping for definitive proof someone's really back there. It's just when I think Stranko's not going to move forward any farther that the screen changes, and we're looking at the side of Adleta's leg, and then there's a blurry rush and the screen fills with light. The picture on the screen jumps so chaotically that I get dizzy. I have no idea what I'm seeing. It's all just fuzzy, nausea-inducing pandemonium.

Then the image completely disappears.

FaceTime Ended

"What happened?" Puma says.

My instinct is to grab Ellie's hand and run, but no, we can't do that. If Stranko has Adleta, there's no way we're leaving him behind. I type a text to Malone and Wheeler reading Abort. My finger goes to Send, but right before I tap it, Ellie says, "Oh!"

FaceTime Request from Tim

"Don't answer it," I say. "It could be Stranko."

"But it could be Tim," she says. "Besides, if it's Stranko, he'll know Tim was FaceTiming me. It'd be in the call history."

She has a point. And if Stranko has Tim, I'm not letting Tim take the fall by himself. So I tell her to go ahead, and Ellie touches the Accept button. There, standing in front of the closed tunnel door, which inexplicably has a large box against it, is Adleta giving us a thumbs-up.

"Awesome," Ellie says, and returns the gesture.

Tim gives us the *one second* finger and starts down the hall. There, outside the noise of the loading dock, he says, "Man, that felt good."

"Nice job, Sluggo!" Ellie says.

"Stranko had no idea what hit him. I shoved him from behind, and it sent him into the tunnel. But I think something broke on the door when I slammed it shut."

"Will it hold?" I ask.

"I think."

"Did he see you?"

"Not a chance."

"Excellent. Get to position two."

"Should I text da Vinci?" Ellie asks.

"Yeah, but here, use the burner."

You're up.

"Do you think the Chaos Club is somewhere nearby, watching?" Ellie says.

"They're here. They have to be."

"And if they're not?"

"Then we're doing all this for nothing."

"Well, not nothing. It's fun. That's something."

Across the lawn, Officer Hale remains planted in his chair on stage. Stranko's been gone for twenty minutes, and I wonder at what point Hale leaves to check on him. No, he'll probably call or text first. Not that it'd help. No signals can escape the concrete tomb Stranko's currently buried in.

Across the parking lot, the flashers on Hale's security car suddenly blaze to life, spinning red-and-blue lights in the dark. Hale jumps to his feet and is quickly down the stage steps.

Then the lights shut off.

"What's she doing?" I say. "He was coming."

"She's messing with him."

"But that's not the plan."

"Relax, Kate knows what she's doing."

Hale stares at his car, probably worried he's hallucinating, then climbs back up the stage steps. But as soon as his butt hits the chair, the light bar explodes again into red-and-blue disco lights. You can practically hear Malone laughing as she does it.

"And there he goes," Ellie says.

You'd never use the word *running* for what Hale does as he heads for the parking lot—his weight makes running impossible—but it's faster than a walk and slower than a jog. It takes him thirty seconds to get to his car, and as he walks around the front to the driver's side, Malone's shadowy figure creeps around the back. At least I assume it's Malone. The ski mask she's wearing makes positive identification impossible.

Hale opens the driver's door and shuts the lights off. He looks around the parking lot, but there's no one to see. From the other side of the car, Malone, still close to the ground, reaches up and opens the back passenger door, tossing something inside. She then scurries around to the back as Hale rushes—more like lumbers—around the back. By the time he gets to the open door, Malone's circled the car. She's flat against the trunk, only a few feet away from Hale. He stands at the open door, looking inside the car, presumably at what's on the seat.

"Get it," Ellie urges.

Malone risks a peek around the trunk and sees Hale move into the back, his fat body climbing across the seat

where he had all five of us sardined after the water tower
and me after my arrest in Stranko's office.

I dig my fingers into the dirt.

"Come on," I say.

When Hale disappears into the backseat, Malone
springs out, slamming the door and trapping Hale in the
back of his own patrol car—or, more accurately, the patrol
car with no door handles in the back and the unnecessary
bulletproof glass that makes it impossible for him to get
to the front seat. Or even more accurately, the patrol car
with the cell phone jammer in it that Hale was once so
proud of that now makes it impossible for him to call
for help. But at least he has the lunch bag Malone threw
inside that he couldn't resist. Inside the bag:

A Chaos Club card.

And a plastic doughnut.

Wheeler's idea—"A fake doughnut for a fake cop."

Hale pounds on the window. Malone's just below him,
and there's no doubt he can see her. She's supposed to run,
but of course being Malone, she doesn't. Instead, she points
her phone at the screaming Hale and takes his picture.

So much for keeping evidence to a minimum.

Malone sprints away from the car, coming our way
fast. But when she reaches the steps on the curb, her body
goes rag doll. She falls, rolling and tumbling in the grass
like her legs have gone boneless. Before I can react, Ellie
breaks from cover. When I catch up, she's helping Malone
limp to the trees.

"Are you okay?" I say.

"That stupid curb," Malone says. "I didn't even see it. I'll live."

"What do you think?" Ellie says to me.

I look at Malone, who gives me a *yes, duh* look.

"Do it, Puma," I say.

Puma stands up and puts on her backpack. From her pocket, she pulls a box cutter and holds it up.

"My weapon of choice," she says.

Then Ellie grabs the front of my shirt and pulls me in, kissing me hard.

"For luck," she says.

⊕

At Puma speed, Ellie covers the distance to the statue in seconds. From where he's trapped, Hale can't see Ellie approaching, but she stays on the opposite side of the patrol car anyway and drops at the base of the curtain. She slices a three-foot incision in the curtain and then pushes her backpack through first before disappearing inside.

"Do we need to get you to a doctor?" I ask Malone.

"I'll be fine. But you'll have to be the one to climb if it comes to that."

I feel real fear for the first time that night.

"No way," I say.

"Don't worry," Kate says. "I'm sure it won't be needed."

It'd better not be.

For the next three minutes, while Ellie is under the

curtain, I make a meal out of my fingernails. My big fears are a car entering the parking lot, an additional security guard on the grounds for the night, or someone simply turning around who Hale might be able to flag down.

But none of that happens. Ellie slips back out from under the curtain and races across the parking lot without any trouble. Malone and I move aside as Ellie crashes back into the trees, out of breath more from excitement than exertion. She rocks back and forth on her toes, not able to keep still.

"Oh my gosh, that was so fun!"

"It went okay?"

"Perfect."

"How's the light in there? Can you see anything?"

"Don't worry," Ellie says. "It should be bright enough."

"And Wheeler?"

"He's fine. Going a bit stir-crazy, but fine."

Since rendezvousing with Boyd nine hours ago, before the statue's delivery, Wheeler's been hiding in the secret compartment in the newly constructed base of the statue. If Wheeler wasn't claustrophobic before, he sure as hell is now.

"Sue me," Wheeler said when defending his wanting a simple job for the caper. "I helped edit the documentary and hacked the sound system. You guys are finished on Friday, but I have summer school starting Monday and that comes with a boatload of assignments due on the first day."

So yeah, Wheeler's been folded up in the statue's base

like a contortionist, reading and working by flashlight. Or, more likely, he's on H8box posting the whole night for millions to follow.

Now with Stranko and Hale gone, the real waiting begins. For the next twenty minutes, Ellie, Kate, and I sit hidden, watching the parking lot and statue for any sign of the Chaos Club.

Nothing.

"Be patient," Ellie says. "They'll be here."

I wish I were as optimistic. The plan's founded on the assumption that the Chaos Club was here to witness Stranko's and Hale's exits, followed by Ellie's assault on the statue. With the coast clear, we're hoping they'll make their move. Now, at 9:45, there's no one, leaving me feeling like a major dumb ass.

Then my phone vibrates in my hand.

Adleta: Movement on south side.

Ellie's squints into the darkness.

"There," she says.

"I can't see anything."

"Me either," Malone says.

Ellie grabs my head and points.

"*There.*"

I strain my eyes and am unable to see anything at first. Then I see them. They're almost impossible to spot, skulking along the building in the shadows, but there they are, two people with backpacks.

"What do you have? Bionic eyes or something?"

"No, silly. Cats have great night vision."

We watch the two intruders as they slowly creep to the statue. At this distance, they appear to be roughly the same size as my two kidnappers from the baseball field. The dark makes it impossible to see their faces.

"What if they're wearing masks again?" I say.

"Shut up," Malone says.

"Yeah, shut up," Ellie says. "This is going to work."

They're right. I see that now. Everything has worked out exactly as planned, minus Malone's twisted ankle. Once the Chaos Club enters the security curtain, it's over for them. And they're less than a minute away. Even when I drew up the plans, I realistically understood it was a long shot. Something would go wrong. Like Stranko wouldn't follow the text bait. Or Hale would call for backup instead of going to his car. But no, it's working. Hell, wrong verb tense. It's worked. We've done it.

Then—

"Oh no," Malone says.

"What?"

And this time it's Malone who grabs my head and points me toward the front of the building to the person standing there.

Stranko.

⊕

Shit.

Double shit.

Triple shit.

The three of us remain frozen, like somehow Stranko will spot us through the camouflage of the trees. He surveys the parking lot with his hands on his hips like a pissed-off drill sergeant. The two Chaos Club members hug the ground along the side of the building, no doubt trying not to vomit.

Ellie speaks barely above a whisper, saying, "He must've Hulked-out or something."

"Adleta said the door was messed up," I say and take out my phone. "We need to get Wheeler out of there before he gets caught. Stranko has to have called the cops. We have to abort."

"No way," Malone says. "You know what you have to do."

Oh man.

Heist Rule #21: *Always have a backup plan.*

That's the one drawback of being the heist team leader. You not only have to memorize everyone's roles, but you have to be able to perform them as well. And that includes the backup plan roles too, unfortunately.

"I can't do it," I say.

"Oh, you can do it, and you will, Maxwell Cobb," Ellie says. "Now hurry up."

She helps Kate up, and after a quick wardrobe switch with Malone, I'm ready.

"Here, don't forget my mask," Malone says.

"Good luck, Mongoose," Ellie says. "You'll be great."

Or paralyzed for life. One of the two.

I step out of the trees and hustle across the parking lot, past booths and rides, toward the lawn and statue. I force myself to keep walking so I don't wuss out. Stranko's away from the building now and approaching the statue when he spots me.

Stranko stops.

I stop.

Fifty yards separate us.

Does he know who he's looking at?

I take a single step back.

Stranko leans forward.

I take two more away.

"Stop!" Stranko shouts.

Three more steps back now.

"I said stop!"

He's coming at me now, moving fast, and I backpedal, but slowly. It's only when Stranko is within thirty yards that I race off. He breaks into a sprint, and I run for my life to the water tower, leading him away from the statue. I sprint around the back of the security fence and crash through the gate. Thanks to Ellie's key, the ladder guard is open. There's no time to think or second-guess myself. There's only time to climb.

I monkey my way up the ladder. I'm a third of the way up when I feel it shake. I don't have to look behind me to know Stranko's following me. I speed up, and my left foot slips off the rung. *This* is exactly why I hate ladders. The only good news is if I fall, I'll probably crash into Stranko and take him with me.

I hear a loud bang from below and look down. Ellie and Malone stand at the base of the ladder, and Malone's putting a lock onto the ladder guard that's just been slammed shut.

Now I'm officially screwed.

I climb onto the metal grating at the top of the tower. The spotlight shining on the tower half blinds me, but I can see I only have about fifteen seconds before Stranko's here. I inch along the rail and find what I'm looking for.

There it is, the clip Malone prepared earlier.

I'm fumbling with my waist when Stranko's head appears.

"Get over here," he says.

I throw one leg over the railing, then the other, until I'm leaning back over the edge. I grip the metal so hard my fingers might break. Even with all the time spent working with Malone this week when she wasn't at Boyd's, I still am nowhere ready for this.

"What are you doing?" Stranko says, panicked. "Stop."

"Do it, Mongoose!" Ellie shouts from below.

And I do, letting go of the rail and free-falling to my death.

Stranko shouts in horror from the top of the tower.

I want to join him, but Heist Rule #2: *Be cool* sort of prohibits screaming.

Instead, I squeeze the handbrake on the rope that has me tethered to the water tower. My falling slows just enough that I don't feel out of control. I use the rappelling tricks Malone has taught me and descend quickly. I even open my eyes once or twice.

Ellie and Malone are waiting for me when I reach the ground. Both of them hug me simultaneously, and I have a terribly dirty thought I'll no doubt revisit tonight when I have some privacy.

"That was amazing!" Ellie says.

"Yeah, you were great," Malone says. "Terrible form, but you didn't die. That's all that matters."

At the top of the water tower, Stranko grips the railing, glaring at us. I don't know if he can see us, but at the moment, I don't care.

"You stay there," Stranko yells back.

The three of us hurry through the security gate and around the corner, out of Stranko's line of sight, just in case he really can see this far down. Malone's moving the fastest of all of us.

"Wait, I thought you hurt your ankle," I say.

She and Ellie start laughing.

"I lied," Malone says. "We just wanted to see you go up and down the tower if it came to that."

"I could've been killed!"

"But you weren't, so shut up."

This has to be why most heist crews don't have many girls on them.

Stranko continues yelling from the top of the tower, his voice echoing across the parking lot. Minus Ellie's quick kiss back in the trees minutes ago, it's the highlight of my entire school year.

"What should we do now?" Malone asks.

I look toward the statue, wondering if the Chaos Club made their move and if we missed it.

"I guess we need to find out from Wheeler if—"

The next two things happen simultaneously.

1. My phone vibrates with a message from Adleta: They split.

2. And in the distance, an approaching police siren wails.

The three of us exchange panicked looks, and this time, I don't text. I call Wheeler directly.

He answers on the first ring.

"The Chaos Club hasn't showed up yet."

"Get out of there," I say. "The cops are coming."

"But—"

"I said get out. It's over. We failed."

CHAPTER 22

Life sucks.

At noon the next day, I'm still in bed with the shades drawn. Since sneaking back in last night, I've barely moved or spoken, and if I have it my way, I won't until I'm thirty. Unfortunately, Mom won't shut up about me going with them to the Asheville Celebration.

"Are you sure?" she says. "From what I saw driving by this morning, it looks like a great time."

And return to the scene of my greatest failure? Why would I do that? Did the guy who captained the *Titanic* ever sail another ship? Of course not. Okay, so yeah, he was among the fifteen hundred plus who drowned that night, but if he'd lived he wouldn't have stepped foot on another boat. Shit, I doubt he'd even want ice in his drink ever again. Failing sucks that much.

"I'll be okay," I say to Mom. "You guys go. I just want to sleep."

That's me—Max Cobb, sore loser.

Of course, Ellie, who pulls up out front ten minutes later, proves to be more of a motivator than Mom.

"Oh, you're going," she says on the phone. "Get out here."

"I don't want to. Why should I?"

"Two reasons. Number one, I look supercute today. And number two, if you don't go, Wheeler said he'll help me ruin your life on H8box."

"How will you do that?"

"Let's just say whatever I do will guarantee you never get any action with the opposite sex ever again."

"Ever again? I haven't had *any* action."

"And you won't for your entire life unless you get out here. So stop being a sourpuss and let's go."

The transformation the school property has undergone since last night is amazing. The once-empty booths are now filled with local food vendors, stuffed animals likely made in Thai sweatshops, and students from clubs like National Honor Society who will paint your face for a dollar. The rides are up and running, the two most popular being a Ferris wheel–like contraption with flipping cages that's pretty much guaranteed to make you puke (no ipecac required) and the Scrambler, which looks like it was designed by chiropractors hoping to induce whiplash.

Ellie and I stand near the front of the stage with the growing crowd. My parents are around here somewhere, which doesn't matter anymore now that we have zero chance of exposing the Chaos Club in public. We spot a few teachers around, and like always, it's weird seeing them out of the classroom. Seeing them in shorts is even weirder—even wrong in Watson's case, with his aqua-blue shorts, sandals, and pasty legs. I love the guy, but, man, there ought to be a law.

"I can't believe how many people are here," I tell Ellie. "There have to be a couple thousand."

"The goal's five thousand over the course of the day," Ellie says.

"Yeah, and just imagine the show we could've given them."

"Oh, cheer up. What's done is done. Besides, in a few minutes, I'll be on stage and you can ogle me with the rest of the men in Asheville."

At least there's that.

From where we stand, we have a clear sightline to Malone at the LGBT booth, where they have a long line of people waiting to get rainbow braids in their hair. Malone's with some of her friends from the art department wearing orange "Some People Are Gay, Get Over It" T-shirts. She waves to us, not looking at all like someone who was part of a failed operation last night.

"So is Malone gay?" I say to Ellie.

"I don't think so. She's just very pro-people. Why? Would it matter?"

"Of course not."

"Right answer," Ellie says.

Nearby, two cameramen shoot footage of the crowd while another has her camera trained on the statue or, more accurately, the curtained tower hiding the statue.

Oh, what might have been.

Or still could be.

Because here's the thing, my prank is still set up and ready to go. I don't see the point though, especially since the Chaos Club didn't vandalize the statue as expected. Finishing my prank now would not only get the five of us in übertrouble but would also leave Boyd with a lot of explaining to do.

At two o'clock, the town dignitaries make their way through the crowd and take the stage. Most of them I don't recognize, but Mrs. B's up there, wearing a bright-blue dress and looking like she's had her hair done for the occasion. Stranko is in an Asheville button-up but is probably dying to get into the yellow-and-black Asheville lacrosse shirt he always wears while coaching. Tonight's the state semifinal, and he has to view this public relations event as a massive inconvenience. Not as inconvenient as being trapped on the water tower, but I doubt much trumps that. I wonder how long he was trapped on the tower. Hours, I hope.

Once everyone is in place, Mayor Hite comes to the front of the stage and taps the microphone.

"Hello, everyone!" she says. "I'd like to welcome all of you to the first annual Celebrate Asheville Festival!"

People applaud, and I roll my eyes. What are they applauding? The festival itself? The mayor? Themselves for showing up? And before you say it, yes, I'm bitter. Sue me.

Mayor Hite drones on about how wonderful Asheville is, what a wonderful history it has, blah, blah, blah. It

might as well be a campaign speech. Get to the statue already and put me out of my misery. She welcomes a kids' choir from the elementary school to the stage, and they sing a couple songs that has the crowd aww-ing their heads off. Stranko is smiling behind them, but like all his smiles, it's forced. Off to the side of the stage, Officer Hale is in full security-guard gear. I was hoping Hale had to gnaw off some fingers to survive in the back of his cruiser, but all ten are there. Life's just one disappointment after another.

Once the kids finish singing, Mayor Hite calls Mrs. B to come stand beside her. The mayor puts an arm around Mrs. B and says, "The humble person she is, Mrs. Barber has asked I keep this short. As most of you may have heard, Mrs. Barber just completed her fortieth year in the Asheville school district. That's twenty-two years in the classroom and eighteen as an administrator. Any celebration of Asheville wouldn't be complete without a few words from one of its most dedicated and beloved servants."

More applause—aren't people's palms getting numb?— and Mrs. B smiles and waves, waiting for the noise to die down. Then she starts thanking people for coming, and that's when I stop paying attention and instead scan the crowd, wondering if the Chaos Club is nearby. It's frustrating, thinking they're possibly within spitting distance, probably laughing at me at this very minute. One of these days, I'll learn to be strong in defeat, but today is not that day.

Mrs. B tells a quick anecdote about her first day as a teacher at AHS and talks about all the fantastic people she's had the pleasure of teaching and working with. It's a nice, short speech that she ends by saying, "And with all of you here, I'd like to announce that next year will be my last as principal."

Even my mouth drops at that.

"Forty years is a long time, and I'd like to retire while I still have the energy and health to do some traveling. It's time someone else takes over and leads this school and these wonderful students."

I immediately look to Stranko, who's as stunned as the rest of us. I'd have thought he'd be doing backflips at Mrs. B announced retirement. Instead, he's slack jawed. When the applause begins, it takes him a few seconds to join in, and even then it's halfhearted.

"Now enough about me," Mrs. B says. "Before we unveil the renovated statue, we'd like to show you a fantastic short documentary about our beloved Zippy made by one of our students, Ellie Wick."

Mrs. B motions to Ellie, who squeezes my arm before stepping onto the stage and waving. She looks great up there, and as instructed, I ogle appropriately. Ellie then motions to a table off to the side, and unexpectedly, there's Wheeler, sitting with one of his stage crew friends at the soundboard. I guess with everything going to shit last night, he still wants a good seat in the house for the unveiling.

Ellie's documentary is shown on the screen behind the stage, and the speakers on both sides boom the sound. Ellie and Wheeler did a private screening for all of us when it was completed. Coming in at just over seven minutes, the film interviews the widow of the eagle's creator, Gregor Hitchens, about the statue's production and gives a detailed travelogue of the various display sites the eagle had before the school was chosen as its permanent location. The video ends with a montage of different Asheville citizens, from the mayor to a local sportscaster to Mrs. B herself, all saying, "We love Zippy!"

We're nearing the start of this montage when I sense movement behind me. Someone's so close I can hear breathing, and I turn, expecting to see some dope crowding me for a better view of the movie. But no, it's not just any random dope.

It's Jeff Benz and Becca Yancey.

And unlike everyone else, they're not looking at the movie.

They're looking at me.

My body goes cold.

"Hi, Max," Becca says. "Can we ask you a question?"

"Um, sure."

Benz leans in with a professional-grade shit-eating grin. "What's it like to fail?"

My brain tries to wrap itself around the revelation, looking for clues in the school year that I should've picked up on or some forgotten history with either of these two that would have led to the water tower setup, but there's nothing.

Benz says, "I mean, you, or whoever, makes that announcement at the assembly, promising to expose us, and now here we are at the celebration, and you can't deliver. That either makes you a failure or a liar. Which is it?"

Becca gives Benz a little shove.

"Knock it off," she says. "Max is a good guy."

"A good guy you got suspended," I say.

"We gave you a choice," Benz says. "Remember that."

The anger I feel is a different, deeper kind of anger—an *I would blow up the world if I could* anger. I've waited nine months to discover who was in the Chaos Club, focused an unhealthy amount of time and thought on the question, and now that I know the answer, I really just want to see the world burn—with Benz as kindling and Becca as the match.

"Why are you revealing yourself to me now?" I say.

"Because it's over," Becca says. "You can't pin anything we've done on us."

"You don't mess with the Chaos Club, Max," Benz adds. "We're too smart to get caught. Why do you think we've lasted this long?"

"Besides, there's nothing you can do about it now. Jeff graduates tomorrow, and I'm moving next month," Becca

says. "He didn't want to tell you, just have it be a mystery you go your entire life without solving, but I thought we should put you out of your misery."

"Wow, thanks. That's really kind of you."

"No, it's us who should be thanking you for getting Stranko and Hale out of our way," Benz says. "If you hadn't, we couldn't have pulled our final prank. But I have to say, I'm a little disappointed in you. You went to those lengths to clear them out, and the best you could do, or whoever that was who cut the curtain, is to drape a 'Chaos Club Sucks' sign over Zippy? That's pretty embarrassing, man. But don't worry, we took yours down and did a prank a bit more memorable for the day."

"But you didn't pull your prank," I say.

"Exactly what world do you live in, Max?" Becca says.

Loud applause erupts from the crowd as *The End* appears on the video screen. Mrs. B pushes Ellie to the front of the stage for a bow, then returns to the microphone.

"No one except our local resident artist and former Asheville High graduate Boyd Phillips has seen the Zippy statue in four months—"

"Not true," Benz whispers, laughing.

"—so without further delay, let's welcome back Zippy, the Asheville Eagle!"

All eyes turn toward the curtains. The media moves in, their cameras ready for the unveiling. Mrs. B pulls a ceremonial rope on stage, and all four curtains hiding the statue simultaneously drop.

It's pretty much one giant, collective gasp from the crowd after that.

Me included.

Parents cover their children's faces and cameras start snapping pictures. Heads turn from the statue to Stranko and back again, laughing harder and harder by the second.

Why?

Because straddling Zippy's back is a naked and anatomically correct mannequin with Stranko's face superimposed on its head. Fake-Stranko's wearing a red-lettered Chaos Club cape and grips Zippy's soaring wings like something out of a dumb kids movie. If I weren't so busy wondering how Becca and Benz pulled it off, I'd probably be impressed.

"Just in case you didn't know," Benz says, "that's what's called writing your name in the wet cement of the universe."

"And to think you could've been a part of this, Max," Becca says. "It would've saved a lot of hassle."

I have regrets, yeah, but not joining the Chaos Club isn't one of them. What I do regret is that this fell apart, because right now, at this very moment, is when we were going to reveal who they were. And now that's not going to happen. I regret not getting to see the looks on their faces the moment they realized they'd been tricked, when all eyes in the crowd fell on them once people discovered the Chaos Club members were right here—and best of all, when Stranko came to take them away. Missing all

of that is what I regret. So much potential unrealized. It's enough to make a sixteen-year-old boy tear up like a little girl.

Then a voice thunders from the speakers.

"Citizens of Asheville, this is Captain Calamity!"

Stranko and the others on stage look to Wheeler and his friend at the soundboard, but both are pantomiming confusion, frantically twisting knobs and flicking switches like they have no control over what's happening.

"For too long, this school has been the victim of the evil Chaos Club. Today, their reign of terror comes to an end. Please direct your attention to the movie screen."

Without anyone at the soundboard doing anything, the documentary picks up where it left off, with *The End* on the screen. Those words then fade.

Last Night.

"What's this shit, Max?"

Benz wants to sound menacing, but his voice is way too shaky. Beside him, Becca is wide-eyed and openmouthed.

The truth is I have no answer for him, but I know to play it cool.

"Shh," I say. "You're going to miss the big twist ending."

The screen fills with the eerie green glow of a recording made with the night vision camera Boyd helped Malone place in Zippy's eye. All anyone can see at the moment is the white curtain shot from inside the statue.

Although most people don't know what they're looking at, Becca and Benz figure it out.

"You set us up?" Benz asks.

"Just like you did with the water tower," I say. "And Stranko's office."

"We need to get out of here," Becca says.

"Sure, leave. It's not going to help though."

At least I don't think it will. I'm still not exactly sure what's going on. Ellie's real job last night was to turn the camera on. The stupid "Chaos Club Sucks" banner was just a diversion. She succeed in her part, but Wheeler never got to fulfill his role, which was to squeeze out of the base and remove the camera, then edit the footage into the end of the documentary. But he never got to do that because the cops showed before Becca and Benz could appear. So if we failed, what exactly are we about to see?

We don't have to wait long for the answer. After a few seconds of nothing on the screen, the curtain suddenly ripples, and we hear a rushed, "Come on, hurry up."

Benz.

"I'm going up," Becca's voice says. "Hand me your pieces."

The camera jiggles a bit as Becca climbs onto the statue's base.

"Weird," she says.

"What?"

"This thing isn't as stable as I thought it'd be."

No one in the crowd moves for the next two minutes

as we hear whispered instructions. Stranko seems the most hypnotized, unblinkingly watching the movie. What's funny is that nothing is happening on screen—we're all just looking at the curtain. And while it's good to hear Benz and Becca's voices, I need them to step in front of the camera at some point.

"I think I hear a siren," Benz says after a minute. "Are we good?"

"Yeah," Becca says. "Let me make sure."

The camera shakes again, and then, for the first time since the film began, there's actually something to look at besides the curtain. Becca and Benz, neither of them in masks, step in front of the camera to admire their work.

"It looks great," Becca says, holding up a hand to Benz.

He high-fives her and says, "The perfect way to end our time in Assville. Crap, that *is* a siren."

The movie freezes on Becca and Benz staring at the camera, the whites of their eyes a creepy green.

Busted.

Somehow.

But the movie isn't over, because as the picture of Becca and Benz slowly dissolves, a different picture—a much older photo—appears: Stranko getting shit on during his senior picnic.

The crowd's laughter starts as a chuckle, then rises to full-on howling. I instinctively look to the soundboard and see Malone, Ellie, and Adleta now standing beside

Wheeler. They're all giving me *sorry we just couldn't resist* shrugs.

Becca grabs Benz's arm and starts for the parking lot.

"Let's go," she says.

"You're dead, Cobb," he says over his shoulder.

I don't say anything.

Heist Rule #22: *Gloating's for amateurs.*

Besides, with the Chaos Club exposed, it's time for my entry in the prank off.

I kneel beside the base of the statue and slide open a small door. I quickly turn the red-handled valve and step away before anyone notices me. Seconds later, a loud hiss erupts from the statue. The noise stops Becca and Benz's escape, and they come back to where I'm standing. People back away from the statue like this might somehow be part of the prank, as if the Chaos Club is now in the poisonous gas business.

They're both right and wrong.

Right in that the hiss is a gas.

Wrong in that it's not poisonous.

Because as even Wheeler can tell you, helium isn't poisonous, but it is excellent for achieving liftoff.

The side panels of the statue's base pop off as the weather balloons inside inflate and fight for room to expand. Then ten balloons permanently borrowed from Mrs. Hansen's science room burst from the statue's base and head for the sky. They lift ten feet into the air before the ropes attached to the statue's base slow them down. Painted on each balloon for everyone in Asheville to see: *The Water Tower 5.*

At the foot of the stage, the members of my crew stand gaping at me. None of them knew about the weather balloons.

It's Heist Rule # 23: *Always know more than everyone else.*

It takes less than a minute for the balloons to inflate to their maximum level, but then Zippy breaks from his base and rises into the air, first slowly, then more quickly, until he's rocketing skyward.

Everyone—Stranko, Mrs. B, my crew, the hundreds of town citizens, even Benz and Becca—watches Zippy take flight, ridden by a naked Fake-Stranko.

It's epic.

It's art.

It's glorious.

I step up to Becca and Benz, their heads staring skyward like everyone else here.

Screw no gloating.

"No, Jeff," I say, "*that's* how you write your name in the wet cement of the universe."

CHAPTER 23

The school conference room is a circus car jammed floor to ceiling with clowns of all ages. Representing Asheville are Officer Hale, Mrs. B, Mayor Hite, and, with hate in his eyes, Stranko. Benz's and Becca's parents are seated beside their criminal children, and Ellie and I are here with our parents after voluntarily giving ourselves up. The only players not present are the three other members of the Water Tower Five, and I'm not about to pull them into this.

"Okay, Max," Mrs. B says. "Let's hear it."

Look, I wholeheartedly believe there's a time in your life when you have to tell the truth. This, however, is not one of those times.

"None of you believed me when I said I'd been set up," I say. "I had to prove to everyone that I wasn't in the Chaos Club, and the only way to do that was to expose them."

"By taking part in felony vandalism?" Stranko says.

"Let Max speak, please," Mrs. B says.

"Elaine, that statue was worth more than $25,000, and those kids—"

"It wasn't the real statue," I say.

Everyone's mouths drop open like they're on wires I just yanked.

"Boyd created a fake statue for me, identical to the first but hollow inside. The whole thing barely weighs thirty pounds."

I hate not giving Malone credit for all her hard work in replicating the original statue, but something tells me she'll be getting lots of recognition for her art in her lifetime.

"So where's the real statue?" Mayor Hite asks.

Ellie's standing near the window and taps the glass.

"It's being installed right now," she says.

Everyone crowds the window where, outside, hundreds of people are cheering Boyd and Mr. Jessup as they transfer Zippy to his rightful perch. The revelation that the actual Zippy statue isn't halfway to Mars lightens the air in the room considerably, which is nice because I haven't started lying yet.

"We installed a camera in the eagle's eye, which directly transferred the video to my phone," I say.

That's Lie #1.

Because, yes, there was a camera in the statue, but Ellie turned it on when she entered the curtains and Wheeler removed the camera once Becca and Benz were gone. At least that was the original plan. I still have no idea what exactly happened after things fell apart last night.

"Then I added the footage of Jeff and Becca to the end of my movie," Ellie says.

"And today I used a remote to turn the projector back on," I say.

That's Lie #2.

"A remote?" Stranko says skeptically.

"Well, if you want to be technical, a remote app."

Which is Lie #3.

Here's a quick tip: If you're ever talking to an adult and need a fast explanation for something unexplainable, say you did it with an app. Adults are awesomely ignorant when it comes to technology.

"Really, we didn't do anything special," I say. "We set up a camera, filmed the Chaos Club, and showed it today. Simple."

This Lie #4.

"That's not true," Benz says. "They were there at the school last night. We saw them."

"Just a moment, Jeffrey. You'll get a chance to speak," Mrs. B says, then turns to me. "If what you're saying is true, Max, why wouldn't you come to us instead of going through with this elaborate display?"

Great question.

Time for my ace in the hole.

"I tried," I say. "I went to Mr. Stranko's office to tell him I was worried the Chaos Club was going to do something at the celebration, but he wouldn't listen."

Mrs. B looks up at a stunned Stranko.

"Is this true?"

"Well..." Stranko says stalling. "He did come by, but I thought he was setting me up somehow."

"Setting you up how?" Dad says.

Stranko's getting whiter by the second.

"I thought he was trying to trick me," he says. "Don't forget that someone did lock me in the loading dock. And on the water tower. If they didn't do it, then who did?"

"Our son came to you with this concern beforehand and you ignored him?" Mom says.

"He screamed at me to get out," I say. "I couldn't get him to believe me, so I had to do something."

Stranko's on the ropes, but Mrs. B saves him.

"We're getting off track," she says. "What I was getting at before is this: Why would you have a fake statue installed and then launch it like that? Why not film the Chaos Club some other way that doesn't involve breaking a dozen FAA laws?"

"We talked about that, Mrs. B," Ellie says, "but we really didn't know what the Chaos Club was going to do to the statue. You've seen their pranks. We were afraid they would do permanent damage, and we didn't want that to happen."

By the way Stranko's grinding his teeth, it's clear he's not believing any of this, but he has no ammo. Any suspicion he has can be explained away by Chaos Club involvement. He knows it, and I know it.

Mrs. B asks a few other detail-y questions that I answer mostly with lies to protect the others. Eventually, she says to Becca and Benz, "So now it's your turn. What would you like to add to this?"

For the last ten minutes, Benz's been squirming hard

in his seat, his body twitching as he fought to keep quiet. Now that he's allowed to tell his side, he vomits it all out in a shout while jabbing a finger at me.

"They're both lying! We saw them last night! They trapped Hale in his car! And Stranko on the tower!"

"And there were others too," Becca says, not as crazed but still as pointed. "It wasn't just them. I don't know who else, but I one hundred percent saw Ellie and Max there."

"That's not true, Mrs. B," Ellie says.

"Which part?"

"Every part. None of it's true. Max and I were nowhere near the school last night."

"Didn't you say you were going to a movie?" Ellie's mom says.

"Yes," Ellie says, her voice trembling a bit, "but that's not what we did."

"What do you mean?"

Ellie stares at her hands.

"Ellie?"

When she looks up, her eyes are wet, and she's blushing. A baseball-sized knot forms in my throat. Ellie's gone completely off script.

"I don't want to say anything with all these people here, but we weren't there. You have to believe me."

"I don't understand," Ellie's mom says.

Ellie looks around the room like she wants to run away. She lets out big deflating sigh.

"We were at the baseball fields having sex. We didn't

mean for it to happen, but it did. So that's how I know we weren't at the school."

Wait, what?

Tears trickle down Ellie's cheeks. She turns away, wiping her eyes with her palms. The entire room is silent, and now it's not just Ellie who's feeling awkward—it's every single one of us. I understand her reasoning, but did she really have to pull the *Max and I had sex* card? I mean, it certainly worked—no one would dare question her story after those dramatics—but it's sure going to make for some awkward conversations with our parents later.

"Do you have anything else?" Mrs. B says to Becca and Benz. "Neither of you appear to deny vandalizing the statue."

It's one of those courtroom drama moments you see in movies where everyone is waiting for the defendant to lose control and confess his crimes. But neither Becca nor Benz is talking because they know they're trapped. The video eliminates any realistic denial. They're busted dead to rights. I wonder if there will be a school-wide field trip to attend their execution at the state penitentiary. The tension in the room continues to rise as everyone stares at Becca and Benz, waiting for some sort of response. Just as I don't think the rising pressure will splinter the windows, there's a knock at the door. Hale looks to Mrs. B for approval before opening it.

It's Mr. Watson.

"I think I can be some help," he says.

"This doesn't concern you," Stranko says. "If we need character witnesses, we'll let you know."

"Do yourself a favor and keep your mouth closed, Dwayne. I'm about to give you what you've wanted for years."

Watson crosses the room and stands behind Becca and Benz, putting his hands on both of their shoulders.

He says, "I'll save you lots of trouble here, Elaine. These students aren't the Chaos Club. I am."

⊕

Watson might as well have hit all of us with sledgehammers.

"I confess to all of it," Watson says. "The statue, the cows on the roof, Stranko's My Little Pony–pink office, everything going back all those years. If anyone is to be punished, it should be me. I'm the guilty one."

"You want us to seriously believe you single-handedly carried out those pranks?" Stranko says.

"Well, of course not, Dwayne. Don't be ridiculous. I have my soldiers, but they're only following my orders. I suppose one could argue they have free will and could've chosen not to join when I invited them, but teenagers are rebellious by nature, and an opportunity like this is just too tempting. Trust me, I should know. I've been direct-ing their pranks for almost forty years now, even back to when you were a student and you were one of the many victims covered in bird droppings."

"Why would you do all that?" Hale asks.

"Let's just say I believe the world is a much more

interesting place with a little chaos thrown in. Admittedly though, things got out of control this year. I apologize for that."

"You're finished here," Stranko says smugly. "I'm going to make sure you're not only fired but also—"

Mrs. B holds up a hand.

"There will be plenty of time to discuss that later," she says. "Right now, we need to deal with the issue at hand, these students."

"Correct," Mr. Watson says, "and I'm here to say they're only guilty of following my directions."

"And these are your only two"—and here Stranko makes quote fingers in the air—"*soldiers* this year?"

Watson nods.

"Not Max?" my mom says.

"No, not Max, although from what I've seen today, he would've been an excellent addition," Watson says and smiles at me. "Mr. Benz and Ms. Yancey were my two club members this year, and they served me well. But I took advantage of their youth, and it's brought them all this trouble. So if you're going to blame anyone, Elaine, blame me. I talked them into it, and they couldn't resist."

Becca says, "That's not true. We—"

Watson cuts her off. "You're a kind soul, Becca, but there's no need to defend me."

Mrs. B says, "John, I think this is a discussion we should finish later, maybe when you have union representation with you."

"I understand, Elaine. I apologize for the trouble I've helped cause today. But we certainly had some fun in our years, didn't we?"

They exchange smiles before Watson leaves the room. He doesn't walk like someone who's probably just lost the job he's had for the last thirty-whatever years, but he has, and I'm the reason for that. Way to go, Max.

"So what does this mean for the kids?" Becca's mom says.

"Yeah, you heard that teacher," Mrs. Benz says. "He manipulated those kids. They didn't have a choice. Those were his words, not mine."

"Mom, it wasn't like that," younger Benz says.

"Shut the hell up, Jeffrey."

"But—"

"You heard your mother," Mr. Benz says. "Keep quiet."

Benz looks down at the table and doesn't say anything else. I guess Adleta's not the only kid in town with idiots for parents. I should consider myself lucky. Mrs. B sighs as she leans back in her chair. I'm pretty sure it's dealing with moments like this that makes retirement pretty appealing.

She says, "I think that's enough drama for one day. No actual harm's been done, and considering Mr. Watson's revelation, I see no point in furthering the bloodshed. So unless anyone has something to add, I think all of you can go."

Wow.

Way to go, Mrs. B—a verdict that's simple, to the point, and agreed upon by everyone in the room.

Minus Stranko.

"Typical," he says.

"Excuse me?" Mrs. B says. There's a dangerous edge to her voice that I've never heard before. It gives me actual goose bumps.

"I said it's typical," Stranko says. "I've watched it for years—the way we coddle these kids, excusing their bad behavior, which does nothing but lead to more bad behavior. We've fostered an environment here where a group like the Chaos Club is cheered for almost four decades, and the result is an embarrassment like what happened out there today."

Mrs. B's face doesn't change, but she gives a slight nod.

"Thank you for your opinion, Mr. Stranko."

"This is precisely why I accepted the principalship in St. Louis. Like I told you the other day, as much as I love this district, I can't continue working in a building with such little discipline. It goes against everything I hold sacred."

Holy shit! I want to open the window like Scrooge on Christmas morning and shout to everyone below that our long, school-wide nightmare is ending.

Mrs. B says, "Well, I'll tell you now like I told you then, we wish you only the best of luck. You'll be missed."

By no one, I think.

CHAPTER 24

Okay, first off, what the hell just happened?" I say to my team. "We were all there last night when it fell apart. So how did it all magically work out? And why didn't any of you tell me?"

The five of us are debriefing in the lobby while the adults mill around the conference room, where they're likely blaming our unruliness on video games or the inability to legally pistol-whip students. The rest of the lobby is empty, and that's a good thing because my questions are met with laughter. And not just laughter but the worst kind of laughter: mocking laughter.

"Oooh, can I tell him?" Ellie says to the others. "Please?"

"Absolutely," Malone says. "It was your idea."

Ellie takes my hand and goes all doe-eyed, her voice exaggeratingly sweet.

"Max, remember when we all agreed to the prank off rules?"

"Yeah."

"Do you remember what I said would happen to the loser?"

My stomach sinks.

"Do you?" she asks.

"Yeah."

"What did I say?"

"That there would be dire consequences."

Ellie squeezes my hand hard and grins.

"Well, consider yourself consequenced."

"But how did I lose? If anything, I should be the winner. My prank was the best."

"Subjective but maybe," Malone says. "Unfortunately, you were disqualified."

"Why?"

"Because school was out," Adleta says. "The rule was by the end of school."

"But I did it that night!"

"Yeah, but we said before school ended," Wheeler answers. "I've said it before and I'll say it again—semantics, man, they're a bitch."

"So that's what you came up with for my punishment? Fifteen hours of feeling like a complete failure? You guys suck."

"She did say dire," Malone says. "You do know that word, right?"

"Yes, smart-ass, I know that word."

"Just be thankful we didn't go with Ellie's first suggestion as a punishment," Adleta says.

"Which was?"

"Having 'Prank War Loser' tattooed on your forehead."

I look at Ellie, not sure if Malone's being serious.

"What can I say?" Ellie smiles. "I take competitions seriously."

"Besides, we couldn't let you get cocky about every-thing," Adleta says.

"Yeah, humility is one of life's greatest virtues," Malone adds.

"Like my balls," Wheeler says.

They're all laughing now—at my expense, I must add—but it's hard to be angry when we've just pulled off the greatest caper in Asheville history.

"Okay, so now that I've suffered, will someone please tell me what happened last night?"

"There's not much to tell, dude," Wheeler says. "Benz and Becca came in, did their little prank—which was hilarious even by my high standards—and then split when the cops got close. Once they were gone, I pulled the camera and took off. After that, I just had to add the video file to the end of the documentary like we planned."

"It all worked perfectly," Ellie says. "Well, except for Stranko getting out of the tunnel."

"Yeah, sorry about that," Adleta says.

"No, it forced Max to rappel off the tower," Malone says. "That was worth it."

"Almost as good as hearing Stranko's taken a job somewhere else," Ellie says.

Adleta and Malone simultaneously shout, "What?"

"Yep," Ellie says. "Stranko quit. He took a job in St. Louis."

I don't think I've ever seen Adleta as happy as he is at this moment. He throws both fists into the air like he's

just won the state championship, was named MVP, and was awarded a full ride to Duke all at the same time.

"This isn't a joke, is it?" he says. "Because if it is—"

"It's no joke," I say. "He told everyone in the meeting."

Adleta pumps his fist again, saying, "The only way this could get better is if my dad were going with him."

"From what I've heard, his job is at a brand-new private school," Wheeler says. "He'll be opening a new building, helping establish the athletic program, everything."

We all slow-turn to Wheeler, and it's Malone who says what we're all thinking.

"Wait a second. How do you know about Stranko leaving?"

Wheeler says nothing. Instead, he just gives us the most satisfied smile I've ever seen.

"Come on, tell us," Ellie says.

"Because I, Dave Wheeler, recruited some H8boxers to headhunt Stranko for a principalship in St. Louis, show him around a new building under construction, and interview him twice for the job. They really made him salivate before making the offer."

A hallelujah choir of "holy shits" and "oh my Gods" ring through the lobby.

"So it's not a real job?" Adleta says.

"Nope."

"And Stranko just quit this one?"

"Apparently."

"But how could he fall for that?" Ellie asks.

"Never underestimate the power of H8box, my dear. We're all ages, all backgrounds, and all anti-asshole. Stranko never had a chance."

"How long ago did you set this up?" Adleta says.

"Three months ago, around the time I had the Secret Service show up. I figured if they weren't going to get rid of him, I'd have to do it myself."

Wheeler's prank is evil, massively so. It's impossible to hide my unease.

"Dude, I told you—I'm an upgrade, not a new install. This is who I am, and I'm cool with that."

"Well, as far as I'm concerned," Ellie says, "you win the prank off."

Wheeler claps his hands.

"So I get the guaranteed yes?"

"Those were the rules," Ellie says.

"Oh man," Wheeler says. "This is way too much power for one person."

"Especially in your case," Adleta says.

"Nothing sexual," Malone warns.

"Wait, that wasn't a rule," Wheeler says.

"Okay, but you'll have a hard time performing if you're in a coma."

Wheeler holds his hands up. "Calm down," he says. "I'm not going to ask for anything like that. I have a better request."

"What is it?" Ellie says.

"That this doesn't end after today," Wheeler says. "I

want us to keep doing things like this next year. We're good at it. Maybe we can even figure out a way to make money from it. If not, no big deal. I just want us to continue. I need this in my life. It helps balance out all the boring stuff, like studying."

When Wheeler finishes, everyone's smiling.

"Does that work for my guaranteed yes?"

"Yeah," Adleta says.

"Of course," I say.

"Yes," Malone says.

"Game on!" Ellie says. "And I have an additional prize for you." She reaches into her pockets with both hands, fishing around before pulling out a double thumbs-up.

"Excellent," Wheeler says. "I'll cherish this forever."

"Like my balls," Ellie says and turns red.

"Wait a second," I say. "I thought we agreed no outside help on the pranks. Doesn't that disqualify him?"

"Oh, don't be such a rule Nazi," Ellie says and winks.

"Look who it is," Adleta says, motioning with his head.

Becca and Benz are out of the office, heading for the front door, when Becca sees us. She says something to Benz and the two come over.

"I guess we should say we're sorry," Becca says. "I'm just glad none of us really got in trouble."

"Yeah, except for Max getting suspended and arrested," Malone says.

"Things got a little out of control," Benz says.

"Is that supposed to be an apology?"

"It's the closest any of you are going to get, Kate, so take it or leave it. I was mostly talking to Max anyhow."

"Why not the rest of us?" Wheeler says.

"Because he's the one we got suspended," Benz says and turns to me. "It was nothing personal, you know. We were just protecting the club."

"You made it personal when you put all of us on the water tower," I say.

Both Becca and Benz stare at me confused for a second before Becca shakes her head and rolls her eyes.

"You're hopeless, Max. Have a good life."

With Benz graduating and Becca moving, I doubt I'll ever see them again. Like that's any big loss.

"What was that about?" Malone says.

"They're just sore losers," Ellie answers. "We won. That's all that matters. The Water Tower Five prevails!"

The first weekend of summer break is spent having long talks with my parents—or more like lectures, rehashing the same ground until I'm certain if I hear "You should have told us from the start" one more time, I may have to hammer pencils into my ears.

When Mom and Dad tag team the lectures, they're on point with:

1. How lucky I am no one else was injured or arrested.

2. How I'll have to rebuild their trust.

3. How sex is nothing to be taken lightly.

4. How they hope I take the summer to really do some
   soul searching, which is ironic since that's what led
   me to finally toppling the Chaos Club.

But privately, one-on-one, when the other is out of the
room, both Mom and Dad tell me they understand why I did
it. Both even say the identical thing, "I'm not saying what
you did was right, but I understand," followed immediately
by, "but don't tell your mother/father I said that."

I'm not officially grounded—it's not like there's a
proclamation nailed to my bedroom door—but it's an
understood grounding. Asking to go out would only
incur another lecture, so I lay low a couple days, sticking
around the house and getting adjusted to the laziness of
summer, which means sleeping in late and binge watching *Leverage* with Dad at night.

It's on Monday evening, two days after the celebration and our complete destruction of the Chaos Club—
hold your applause, please—that I receive an email from
Mr. Watson.

I'll be in my room all day tomorrow. Come see me if
you get a chance.

Mom and Dad have a private conversation about my request before agreeing to let me go. The next morning, I find Watson in his room, loading books into a box on his desk. The room looks like a tornado hit it, with files and poster boards from old projects covering the floor. Sitting atop most desks are boxes—some empty, some half-filled, some taped and ready to be moved. I join in at a bookshelf, packing up books from his personal library.

"So you got fired?"

"We've agreed to early retirement. Easier on this district publicity wise, and it allows me to keep my entire pension. Everyone wins this way."

He doesn't sound sad when he says it, only resigned.

"I'm sorry," I say. "I didn't mean for this to happen."

"I thought you might be feeling guilty. That's why I asked you to come. You don't need to apologize to me, Max. My actions are my responsibility, not yours. In fact, I'm proud of you for doing what I suggested you do at the beginning of the year—you made your mark in the wet cement of the universe. You ended a tradition that's lasted for almost forty years. How many people can say that?"

"Then why don't I feel better about it?"

"Because most triumphs are never clean. Have you ever heard of a Pyrrhic victory?"

I shake my head.

"It's a victory that comes at a great cost. You win, but you pay a great price. For you, it's the guilt you're feeling

that I'm finished here. That'll pass though, especially since I assure you none of this is your fault."

"Well, I'm sorry just the same."

"I accept your apology, Max, as unnecessary as it is."

This is likely the last time I'll ever see Mr. Watson. If that's the case, I have one question that has been bothering me for months.

"With all the running around that's happened in this building after hours, how did you work it that the Chaos Club was never caught?"

"That's a great question, Max. You're definitely my kind of thinker. Can you keep a secret?"

"Of course."

"Well, so can I," Watson says and winks. "Let's just say that Becca and Benz aren't the only ones I protected by confessing."

Great, just what I need—a new mystery to solve.

"What will you do now?" I say.

"Oh, I have friends across the country I plan on visiting for the next couple months. After that, who knows? Now that I'm no longer a teacher, I'll have to discover a new me."

We spend the next half hour packing boxes together. Thirty-nine years of teaching in the same classroom can amass a great deal of junk, a whole lifetime really, and Watson's room is evidence of that. I find reports written in the eighties, pictures of Watson at least twenty years younger and fifty pounds lighter, football programs with yellowed pages, and files of newspaper articles about individual students Watson taught going back to his first year. There's so much to pack that it seems as if we're not making any progress, but I'm fine with that.

"You don't need to stay here all day, Max. I appreciate the help, but I'd sort of like some time alone with my memories."

"Okay," I say, feeling awkward. "I guess I'll see you around."

"You have my email, Max. Feel free to use it anytime."

We shake hands, and Mr. Watson returns to his closet—itself a cluttered mess of memories. I head for the door, and really, this is where the story should end—with the Chaos Club destroyed, Stranko leaving, Watson retiring, and me discovering who I really am. But it's not the end.

I'm on my way to the door when Watson stops me.

"Max, before you go, there's one more thing."

I look back.

"I've debated whether or not to tell you this, and I'm still not sure I should, but I'm going to anyway. As ironic as it sounds, I believe in the truth, and I think you need to know it in this case."

Then Watson tells me, and my world turns upside down.

CHAPTER 25

My fingers tap nervously on the steering wheel as I drive through the wooded hills, trying not to think about that night in October when I first came here with Ellie. I park the car on the side of the road and hike among the trees toward the clearing. It's June, and summer's in full swing, the woods cool and alive with the buzz of a million insects. I slow at the edge of the clearing, then stop completely before stepping out of the trees.

Am I ready for this?

Probably not.

But will I ever be?

I emerge from the trees, and Ellie immediately jumps to her feet on the radar dish, raising both arms over her head, her fists clinched.

"Victory!" she shouts.

She's wearing cutoff jean shorts and a vintage white Rolling Stones concert T-shirt. She couldn't look any more beautiful if she tried.

God, this sucks already.

I walk up the hill to the dish and climb the ladder, poking my head through the hole in the mesh floor.

"So the grounding's over?" she says.

"I'm officially free."

"Excellent! Did you talk them into letting you out?"

"Something like that."

"Me too. I mean, after that meeting, my parents were ready to put me in a convent, but then I..."

Ellie's mouth is moving, but I'm not hearing her. It's something about her parents lecturing her about sex. Yesterday, after leaving Watson's room shell-shocked, I went home and told my parents about everything— the pranks, everyone's involvement, even about my field trip with Boyd to see his archway. Everything. Through all of it, Mom and Dad only made a sound once, giving audible sighs of relief when I told them Ellie and I hadn't had sex. After that, I probably could have told them I'd decided to drop out of school to become a white supremacist and they'd have been okay with it.

Ellie snaps her fingers in front of my eyes.

"Hello? Max? You look about a thousand miles away. What are you thinking about?"

What I'm thinking about but don't tell her is this— how could I have been so stupid?

"I went to see Watson yesterday," I say. "I helped him pack up his classroom."

"Yeah, I heard he retired. That's too bad. Was he mad at us?"

"No, in fact, I think he sort of respects us for what we did."

Ellie smiles proudly. "It is sort of cool, right? We really did make our mark like he wanted us to."

"We're sure did that. But what's funny is that when I was leaving, Watson told me something I didn't know."

"What was that?"

On the drive here, I practiced saying the words aloud, but now in the moment, I have a hard getting them out.

"Watson told me the Chaos Club didn't set us up at the water tower."

Ellie doesn't move. It's exactly how I reacted when I heard the news.

"That's why we never could figure out why the Chaos Club chose us. Because they didn't," I say. "And now that we know Becca and Benz were this year's members, it makes even less sense. They had no reason to target us. Becca even told me in Stranko's office they didn't set us up, and I didn't believe her."

"That doesn't mean—"

"That's why the water tower was never mentioned on their website—because the Chaos Club didn't have anything to do with it. The Chaos Club goes for the big spectacle, not individual vendettas. I should've known it wasn't them from the start."

Ellie frowns.

"Why are you talking to me like that?"

"Like what?"

"Like you're angry with me."

Because I am angry. Pissed even. I look at Ellie, all

summery and beautiful, and there's an instant when I consider not saying anything else and just enjoying the rest of my life. It would definitely be the easier path to choose. But I know too much now to do that. It's entirely my fault for forgetting Heist Rule #24: *Beware the double cross.*

"Here's what I've figured out: if the Chaos Club didn't set us up, that only leaves the four of you. And nothing against the other three, but they don't have the abilities and drive to pull off everything that's happened," I say, "but you do."

Ellie goes wide-eyed.

"What?" she says.

"You set us up at the water tower."

Ellie blinks twice before her laughter echoes across the open field.

"Maxwell Cobb, you're not serious? There are two thousand students in our school. It could have been any one of them."

"Not that has your access to the building and lockers—"

"Max—"

"Or who I saw send a text minutes before Hale showed up."

"This is crazy."

"Maybe, but what really seals it is the picture of me on the football field. You were the only person who knew we'd be there that night. If you're right and it was one of the other kids in the building who set us up, did they also

just happen to know we'd be at the football field? That's too big of a coincidence."

"I'm not sure where you came up with this, but—"

"You'd like everyone to believe you're the naive preacher's daughter, but you're not. Not by a mile. You're probably the smartest of all of us. I'm right about this. Just admit it."

Ellie goes quiet, staring at some place far behind me. I prepare myself for more arguing, but then her body sags like warm wax.

"I shouldn't have let it get as far as it did. That was never my plan," she says. "I didn't think anyone would ever find out."

Oh God, I was right. It was one thing to think Ellie set us up. It's another thing entirely to hear her admit it. Every part of me hoped she'd be able to prove me wrong, to offer up an alternative that made sense. But no.

I blink away the tears forming.

"Why did you do it?"

Ellie sighs, saying, "At first, it was like I said—I wanted the Chaos Club to pay for what they did to me last year. And to do that, I needed a team. Obviously I picked the right people too. But eventually, it became more fun than anything. I wasn't even mad at the Chaos Club after a while, even if I acted like it. I just wanted to see if we could pull it off, and we did."

"By using us."

"We all used each other, Max. Don't try to tell me we

didn't all have a great time. The five of us made a great team. Look at what we achieved."

"By lying to us."

"And I'm sorry about that. I really am. But just for a second, try to see the big picture—everything worked out for the best. I'm not just talking the Chaos Club. I'm talking about everyone. We're all better for what's happened this year. And somehow we even got rid of Stranko. None of that would've happened if I hadn't done what I did."

Now it's my turn to be quiet. Everything she's saying makes sense in a slanted, blurry way. If she keeps talking like this, I'll cave.

"Who took the picture of us at the football field?" I say.

"Well, like Dave said, you can learn how to do anything on H8box."

"And you doughed our lockers too?"

"Max, why are you getting caught up in the details? Yes, I did it, okay? Is that what you want me to say? But you were talking about giving up. And it worked. You stayed with it, and we accomplished our goal. The specifics don't matter."

"Don't matter? I got arrested, Ellie. And suspended. My parents were ready to disown me!"

"That wasn't the plan. I just wanted to keep you in the game. It was the worst night of my life when I found out what the Chaos Club did to you."

"What did you think would happen?"

"Honestly? That they'd threaten you or pull a different prank—something that would get you pissed and focused again. I never imagined they'd set you up like that."

"So what about Watson? He basically got fired over this. Not to mention we destroyed the Chaos Club, and they didn't do anything to deserve it."

"You mean besides the scoreboard prank last year? And how they got you arrested?"

"No, Ellie, you got me arrested. Not them."

She doesn't say anything.

"You led me on," I say.

"No, that's not fair. I may have lied to get everything started, but you can't ever say I led you on. I made it clear the first time we came here that this was about destroying the Chaos Club, not about us being together. That just ended up being a bonus."

Um.

"A bonus?"

"Yes, silly. Why do you think I had us meet here today? When we came here the first time, I told you *maybe* when the year was over we could go out. Well, what was a *maybe* is now a *definitely*. It was never my plan, but I like you now, Max. As in like-like you."

Then Ellie kisses me, and the world collapses in on itself. Her lips are soft and warm and perfect, and I'm so shocked, so stunned, I don't immediately kiss her back. This isn't like the quick "for luck" kiss she gave me before.

This is a universe destroyer. Then her fingers begin tracing the back of my neck up into my hair, and oh God, there's her tongue on mine. And now I'm kissing her back with my hands on her hips, and she's not stopping me. We fall and become entwined on the radar dish, our mouths together, our hands on each other. The hot summer sun overhead could supernova right now and I wouldn't care. Because Ellie's right. Any lies she may have told led us to this perfect moment. I can leave here with her, the two of us a couple, and return to Asheville and my friends and not tell anyone what I know. Because, man, I've wanted this for so long, and Ellie's mouth is amazing, and her hands are moving to all the right places.

I mean, I could do all that, right? Not tell the other three what I know? Isn't it only a betrayal if someone gets hurt? I mean, yeah, it'll be hard knowing Ellie set up Wheeler, Malone, and Adleta, but doesn't the mastermind have to carry the heaviest weight? And isn't your crew only your crew as long as there's a job to pull?

Aren't they?

Please?

Shit.

I pull away, and Ellie leans farther in. If she gets her mouth on mine again, I'm a goner. So I back safely out of the kissing zone and hold out a hand to stop her from advancing.

"I'm leaving," I say.

"Max," she says, taking my arm. "Everything's fine.

It all worked out for every one of us. If the phrase 'the end justifies the means' was ever fitting, it's here. Yes, bad things happened, but we can forget about that and move on—together. The two of us."

Ellie sounds sincere, but I can't be sure if she really is. She's that good of an actress. That's the problem with liars—you never know if what you're hearing is the truth.

"Come on, Max, admit it. You've had more fun this year than you've ever had, haven't you?"

"Yeah, but—"

"Then why end it?" she says. "Who cares how we got started? What matters is what we became. We're an amazing team. What just happened proves it. And imagine what the five of us can achieve next year...and the fun you and I can have this summer."

I see it all clearly now—Ellie Wick is the devil.

I stand up and step toward the ladder.

"So let me get this straight," she says, standing too. "We had an awesome year, and I'm telling you I want us to be together, but you're turning me down?"

"I can't trust you."

It's a few seconds before Ellie says anything. "Have you told the others yet?"

"No, but they deserve to know."

"They'll hate me."

"Maybe."

Ellie's eyes go slowly cold. It's a disturbing, frightening shift. I swear the temperature drops twenty degrees.

"I can't just let you ruin my life like that," she says. "If you go through with it, then you're my mortal enemy, Maxwell Cobb. Isn't that what would happen in one of your little heist films? The crew leader kicks someone out and that person comes back for revenge?"

If she's trying to shrink my balls, she's succeeded.

"You don't need to do that," I say.

"No, I don't. But think of the fun I can have. Or"—and she puts on a voice that could make cartoon birds flock to her—"you can forget everything and we can rule the school next year as a couple. It's up to you."

I understand now this was all a game to her. She's even used that very word. Was she ever really as tortured by the Chaos Club's prank on her dad as she said or was that just a convenient excuse to get us to play her game? I'll probably never know. Heist victims are always left with unanswered questions. But if I've learned anything from this, it's that I have the strength to handle whatever Ellie can throw at me.

"I can't have a supervillain for a girlfriend," I say.

"Oh, Max, you don't know the meaning of supervillain yet."

I start down the ladder, feeling her eyes on me.

"I can't wait to hear you try to sell this story to people," she says. "They're going to put you in a mental hospital."

"It doesn't matter, Ellie. The right people will believe me."

At the base of the tower, I wipe the rust off my hands.

"This is your last chance, Max," Ellie says. "Summer fun with me or complete chaos. It's up to you."

But there's no real choice here.

There never was.

Someone else might get scared and give in, but not me. Not anymore. Whatever I'm giving up with Ellie is nothing compared to what I've gained. With my crew on my side, nothing can touch me. Besides, every mastermind knows Heist Rule #25: *Know when to walk away.*

Before starting down the hill, I return Ellie's smile.

"Game on."

Acknowledgments

Writing a novel is a lot more collaborative than I ever knew. I'm forever thankful to the following people for their help and support:

First and foremost, thanks to my wonderful, supportive, and brilliant wife, Jen, who started me on this adventure by not-so-subtly convincing me to attend my first writing conference by saying, "Oh, you *are* going." She's not only my biggest champion and best friend, but she also gave me the four most wonderful reasons to exist: Brody, Sam, Charlie, and Murphy. I love you all.

My brother-in-arms John Mantooth deserves a warehouse of craft beer for reading all eight drafts and talking me off the ledge hundreds of times. Early readers Sam W. Anderson, Kim Despins, Daryl Gregory, Josh Penzone, and Kimberly Gabriel (Your turn's next!) helped get this book out of the trenches with their notes and friendship.

Kerry Sparks is a true badass who gave me the chance no one else would. If you look up *literary superagent* in the dictionary, there's a picture of Kerry carrying all her writers on her back while she stands on a pile of bloodied and beaten foes foolish enough to get in her way.

Editor extraordinaire Aubrey Poole had the razor-sharp insight and enthusiasm I needed to make this book as good as it could possibly be. I'm thankful to her and the rest of the Sourcebooks team for their incredible support and hospitality.

Writers Josh Berk, Michael Cook, John Langan, Petra Miller, John Rector, Ian Rogers, Lance Rubin, Brett Savory, Paul Tremblay, Fred Venturini, and Erik Williams probably aren't aware of how helpful and motivating they've been, but hopefully, now they know. Andrew Smith graciously gave me a kick in the ass precisely when I needed it. Thanks to Mac McCaughan of Superchunk for permission to use his lyrics.

My mom and dad let me read and watch whatever I wanted while growing up, which is questionable parenting at best, but forever appreciated. My brothers, Eric, Brent, and Jay, were always better at sports than I was, so this novel is probably just a thinly masked attempt at showing off in the only way I can.

On occasion, I had to turn to the experts for their brilliance: Pat George is a grammar goddess; Kristi Stephens is a math nerd; Halie Limpert is a lacrosse beast; Matt MacNish is a query letter master; Aaron Roberts is a design guru; Whitney Ballentine is a photography wizard; and Amanda and Julie are Panera rock stars for sneaking me free coffee. Extra special thanks to Barbara and John Miller, who, among a million other things, graciously watched the kids when I needed extra writing time.

My students over the last twenty-one years have given me plenty of inspiration, laughs, and headaches. I expect a three-page review of this novel on my desk by Monday.

And finally, a special thanks to my oldest brother, Eric, who passed away before this was published. If he hadn't let me read his books and listen to his albums when I was growing up, this novel wouldn't exist. He never got a chance to read this, but I'd like to think he would've gotten a kick out of it.

About the Author

Kurt Dinan has taught high school English for more than twenty-one years, and while he's never pulled any of the pranks detailed in this novel, he was once almost arrested in college for blizzarding the campus with fliers promoting a fake concert. He lives and works in the suburbs of Cincinnati with his wife and his four children, whom he affectionately refers to as "the Crime Spree." *Don't Get Caught* is his first novel.